WILDFIRE

A Kelly Turnbull Novel

By

Kurt Schlichter

Putin had wasted no time in once again making all of Ukraine a Russian brand once again. "Sadly, this sort of business is better conducted discretely."

Bullethead stood silently, unsmiling, watching.

"Discretion is important," Turnbull said. "Shall we get on with it?"

"Of course, but where are your friends? I understand there were to be three of you."

"Where do you think they are?"

"Probably in the trees pointing nice new weapons like that one at my head," the boss replied. "Even my men aren't equipped with such quality arms as yours, and we are the sword and the shield of the state."

"You'll be able to buy them whatever you like once we conclude our business."

"Of course, of course. Now this business – tell me about it. Our mutual friend Vasily, he was less than clear on your business in my *oblast.* I think the English word is 'opaque.'"

"My business is *my* business. We're paying for confidentiality, as well as safe passage out."

"Of course, of course, but I need assurances that you and your friends won't be – disruptive to the public peace, if those are the right words."

"We're not here to be disruptive. In a few hours, we will be gone just as if we had never been here," Turnbull said. "And you will be considerably wealthier."

"That's reassuring, my friend. But I must know, from your mouth – is this business something that might harm the security of the

His improvised killing plan complete, Turnbull relaxed and waited, moving the index finger of his right hand almost imperceptibly to manipulate the selector switch on his rifle from semiauto to two-round burst.

Only the boss and Bullethead came forward; they knew enough not to mob the American. This was supposed to be peaceful, a simple business transaction.

Turnbull came up to the front of the Land Rover, his boots crunching the filthy snow, and gestured at Vasily to join him. The Russian fixer swallowed again and joined him.

The boss stepped up to about three meters from the American, while Bullethead lingered a couple meters back, staring dully. This dude definitely had to be fun at parties.

"Welcome to Russia," said the boss in an accent that sounded a bit like Dracula, if Dracula had spent the prior evening pounding vodka instead of hemoglobin. "Or, welcome *back*. I assume you have been here before."

Turnbull was mildly pleased that the man spoke English, and they would not have to do the translation kabuki dance. Plus, Vasily might screw up the words, which could be seriously bad, because he was clearly terrified of the guy – as he should be. This was no ordinary thug. This was an extraordinary thug, the head of the *Federal'naya sluzhba bezopasnosti Rossiyskoy Federatsii* (FSB) in the Novosibirsk region, and Vasily had to stick around and deal with these guys after the Americans were long gone.

"Russian hospitality is always a pleasure." Turnbull replied, the memory of several notable hangovers bubbling up from his deep subconscious where he had forcibly suppressed them.

"I would prefer we would meet and share a bottle of *Hetman*, like civilized folk," the boss said. *Hetman* was a premium Ukrainian brand; when the United States split apart, the now-elderly Vladimir

"I'm losing the mic, over," Turnbull replied.

"You going to do that hand in the air thing?" Hiroshi asked. "I *love* that thing, over."

"Nah. If I start shooting, or they start shooting, *you* start shooting," Turnbull said quietly. "Out."

He took the throat mic and earpiece off and tossed them onto the passenger seat. Across the hood, Vasily looked around, skittish. He started reaching for his Marlboros.

"Don't," Turnbull hissed. No sudden moves. Not around these guys.

The twelve doors on the sedans opened almost simultaneously, but slowly, deliberately, in a manner that demonstrated their intent not to spook the big American with the assault rifle.

Ten of them were typical Russian thugs, dull-eyed and broad shouldered, wearing back of the rack grey suits and each clutching some elderly member of the Kalashnikov clan of killing tools. Another was especially big, really big, with a smooth, hairless head like a .45 ball round and eyes even deader than dead. He had been riding in the passenger seat of the front sedan and right behind him was the boss. You could tell the boss because he didn't have an AK, and because his black suit fit. Sort of.

Back in the day, communist flunkies wore the grey suits; now grey was for the *assosiyatniki.*

Okay, Bullethead would get two caps in the noggin first, then the front driver, and then Turnbull would move fast to try and take the boss hostage while Hiroshi and McCluskey dropped as many of the others as they could. Maybe the survivors would stand down if their fearless leader had a flash suppressor pressed up under his double chin.

Turnbull would have preferred a different gun, but the Americans already stood out like sore thumbs, which is why they were rendezvousing out here in the midst of nowhere with the three Mercedes sedans now approaching up the empty country road. Anyway, there wasn't supposed to be shooting.

Of course, there was almost never *supposed* to be any shooting.

This was a pretty routine gig – or seemed to be when he heard it laid out. Still, the question of why Clay Deeds had sent three top-shelf operators in for a simple whisk-away mission was always there, bobbing and weaving, in the back of his head. And Turnbull wondered why Deeds had so quickly met his grossly inflated price – getting him out of retirement for four day's work had cost plenty to whoever was writing checks for the spook's project. Why him though? There were plenty of salty-enough guys who hadn't had a billionaire fork over several million bucks for rescuing his little girl from deep inside the blue and who couldn't afford to run out the clock kicking back and swilling Shiners on their porch until they vapor locked. No, there was more to this one than Deeds was letting on. But then there was always more than Deeds let on.

Enough of that, Turnbull thought, clearing his mind. The three black sedans – they cried out "government bad guys" – were pulling to the shoulder and it was time to focus.

"Come on," Turnbull said, opening the passenger door. He and Vasily were parked on the shoulder of the wrong side of the road, and the other cars were lined up about 20 meters to their front. Vasily swallowed, then crushed out his cigarette in the overflowing ash tray and popped his own door.

Turnbull's boot hit pavement, and he brought the AK-12 with him as he stepped up to his full height. The three black vehicles to his front idled, their windshields tinted and inscrutable.

"Got 'em, over," Hiroshi said.

that wizard kid now anyway? Fifty-something? *Harry Potter and the Crushing Mortgage, Enlarged Prostate, and Bitter, Unfulfilled Wife?*

Turnbull had dodged a lot of bullets in his day, and *that* life was the one he was most grateful for dodging. Most of the time, anyway.

He wondered how his dog was doing back in Texas. Probably hadn't even noticed his alleged master was gone.

Vasily blew a long stream of used Marlboro smoke from out the driver's window. Though he was ripping through them, he still tried to take his time exhaling; the American cigs Turnbull brought him were a delicacy. Usually, he puffed on evil Balkan tobacco. Even an ace fixer like Vasily had trouble getting real American smokes in a frozen backwater hellhole like Novosibirsk.

Movement on the road, out 500 meters.

"Car," Turnbull said suddenly into his throat mic. "No, three cars, black sedans, in line. It's them, over."

"I'm gold, over" Hiroshi replied.

"Me too, over," Dave McCluskey added, his Tennessee accent coming through.

When they said they were gold, they meant that they were ready to engage with their black Dragunov SVDM sniper rifles from their respective hide positions in the wood line on opposite sides of the deserted road. By force of habit, Turnbull confirmed that his plastic mag was fully loaded with 5.45 x 39mm rounds, and that it was snuggly fitted into the well of his AK-12C assault rifle. The black gun was the newest model in the Kalashnikov family, heir to the King of Commie Rifles, the venerable but deadly AK-47. With a close quarter optic on a Picatinny rail, it was a solid weapon system, though not his favorite. But when in Rome, do as the Romanoffs do.

1.

"Remaining golden, Ponyboy, over," Kelly Turnbull said into his throat mic.

That would irritate Ted Hiroshi but good, and irritating him was always amusing. A skinny Japanese-American skate punk from the Pacific coastal burg of Encinitas turned Air Force para-rescueman turned private contractor, Hiroshi could be fussy. Pissing him off helped Turnbull ignore the gnawing Siberian cold.

Turnbull awaited the response as he continued watching the long, empty stretch of two-lane blacktop through the dirty windshield of the idling Land Rover. Next to him, in the driver's seat, Vasily's trembling hands lit yet another cigarette. The guy must have already gone through one of the dozen packs of American Marlboros Turnbull had brought him, and they'd only been there a half hour max.

The static broke. Turnbull cupped his earpiece to block out the rush of the frigid Russian wind.

"*Stay*," Hiroshi corrected him, his annoyance coming over the radio lima charlie. "*Stay* gold, over."

Turnbull smiled. Whenever they worked together, Hiroshi always handled the team's commo, and for some reason he always insisted on picking lines from one of his favorite old books to use for their code phrases. This one was from a young adult novel about teen gang kids back when America was still America – *The Insiders*, maybe *The Outsiders*, definitely some kind of *-siders*. Goofy, sure, but it could have been worse. The last time time they worked together, Hiroshi had selected code phrases from the latest Harry Potter book. It was 2035, so how old was

I will say of the LORD, "He is my refuge and my fortress, my God, in whom I trust."

Surely he will save you from the fowler's snare and from the deadly pestilence.

Psalm 91

PREFACE

This is the third book in the Kelly Turnbull series, and if you have come this far I want to thank you for sticking it out.

If you are new to the series, well, welcome. Hopefully you won't find it too confusing. If you do, start with *People's Republic* and read both older ones.

Sadly, I keep having people tell me that my books seem to be coming true. That's not good. These novels are cautionary tales, not how-to guides.

Here's the thing – since *Indian Country* came out in May 2017, the situation has only gotten darker. Americans seem bound and determined to throw away what the Founders gave them in exchange for short term political advantage – and the returns on this investment are diminishing as both sides adapt to the new rules.

To reiterate, this new book is a warning, like its two predecessors. Yeah, I know what the hacks and liars will say – that this is some sort of eager fantasy. Nope. It's a warning, but one that I hope you find entertaining.

So, enjoy *Wildfire*, but also take heed, and do what needs to be done to ensure it never comes true.

KAS
November 2018

ACKNOWLEDGEMENTS

Many people helped make this novel possible, but most of all my hot wife Irina Moises, who was there from the beginning. She helped at every stage, in the development and drafting of the manuscript, and in polishing up the end product.

Lots of other folks helped out in various ways. I can't list them all so I won't try. But I'll list some:

I got plenty of support from my friends like Cam Edwards, Cameron Gray, Drew Matich, Robert O'Brien, Matthew Betley, Jim Geraghty, and others. Big supporters include Larry O'Connor, Glenn Reynolds, Chris Stigall, Hugh Hewitt, John Gibson, WarrenPeas64, Big Pete, and many more.

A special thanks to all my Twitter pals. A lot of them have been demanding that I finish this third book ever since I put out *Indian Country* in May 2017. I appreciate all your support. I'll try to get the fourth one written faster – I'm channeling that weird *Game of Thrones* writer guy, I guess – but I did kind of write a whole other book, *Militant Normals: How Regular Americans Are Rebelling Against the Elite to Reclaim Our Democracy*, in the meantime, so I have an excuse.

Keith Urbahn of Javelin is my traditional agent for traditional books, and he is awesome. This book is totally not his fault.

Of course, there's my cover artist J.R. Hawthorne *aka* Salty Hollywood – he rocks.

And, as always, a shout-out to Andrew Breitbart, who pointed out that if we want to win the culture war, we need to put up a fight. He's the one who sucked me back into writing. Accordingly, if *Wildfire* is awful, blame him!

Kurt Schlichter

Paperback Edition ISBN: 978-0-9884029-8-0
Paperback Version: Final - Wildfire - Draft -112318 v58

State? You see, I am a patriot, and the interests of the *Rodina* must come before my own interests."

Turnbull smiled. The interests of Mother Russia were inextricably bound up with those of the elderly Vladimir Putin to the point that they were essentially one and the same. This guy would not have gotten his position within the successor to the KGB if the old *chekist* in the Kremlin was not convinced of his absolute loyalty. Putin would see his cut of the deal, just as he saw his cut of all the deals cut by all the corrupt *apparatchiks* across the largest country on earth from the Baltic to the Pacific. And Putin needed every ruble. He had just married his fourth wife, a blonde 23-year old Byelorussian pop star named Tatiana Sexxxy who was equally notable for her enormously inflated fake breasts and her auto-tuned dance hit "Touch My Horny."

"This has nothing to do with the State."

"Oh, a private business matter then?" asked the Russian. Behind him, Bullethead remained immobile and as expressive as a gray hunk of boiled beef.

"It has nothing to do with your government. As Vasily explained, we are simply escorting someone elsewhere."

"In a private jet that is landing at an airfield in my jurisdiction. I should ask you how you arranged overflight clearance for it to come in and out through Russian airspace."

"No," Turnbull said. "You shouldn't."

"Of course. My concern is only that no one interferes with your takeoff."

"That's right. And once we depart, Vasily will deliver the other half."

"And if he doesn't?" asked the FSB colonel. Vasily swallowed.

"Then I assume you will be extremely upset with him. But I kind of like him, so I'll make sure he doesn't disappoint you."

"Of course. But I am still...concerned about all of this secrecy. This is a lot of money, and you're so well-equipped. Then there is the airplane. Forgive me, but it seems like you may be here representing not a private company but one of the American governments. I would like to know which one."

"Does it matter?"

"I prefer to know who I am conducting business with. But I must confess that these two Americas confuse me. The United States, the People's Republic. For us, it is sometimes hard to tell them apart. They say that in one of them, men must be only with other men. Is that so?"

"I'm from the one where it's merely optional," Turnbull said. "Are we going to talk all afternoon in the cold, or are we going to do this?"

"You Americans, always down to business. Yes, let's complete our business together and you can do what you are here to do without interference."

Turnbull looked over at Vasily and nodded. The young Russian went to the rear seat of the Land Rover and retrieved one of the two worn brown leather bags. All the while, Turnbull smiled as he stared into the blank, empty eyes of the giant Slavic slab.

Vasily offered the bag to the boss, who scowled and said something sharp in Russian. Chastened, Vasily took a few more steps and put it in Bullethead's outstretched paw. No one checked the cash, at least not there and then.

"Anything else?" Turnbull asked. The boss smiled.

"I think our business is done, for now. I expect Vasily will deliver the other half once you have departed."

"He will."

"Then we will be on our way," said the boss. "Enjoy your time in Novobirsk, and I very much hope that I will hear nothing else about your visit."

"As do I," Turnbull said.

The boss smiled, turned on his heel and walked to the FSB cars. Bullethead paused for a moment, eyes locked on Turnbull's, then turned and followed with the money bag. But Turnbull didn't relax yet. He stared at them until they got back in their sedans and U-turned around and went back the way they came. Then he relaxed, but only a little.

Turnbull waited in the passenger seat for five minutes to see if the bad guys would come back. They didn't. He still hurt a little where he had caught some lead during that Los Angeles op a few months before – luckily the People's Security Force body armor he had worn had sapped enough energy from the rounds so that he wasn't killed outright. It occurred to him that one of these days, a bullet was going to hit something that wouldn't heal and that would be it. And then who would take care of his useless dog?

Focus. Just a couple more hours and it was on the way home. There will be plenty of time for taking a personal inventory back in Texas.

"Okay Ponyboy, time to come back to the corral. And you too…." Turnbull paused, trying to remember what stupid code name Hiroshi had given McCluskey. He couldn't. "Uh, Otherboy. Out."

"They'll be waiting along the road in front of the compound," Vasily said. Turnbull was looking through photos on his iPad 27 again, making sure he knew the layout. Hiroshi, in the backseat, was staring over his shoulder.

"This guard post at the gate," Turnbull said. "You sure it won't be a problem?"

"No, my cousin Dimitri will walk the professor out of the building for a smoke, and then they will go out through the gate and walk down the road and we will pick them up and we will go."

"But will the guards try and stop him from leaving?" asked Hiroshi.

"No, they stop people from coming *into* the compound. It's the men inside the building who would stop the professor from leaving, if they knew, but he and Dimitri go outside to smoke all the time. No one will be suspicious."

"What exactly do they do in that building, Vasily?" asked Turnbull.

"I do not know," said their fixer, swerving gently to avoid a slow-moving tractor half in the road and half on the shoulder.

"Well, what's your cousin Dimitri say? He works there," asked Turnbull.

"He doesn't really work there. He helps the men who do. They are foreigners."

"So, Dimitri is basically you, except working for the assholes."

"Yes, that's right."

"So what's he *think* they do?" pressed Turnbull.

"Science things, I think."

"Of course." Turnbull went back to swiping through the photos of the pick-up point. Novosibirsk had been a center for military research during the Soviet Era, and even 45 years later there were plenty of facilities and plenty of trained scientists willing to earn their vodka rubles doing whatever someone was willing to pay them to do. This Professor Ivan Maksimov, he was clearly one of these guys, and Clay Deeds wanted him out. Exactly what he was doing was not particularly relevant to the task of getting him out cleanly and quietly.

But Clay had been clear. "You get him out, Kelly. You do whatever it takes. Just get him out and back here."

Turnbull's burner cell phone vibrated. It was a text message. "Sunset." Another code phrase Hiroshi chose – he was back behind Vasily grinning.

"The plane is sixty minutes out," Turnbull announced. "Let's get this done and go home."

"Think there's beer on the plane?" McCluskey asked from behind Turnbull. He first grew out his brushy beard traipsing around Helmand killing Taliban and never trimmed it back since. He looked like a grizzly bear in dark shades and web gear.

No one answered him; it was pretty much a rhetorical question anyway. Turnbull was still skimming through the photos and Hiroshi was looking over his AK-12 one last time. The sniper rifles were in the back now, and they'd leave them with Vasily as a tip if everything went off well.

"Okay, it is up ahead and around the corner," Vasily said as they approached an intersection a hundred meters north. It was a wooded industrial area, with most of the buildings set back behind fences and trees. The whole area was shabby too – the entire region needed to be hosed down and repainted. Even the snow looked drab.

Turnbull checked his watch. It read "15:03." Two minutes to go.

"Hold up," Turnbull said, and Vasily pulled to the shoulder and let the SUV idle. A silver Subaru sedan passed by them, oblivious. They all put their windows down.

"Dave, you help them get inside – with extreme prejudice if necessary. Ted, head on a swivel," Turnbull said.

"Roger," replied the human bear. Hiroshi just nodded and lay the rifle across his lap.

"Okay," Turnbull said, glancing at the watch. "Drive."

"They should be out on the road on the right side," the fixer said confidently.

Vasily pulled out into the road again and accelerated north to the intersection. He paused at the stop for a moment, and spit his Marlboro out his window. Hitting the gas, he turned right onto the main road. It was straight and lined with trees for a kilometer ahead. About 200 meters up, on the right, there was a driveway.

Otherwise, the stretch was empty.

"Where are your friends, Vasily?" Turnbull asked.

Vasily seemed confused. "They were supposed to be here on the road."

The vehicle started to slow.

"No, keep going. Don't slow down," Turnbull barked. Vasily obeyed. The driveway was approaching fast.

"They might be off the road in the trees," Turnbull said.

"I got nothing," McCluskey said from the back seat, scanning from the wood line to the high barbed-wire fence set back a dozen meters in.

They passed by the driveway in a flash. There was a guard shack with a gate – closed – and beyond it a large gray building behind a nearly empty parking lot. There was also an old sign. The words were in Russian and they flashed by too fast for Turnbull to make them out.

No people.

"Tell me we got the right day and time," Turnbull said.

"Yes, today, and right now," said Vasily nervously. Turnbull scrutinized the young Russian fixer. He seemed truly nervous and concerned – but Turnbull gripped his rifle just a little tighter anyway in case this turned out to be a double-cross. If it did, chain-smoking Vasily was going to get himself smoked first.

"Call him on your cell. And keep going up to the next intersection, then flip a huey and come back," Turnbull ordered.

"A 'huey'?"

"U-turn. Come back the way we came and we'll make another pass."

Vasily nodded and complied. He drove one-handed with the cell pressed to his ear.

"Nothing," he said after a moment. He completed the U-turn.

On the way back, the Land Rover was silent except for the hum of the engine as they passed the entrance to the compound again heading west.

"Nothing at all," Hiroshi said. "Nobody, not even guards."

But Turnbull had seen something – the old, faded sign. He caught one word – "*Biopreparat*."

"Ah, shit," Turnbull said. "Our professor is a bio weapons guy."

"You're kidding," Hiroshi said.

"That's gotta be it," Turnbull said. The Land Rover was now approaching the intersection where they had first turned onto the main road. "Look, if he's not coming out…"

"You want to go in there?" McCluskey asked. "Clay promised this was a simple pick-up job…"

"Clay said we had to get him, and he's got to be inside," Turnbull said. "Our plane takes off with us or without us in T-minus 55 minutes. I'm open to any other good ideas."

"We could say 'Screw it,'" and punch out now," McCluskey replied bitterly.

"I've never seen you walk away from trouble before," Turnbull said.

"I hate that bio weapons shit," the bear replied. "But screw it, let's go in and get him."

"Ted?"

"I'm in," he said, cradling his rifle.

"Vasily, flip another huey and roll up to the gate."

The Land Rover pulled up to the guard shack and Hiroshi was out the door in a half-second with his AK-12 ready. He rushed the shack, paused, then announced, "Clear!"

"Hit the button," Turnbull yelled. Hiroshi disappeared inside and a moment later the gate began sliding open.

They rolled through the nearly empty parking lot to the front steps of the three-story, gray building, and as soon as the Land Rover paused, the three operators were out with AKs ready. Vasily stayed at the wheel, but only for a moment. Turnbull pointed at him and curled his finger. Vasily was coming along.

Dave was first at the front doors, and he halted, puzzled.

"Is it locked?" Turnbull yelled, frog marching Vasily up the stairs.

"No," McCluskey shouted. "It's got a metal bar holding the doors shut."

"Can we break a window or are they reinforced?" Turnbull said, reaching the top and then immediately seeing that he had misunderstood.

The metal bar was through the handles on the *outside* of the building.

"Oh, this is so wrong," Hiroshi said from his position covering the rear.

"What the hell were they trying to lock *in*?" asked McCluskey, his weapon ready.

"Blood splatter," Turnbull said, pointing to a crimson streak on the inside of the glass windows.

McCluskey cupped his hands on the glass and peered through into the dank interior. "No bodies."

"That's something," Turnbull said. "Now pull out that bar and let's do this."

The power was still on, and they were able to turn on the lights. On both sides of the building were stairways up – they did not even consider the elevators. The east side stairs were dusty and the landing to the second floor seemed to have been converted in to a storage area for old furniture and random boxes. The west side stairwell seemed to be the only one in current use. Turnbull waved them up.

He led, rifle ready. McCluskey was next, beside Vasily, and Hiroshi took the rear. They hadn't needed to discuss it – they'd worked together enough that they simply fell into their accustomed movement pattern.

The second floor was dark, and it was fairly quiet – there were clangs and occasional noises, but it was hard to tell if the sounds were organic or if the dilapidated old building was just falling apart. At the landing, Turnbull felt for a light switch and when he found it, he tripped it. The fluorescent ceiling lights flickered on down a long hallway lined with closed doors, bathing it in a vaguely nauseating greenish glow. The far eastern end of the hall was somewhere in the darkness past where the lights worked.

It also illuminated a large biohazard warning sign with Cyrillic words in a font that screamed, "We're serious!"

"Come on," Turnbull said. They moved down the hall. Many of the doors had obviously not been opened for some time. Whoever was using this place was only using some of it. The door marked "2345" was clearly one of the parts that was still viable. The deadbolt was engaged outside the lock to hold it open.

"Like they want us to go in," McCluskey said.

"Me first," Turnbull replied. They set, with McCluskey pulling the door open fast and Turnbull and Hiroshi rushing in, Turnbull clearing left, Hiroshi right.

After both men announced their sector clear, they took a moment to look around as the ceiling lights began to flicker. It was a lab, or had been. There was a variety of modern equipment, and lots of smashed glassware. There were cords that had clearly been attached to missing computers that lay forlorn across the tables. And there was a freezer unit.

"Empty," Hiroshi announced. "Whoever was here is gone, and took whatever they were working on."

"Ted, take some video of this place. Dave, look for anything that looks like intel – disks, thumbdrives, notes. Especially those machines, whatever they are. Look, but don't touch *nothing*."

Hiroshi hung his weapon around his neck and lifted his phone up to the metal label that was fixed to most of the equipment: "Feldschall Fabrik Gmbh, Hebertshausen, Deutschland." He snapped a couple of photos.

McCluskey was at an interior door, weapon up. A Russian sign on it told him to keep out. He opened it, gun up, and hit the lights.

"Shit, Kelly, you gotta see this," he shouted.

"Quiet!" Turnbull hissed as he moved toward the door. McCluskey stepped aside and he peered in.

It was a long room, lined with what appeared to be cages. Big cages – man-sized cages, at least two dozen. Slumped on the floor of each of them was a shape, unmoving. Streams of red trickled from each to a drain set in the center of the floor.

Turnbull shut the door and turned to Vasily.

"What the hell is going on here?" he asked, and not nicely.

"I do not know, Kelly. Dimitri said he would be outside with the professor." Vasily was plainly miserable. To the extent Turnbull ever believed anyone about anything, he was starting to believe that Vasily really had no idea what was happening.

"Would Dimitri sell us out? Sell *you* out?"

"No, he is my cousin. We have known each other all our lives!"

"Maybe someone else made him a better offer."

"No, not Dimitri."

"If not Dimitri, who else knew we were coming?"

"No one, Kelly. No one."

Noise, in the hallway outside. Footsteps, fast. Running.

Turnbull was up with his weapon, trained on the door. Hiroshi unlimbered his rifle, and McCluskey was on it too.

A howl, like an animal's, of pain and anger.

The door flew open, and a man stood there, breathing hard, eyes red and fierce. Blood streamed from his mouth, nose, ears and the corners of his wild, unfocused eyes.

"Dimitri?" Vasily said, as if he was unsure.

The man's eyes now locked on Hiroshi, who was closest, and he gritted his red-stained teeth even as his throat issued a guttural cry of rage. The man ran at Hiroshi, fast but uncoordinated, bloody hands outstretched.

It was three meters to his target, and he took three rounds before he reached Ted Hiroshi and began clawing and biting at his face. Hiroshi struggled to avoid the flailing windmill of grabbing hands and kicked his attacker hard in the patella. The snap was audible, but Dimitri did not stop. Hiroshi swung the butt of his rifle hard into Dimitri's side, forcing the madman back and far enough away for Turnbull to step up with his weapon.

Turnbull put two rounds into Dimitri's face, blowing the back of his head all over the lab's dingy wall. The man finally went down.

"Damn it!" Hiroshi shouted, but Turnbull grabbed him, forcing his friend's bloody face into a sink and turning on the water, washing away Dimitri's blood.

"Did you see that?" shouted McCluskey, covering the door. "He took a three rounds center mass and kept coming!"

"I saw," Turnbull said, finishing with Hiroshi, who was spitting out water. "We need to go. Now."

Vasily stood shaking, staring at the body of his dead cousin, eyes beginning to water. Turnbull grabbed him.

"He's a fucking zombie, man. You had to shoot him in the head! Like on that show." McCluskey yelled.

"He's not a fucking zombie!" Turnbull yelled, as he pulled the Russian with them into the hall. "Come on!"

More footsteps. A lot more.

Down the hall, several figures sprinted toward them, uncoordinated and howling, running as fast as they could. They were wearing security guard uniforms, and blood was flowing red from every orifice.

"Shoot them in the head!" Turnbull ordered. No sense in taking chances.

The three operators aimed and fired a fusillade. The runners dropped in heaps.

"How about that, assholes?" asked Hiroshi, breathing hard and lowering his smoking AK. His face was scratched up pretty bad.

More noise from the dark end of the hallway. A lot more.

"Let's go!" Turnbull yelled as they turned and ran the way they came.

The four sprinted hard for the stairway. At the top was another bloody security guard, this one with an old AK-74. He raised it clumsily and pulled the trigger without aiming, then took one step forward before two rounds from Turnbull's weapon slammed into his forehead and dumped him backwards down into the stairwell.

They barreled forward and down the steps, the rambling, howling chaos behind them drawing closer. Hiroshi was stumbling, and Vasily and McCluskey each took a shoulder.

They didn't pause on the first floor – instead, they ran straight outside into the cold toward the vehicle.

"Get in," Turnbull shouted, still by the door and picking up the discarded iron bar. Inside, a mass of bodies was tearing down the stairway, shrieking and whirling. Turnbull flipped his selector switch to "Auto" and slipped the barrel back inside through the cracked door one-handed. He pulled the trigger, emptying the mag and sending several of the madmen sprawling. Then he pulled the gun out and barred the door. The survivors, bloody and mindless, pounded and tore at the reinforced glass as he backed away, unconsciously dropping his empty mag and reloading. Then he ran to the Land Rover and got in.

The airport was on the north side of Novobirsk, near where the more equal than others class of old Soviet *apparatchiks* had their *dachas*. No one flew in or out of there much anymore, but someone was paid to keep the weeds from growing in the runway just in case someone who mattered decided to. It was remote, quiet, and therefore perfect.

They sat waiting in the idling Land Rover. After a couple of long minutes, Turnbull's burner vibrated. Another text. "Sunset Sunset."

"Okay, it is five minutes away," Turnbull said. "When it lands, Vasily, you drive us up, we get on and you get out of here. Keep the car and the guns and make sure the FSB guy gets his cash."

"What was wrong with Dimitri?" Vasily asked. Turnbull did not answer.

"Did you see them?" asked McCluskey. "Man, they were totally zombies."

"Can you stop with the zombies?" shouted Turnbull.

"You got to shoot them in the head or they won't die," McCluskey said.

"No, they just didn't die *right then*. Okay, they would have died soon enough," said Turnbull. "The problem is that you've been watching that stupid *The Walking Dead* show for twenty-five years."

"You watch it, Dave?" Hiroshi asked. "What happened last week?"

"Carl III got lost again," McCluskey said. "And cloned Glenn finally died for real."

"Does that look like a plane?" Turnbull asked, pointing out the window. In the western sky there was a small black dot.

"Yeah," Hiroshi said. He looked down. "Shit, I got that asshole's blood all over my shirt."

"We're all nasty from carrying you," McCluskey said.

The plane started its approach.

"Let's go," Turnbull said. Vasily accelerated into the airport. There was no fence. He drove directly onto the tarmac as the unmarked and modified Gulfstream G650D landed. The white aircraft rolled to a stop several hundred yards out on the runway and turned around for take-off.

"Hey, Kelly," said Hiroshi. "Our FSB pals are here."

Turnbull looked out and saw three black sedans hauling ass up the road. He picked up his rifle.

"This is not good. Vasily, let's get to the aircraft. You're coming."

"No," Vasily said. "I will stay here, with the money. They only want the money. You take the Land Rover out to the plane. Just leave the keys in it for me." He smiled nervously.

"You can come with us," Turnbull said.

"No, I will take care of them. They only want their money. You go. I will be fine." He stepped out of the Land Rover and Turnbull climbed into the driver's seat. McCluskey handed him the bag of money through the passenger window. Vasily waved, and began walking toward the oncoming vehicles.

Turnbull hit the gas and started driving out toward the plane. Its door was open and a small ladder dropped to the tarmac. In the rear-view, Turnbull watched Vasily walking and waving to the sedans.

The FSB convoy slowed to a stop and their doors opened. Bullethead stepped out and shot Vasily in the forehead. He went down, sprawling, the bag opening and the cash falling out and blowing across the runway in the wind.

No one went near it.

Turnbull hit the brakes, rammed it into "Park" and spun out the door, rifle in hand. The Russians were all shooting now, but he ignored them and brought the rifle up and the optic to his eye. The designator was right on Bullethead's bald pate. Turnbull squeezed, firing semiauto, and the slugs marred the thug's perfect sphere in a splatter of red goo.

The Russians gunned their engines.

Turnbull flipped the selector switch to full auto, and joined Hiroshi and McCluskey in blowing off a magazine each on full auto to suppress their pursuers.

Two of the sedans were still operational when he slipped back behind the wheel. Hiroshi and McCluskey continued to fire at their pursuers out the windows as Turnbull roared off, pedal to the metal, toward the waiting aircraft.

Another sedan wobbled and flipped over. The last one continued after them, a thug and what appeared to be the boss spraying and praying out of opposite rear windows. Turnbull skidded to a stop at the bottom of the steps and both Hiroshi and McCluskey reloaded as he stepped out.

The last car's windshield was shattered, steam was hissing out of its punctured radiator and lines of holes had erupted across the hood. But the FSB car was still coming.

Turnbull raised his rifle to his shoulder and took aim, the designator dancing on his target. He fired. The boss caught one in the face and went limp hanging out the window. Turnbull pivoted a bit and put three into the driver while McCluskey finished the third thug. The sedan slowed and then just rolled ahead aimlessly.

"Get in!" Turnbull yelled, covering their retreat. When McCluskey was inside, he followed and the jet's door closed behind him. The aircraft began to roll down the runway. They strapped themselves into the seats – very comfortable seats – as the plane picked up speed and took off.

"Anyone hit?" Hiroshi asked. No one had been.

The plane gained altitude and leveled off before Turnbull said what they were all thinking.

"They didn't stop."

"No," McCluskey said. "And they didn't care about the money."

"They *always* care about the money," Hiroshi said.

"They wanted *us*. No matter what. They were going to stop us or die trying," McCluskey said.

"And they did," said Turnbull. Movement to the front – he looked up. The cockpit door was opening. The face of one of the pilots appeared.

"Shut that door now!" Turnbull yelled. He emphasized his point with the barrel of his AK-12. The door slammed shut.

The intercom came alive. "What the hell is going on?" asked a perturbed voice.

Turnbull popped his seat belt, stepped over and took the cabin mic in hand.

"Stay in the cockpit. Don't come out. No matter what."

"What do you mean don't come out? We've got a thirteen-hour flight! How are we going to piss?"

"Piss on the floor. You open that door and you're dead." Turnbull hung up the handset. Hiroshi was looking at him.

"You think I'm infected?"

"I don't know," Turnbull said, shaking his head. He held up his rifle. "I do think we need to disassemble these. Just in case."

Hiroshi nodded, and began breaking down his rifle.

They dodged a big bullet getting out of Russian airspace – though safe passage had been purchased, the pilots still turned on their electronic warfare suite just in case someone started looking for them. The airfield shootout had spooked them good, and they deviated from their agreed flight plan. They were nearly out of Russian airspace when it became clear from the way the radar detection indicators were lighting up that they were being hunted. They got away clean.

With the extra tanks built into this customized aircraft, there would be no need to land to refuel. The fastest way to Dallas was north over the pole and south through Canada and then some zig zagging around People's Republic airspace. Turnbull's headache started over the Arctic.

It began as a pain in the front of his skull, a dull, thudding pain that he at first dismissed as a figment of his imagination, and then as the normal discomfort inherent in air travel. But it got progressively worse. And there was the nausea, a roiling, clamping pain in the gut.

Hiroshi was feeling it bad too. He had stumbled to the lavatory a few minutes before and had not come out. Turnbull felt his guts turning. He got up, staggered down the aisle past a groaning McCluskey, and pounded on the door.

"Ted, I need in," he managed to say. The door opened. Hiroshi's eyes vacant and bloodshot. Red stained his teeth.

"I just shit blood, Kelly," he said. "Puked it too. A lot of blood."

Turnbull pulled him out of the way and vomited a huge splash of red into the toilet. He steadied himself on the sink and looked in the mirror. Blood coated his lips, and a trickle drained from his left nostril. The cabin began to spin counter-clockwise.

He staggered out, past Hiroshi, who was shaking on the floor, to the intercom mic. Turnbull managed to get it off the hook and key it.

"You tell them we're infected. You tell them to quarantine us. You tell them...," he gasped for breath. "You tell them we're dangerous."

He dropped the mic and slumped to the floor.

They were coming for him, the bastards, the fucking bastards, but they wouldn't get him. They wanted to kill him but he was going to kill them first. He was going to kill them all, the bastards, the bastards...

Light! Bright, in his face. Hot air from outside! They were coming now – a weapon? Where were the weapons? No weapons, so he'd use his hands and teeth. He'd go for their throats, their eyes, he'd rip them apart!

All white, their suits were all white, like armor, but soft, not armor, it wouldn't protect them. And the masks – the faceplates couldn't stop him from reaching and tearing their soft eyes, their soft ears, their lips their cheeks, oh he would rip them and bite them grabbing grabbing grabbing, now they were on top of him, holding him down, grab something, tear at them, kill them kill them kill them all....

2.

Nope, no ketchup.

Not anymore. Turnbull would take his scrambled eggs straight up. The red, well, it evoked memories he'd prefer to forget.

He was seated at the back of the room, alone, facing the door. His black Wilson Combat X-TAC Elite .45 was on his thigh; that was his go-to-town piece. Underneath the table his dog growled, and Turnbull brushed him with his shoe. The dog sat in sullen silence, assessing the other diners. There were maybe a dozen, enjoying a Saturday breakfast, most armed, all polite.

"More coffee, Kelly?" Lorna asked. She was holding a pot and wearing her waitress gear – they still called them "waitresses" in Texas. Being home was always so much easier since you didn't have to constantly navigate through the verbal minefields that surrounded every human interaction in the People's Republic. Just having a limited number of pronouns to worry about made life exponentially simpler.

"Uh, yeah," Turnbull replied. "Sure." *Not the right moment.*

She smiled and poured.

"Are you settled back in yet?" she asked. "You've been home what – a month?" Turnbull stared blankly.

"Are you happy to be home again, Kelly?" she said patiently. Every interaction with him seemed to go like this.

"Oh, yeah," he said.

"Well, where were you this last time?"

"Business," Turnbull said.

"I figured that," Lorna said. "Are you ever going to tell me what kind of business?"

"It's," Turnbull stammered, "boring."

"I'm a divorced 29-year old waitress in a diner in Bumfuck, Egypt, Texas, Kelly. You think anything you can say can possibly bore me?"

The "Bumfuck, Egypt" reference gave it away – she had done a military service hitch and was a full citizen.

"Reserve duty," he said.

"Well, why didn't you just say so? No wonder you looked like shit when you first came back. Were you out in the field on an FTX or on a real op?"

Turnbull shrugged. "Just stuff."

"Classified. I get it. I'm a 35-Fox, intel analyst. I do my three weeks active duty next October. So, you'll have to find someone else to try to pull you out of your shell while I'm gone."

Turnbull wasn't sure how to respond.

"That was a joke, Kelly," she said, still patient. She waited while Turnbull processed, then said, "You know, next time I'll tell the dog the joke."

"He's kind of slow too," Turnbull said.

"No, he's a good dog." Lorna put the pot on his table and knelt down, petting the furry beast. The dog ate it up. "What's his name again?"

"Jeff."

"Hi, Jeff. Did your daddy leave you all alone while he went off to play army?" The dog didn't answer, but he didn't growl, which was something.

"I left him with my neighbor, next ranch over. They have kids. He's always bummed out when I come home."

"Just you and Jeff, huh?

"Just us," Turnbull said. *Ask her, damn it.*

"Surprised some lucky girl hasn't already swooped up a guy who's never home and has no sense of humor," she said, smiling. "But you like dogs. You got that going for you."

"I'm still not sure I like this one."

"Well, that was sort of like a joke..." she replied, standing.

But Turnbull wasn't looking at her anymore; he was fixed on the two black SUVs that had pulled up on the street outside the diner. Lorna followed his eyes to the front window, then back to Turnbull.

"Are they here for you?"

"I hope not." But then he saw Clay Deeds step out, in an exquisite suit, surrounded by security guys in dark glasses wearing jackets that bulged over their gear.

"Crap," Kelly muttered. There went breakfast.

Deeds walked into the diner, which had grown quiet. His eyes settled on Turnbull and he smiled and walked over. The security men lingered out front.

"Kelly," he said.

"Clay."

"Who is your friend?" Deeds asked, looking at the waitress.

"I'm Lorna," she said. He took her hand and shook it.

"Lorna Dickinson. You're a staff sergeant in the 193rd MI Battalion."

"And you're definitely a spook. I should probably leave you two alone."

"Could I get a cup of coffee while Kelly and I talk?" Deeds asked. Lorna looked at Turnbull, who nodded.

"Any friend of Kelly's..." She walked away. Under the table, the dog growled.

"Your dog still hates me, I see," Deeds said, sitting across from Turnbull.

"He associates you with me going away," replied Turnbull. "I tried to explain that I'm not going away anymore, but, you know, he's a dog."

"About that..."

"Nope. I'm busy."

"Doing what?"

"Well, last night I watched *Where Eagles Dare* for the seventieth time."

"Broadsword calling Danny Boy."

"Exactly. I'd like to be around to make it to the seventy-first."

"I need you, Kelly. You're my Broadsword."

"Look, I'm nobody's Broadsword anymore. How did you even find me?" Turnbull said. "Did you track my phone? And then run a check on everyone working here so you could come in and freak Lorna out?

"I've read her file. I don't think Staff Sergeant Dickinson freaks out easily. By the way, did you know Juan Velasquez, the cook, won a Bronze Star with 'V' device at Cajon Pass?"

"Really? I don't remember him, but I was kinda busy that day. He does scramble a good egg. Why are you screwing up my breakfast, Clay?"

"How are you feeling?"

"Increasingly pissed off."

"I'm serious, Kelly. How are you *feeling*?"

"I'm fine, Clay. The docs cleared me. I've been off antivirals for a month. There's no more virus in my blood, but you knew all that already, didn't you?"

"I did. But it isn't over. The virus is still out there."

Deeds was quiet. He licked his lips.

"You're kidding me," Turnbull said.

Lorna appeared and they went silent. She left Deeds a cup of coffee and walked away.

"You really learn to appreciate irresponsible coffee living here in the red," Turnbull said.

"Kelly, we have intel that says…"

"You have intel?" asked Turnbull, raising his voice enough that Lorna looked back over her shoulder. He lowered his voice a few decibels. "Clay, the last time you had intel, me and my guys walked into a trap. The target was gone, but they left a little surprise for us. Freaking zombies. My men are all dead. I almost died. I was two months in the ICU."

"Think about what happens if Wildfire gets loose in the population," Deeds said quietly.

"Wildfire?"

"Our code name for the Marburg X virus. Think about it. An old Soviet bioweapon that takes an African hemorrhagic fever closely related to ebola and mates it with rabies. The hosts actively spread it, and if you don't get infected with the bug, you still get infected with the panic. It was designed to tear out the foundations of a society, and that's what it will do if it ever gets out. That's why the Russians went full bore to wax you guys. We're just lucky it's so hard to make."

"You need people. Live subjects," Turnbull said, remembering the cages.

"The virus is alive while the victim is in the psychotic phase and only when it dies does the victim lapse into the final coma, bleed out, and expire," said Deeds. "We got to you before then. I saw you in the psychotic phase when we opened the door to the aircraft, Kelly. It took eight men to hold you down and sedate you."

"I like to think I can handle myself."

"You tried to rip my face mask off and tear my eyes out."

"That wasn't necessarily because of the bug."

"Whoever has Professor Maksimov got him out before you got there. Now they're setting up shop again, somewhere else. Somewhere they can build up enough vectors."

"Vectors?"

"Carriers. Infected carriers."

"Great. Go hire some other guys and kill them all."

"We don't know where they are. Not exactly. But we have leads."

"I don't understand why you're here telling me this, Clay. I'm out. Remember, I'm rich, thanks to your pal George Ryan and his millions of dollars."

"It's got to be you."

"It doesn't have to be me. It isn't going to be me."

"Kelly, they did some other tests on you. Really, on your blood. You have antibodies to Marburg X. Nobody's ever had antibodies to it before. Nobody's ever survived it before."

"I don't like where this is going."

"You may be immune," Deeds said.

"May?"

"We think. Nobody knows. We don't have any live virus. That's part of Marburg X's charm – it dies before you can study it. That's why we need Professor Maksimov. He's the only one who's studied it through its entire life cycle."

"He infects people in experiments?" asked Turnbull.

"Yes."

"And you tried to buy him off and get him here to tell you everything he knows?"

"Yes."

"I'm not a big philosophical guy, but that's pretty 'ed up."

"He's the only one who might be able to help us find a vaccine."

"The old Soviet records…"

"Are incomplete. We've known this was out there for decades, and it terrified us. We assumed it was flushed away when the Soviet Union fell and it never reappeared for decades. But apparently, it was still there, frozen. Someone paid Maksimov to resurrect it."

"Who?"

"We have some ideas."

"Good luck."

"Kelly, this is serious. I need you. I need you *now*."

"What, like this minute?"

"Yeah. We have a plane to catch."

"What if I say 'No'?"

"Then everyone you ever met might well die. Wildfire is the big one, the worst-case scenario."

"And someone plans to use it on us? I'm guessing the PR."

"Wrong," Deeds said. "No, the People's Republic is the target."

"The target?"

"Yes, but don't think we're safe. You and I know what Wildfire does. When it hits, people run, and they bring the disease along with them. And they're going to run right into the United States. We need to fight the battle there, on the PR's ground. And no one on our side knows better how to survive on their side."

"Sheesh," said Turnbull. "You've totally ruined my breakfast."

"You'll never have a chance to ask Lorna out if Wildfire comes."

"How…?"

"How long have I known you?"

"Too long."

Deeds turned and motioned for Lorna, who came over cautiously.

"Sergeant Dickinson, can I ask you a favor? Not for me. For Kelly here."

"A favor?"

"Yes," said Deeds. "Can you watch his miserable dog for a while? When he gets back, he can take you out to dinner. On me."

Lorna looked at Turnbull, who started to say something and then stopped.

"Sure," she said. "I like strays. And doggies."

"Then it's settled," Deeds said. "Thank you." Lorna understood it was time for her to step away again and did.

"I don't understand why you think 'no' means 'yes,'" Turnbull said.

"How's your Spanish?"

"My what?"

"Your Spanish."

"*Frutas, frutas, quien quiere frutas. Tengo muchas frutas.* I learned that in second grade. Also, I can order a beer and hire a...," Turnbull paused. "Cab."

"It doesn't really matter if you know Spanish anyway," said Deeds. "Not where we're going."

"And where's that? Los Angeles?"

"Mexico City."

3.

The Hofbrauhaus had been gutted in a fire and never rebuilt, but that passive description does not provide the full context. The famous German temple to hops and barley had survived the centuries and two world wars, quenching the thirst of Munich's burghers and foreign tourists alike. But it could not survive the mob of Middle Eastern refugees that had appeared around it one evening in 2027, and driven most of the customers, staff, and the odd tuba player out before setting it on fire.

As the flames rose high out of the Bavarian-style windows, the streets echoed with the cries "Allah Akbar!" After watching for a while, they then marched over to the Marienplatz and pulled down the statue of the Virgin Mary from the top of the *Mariensäule*, where it had been placed in 1638 to celebrate the city's freedom from foreign occupation.

That night, the Germans understood that Munich was no longer free of foreign occupation.

Instead, Munich belonged to the most vicious of the millions of foreigners Angela Merkel had invited into the country as penance for crimes committed long before those who would pay the penalty had even been born. But there was no statue to Merkel in Munich, nor any gratitude. The relatively few of those she had saved from poverty and tyranny by inviting them into Germany, where they created their own poverty and tyranny, who bothered to learn German called her "*Die alt Hure.*"

The Old Whore.

Hamid al-Afridi walked east from the Marienplatz – it was no longer called that, of course – his four body guards in pairs five meters forward and five meters back. There were no tourists and, except for a few gaunt male addicts, no ethnic Germans in the heart of the city. But they had their uses and so, for now, they were tolerated. Otherwise, it was almost solely Africans, Middle Easterners, Afghans, and Pakistanis, with the men often in robes and the women always covered.

Rickety wooden stands lined the buildings selling fruits and vegetables; most of the old shops were shuttered. Truckers could not, or would not, go this deep into the city anymore, so instead these vendors would travel to the outskirts of town, make their purchases then haul them back for resale to the locals. The sidewalks were filthy; the city fathers simply stopped providing most services in the city center years before. There was a government somewhere, but it was mostly concerned with distributing dole checks. The *polizei* stayed away, so there were no official police in sight, but the Morality Patrol – composed of angry men with scraggly beards carrying long sticks – kept their own brand of order.

There were a number of coffee houses, men only, and no bars, of course. There were no clubs either, and no music. The last busker had tried to play for euros four or five years before and ended up hanging from the Glockenspiel with a sign around his neck that read, "He blasphemed the prophet."

But Munich was still too degenerate for Hamid al-Afridi. Even these people were dirty and ignorant, lost in their own struggle to survive, ignorant of the Prophet's commands, refusing to do the will of Allah.

He looked into their faces as they passed, and they looked away and walked faster. He could see their hidden sins. That one no doubt played music behind the closed doors of his flat, that woman removed her coverings to tempt men, and that man sat at his table and drank schnapps. They could see in his eyes that he knew their sins. And it was right for them to fear him, for he was an instrument of justice and they were all of insufficient faith.

They would repent or pay, but that accounting would come later. Their little sins could await expiation. It was the truly satanic that Hamid al-Afridi was concerned with now.

The group moved through the crowd, with the people parting before them. It was good for him to be seen in public, not merely talked about in whispers. It rubbed the infidels' noses in their own impotence that he would walk through their country unimpeded.

The cars, a black AMG and several Mercedes sedans, sat idling at the end of a cross-street in a red zone, waiting for him. He took his time walking to them; those he was going to meet could wait for him.

One of the bodyguards opened the rear passenger door for him, but a hand on his shoulder stopped him. It was Azzam, looking determined, just like his name. Behind him, two of his men held down a pair of kneeling captives who Hamid recognized as petty dealers at the fringes of his organization. They were Nigerian, and sold his heroin to German addicts mostly out in the suburbs. Hamid did not remember their names.

They looked terrified.

"So?" Hamid said, indifferently.

"We caught them selling to the brothers," Azzam said. That was bad. The poison Hamid distributed was solely for the infidels. Their souls were already corrupted, so why not their bodies? But to corrupt the faithful?

Unforgiveable.

Hamid looked them over. One of them was silent, the other babbling in his native African tongue.

"Cut their throats," he said. "Right now. Leave their carcasses here, as a warning."

Azzam nodded and pulled a knife from his coat as Hamid got into the waiting car.

The small convoy drove west, out of the foreign enclave at the city center into a more neutral zone where ethnic Germans became common on the streets again. There were *polizei* too, all armed with G36 rifles, all looking skeptically at the Arabs in the expensive vehicles, but not interfering.

Gasthaus Leiber was inside a well-kept white old building on the *Verdistrasse* not far from the Schloss Blutenburg. The street was busy, but the *gasthaus* was closed, at least to the public. There were a half-dozen BMWs already there, and a bunch of hard-looking German men in civilian clothes doing a bad job of hiding who they were.

Hamid's vehicle pulled to the front and he stepped out. Two blonde heads were on the roof of the inn above him. Several more stood about in the garden out front of the restaurant. He leaned back inside the car and ordered "Wait," then shut the door.

Hamid walked toward the door, only to be halted by a severe-looking German holding up his hand. The agent was barely bothering to hide his contempt. Hamid smiled a little smile. Time was on his side.

The agent patted him down, and removed the SIG Sauer P226 Hamid carried under his shoulder as well as the large knife the Arab kept for unpleasant but necessary duties. The German gave a jerk of his head toward the door and Hamid went inside.

It was dark, but Hamid could see a long bar at the north wall and a dozen small tables with their napkins and utensils laid out neatly for the coming evening rush. The paneling was dark wood, evocative of a country hunting lodge, and the walls were decorated with paintings of various seventeenth century *jaegers* stalking elk, deer and boars with muskets and pikes. The dining room was entirely empty except for one portly German man with the red face of an exasperated Bavarian *burgermeister.* He had a blank manila envelope and a glass of Spaten *pils* in front of him, the latter no doubt a calculated insult. Hamid did not acknowledge it. He walked between the empty tables, pulled out his chair and sat.

"Herr Spetters," Hamid said in passable German. The chief of Department 6 of the *Bundesamt für Verfassungsschutz*, abbreviated "BfV," looked him over. It was the component Federal Office for the Protection of the Constitution responsible for domestic intelligence regarding Islamic terrorism in the Federal Republic of German.

"Herr al-Afridi. Always good to see you." Franz Spetters reached out, took his glass and drank a long swig, then put it back on the table. The better to show who was boss.

"Do you enjoy bringing me to a place like this?" Hamid asked. "Your dirty beer hall. Do you think it is wise to insult me, Herr Spetters?"

"I think it wise for you to realize whose country you are in."

Hamid laughed. "I know whose country I am in, Herr Spetters. And I think you do too. Do you have children?"

Anything like a smile vanished from the chief's face.

"Come, Herr Spetters. Children. Do you have any? You don't, do you? I have nine. Sons who will carry on my struggle. Who will carry on yours?"

"Don't over estimate your position, Herr al-Afridi. There are still more of us than there are of you."

"True, but the difference is that we do not fear you because we know how far we can push you. You love your quiet and your vacations to Mykonos and your pornography and your *pils*, but you won't fight for them, not if we don't push you too far. Not even those revanchists out in the countryside that you cannot control. They only fight when we go to them. You Germans fear us. That's why I am here. You fear me and mine and wish to continue our truce, our *hudna*."

Spetters knew that Arabic word – a truce, one intended to last just long enough for the *jihadi* to prepare to retake the offensive.

"Careful. You may be surprised what Germans are capable of."

"I would be surprised, Herr Spetters. Very surprised. You Germans, you believe in nothing – no God, no future, nothing but right now and your next beer to deaden your pain. So, yes, I would be very surprised if you found the strength, the will to resist."

"Enough of this."

"As you wish, Herr Spetters." Hamid smiled.

"The shipment is approved. The export license is issued and the goods will be allowed to be air-shipped to Washington," Spetters said, using the obsolete name for the former capital. He slid over the manila envelope. "The transportation documents are here. You must still make the payment or the factory will not ship the goods."

"I will. Money is not an issue."

"And whatever devilry you are up to, it stays in North America."

"You have kept your part of the bargain, and I shall keep mine. There will be no violence in Germany. You and your people are safe, for a while longer." Hamid smiled. "Who knows, Herr Spetters, perhaps before we raise the black flag of the caliphate in Berlin, and the Islamic State of Germany arises forever, you'll be long dead."

"It will be after I am dead," Spetters said.

"Oh, one way or the other that is true. You know, you should have stopped us when you could."

Spetters assessed the man across the table. He knew everything about the Arab, including his background as the scion of a family of Iraqi criminals who managed to always align themselves with the most brutal thugs of the era. Educated in the United States before the country broke apart a decade before, al-Afridi could speak several languages and move in any Western circle he chose, his familiarity with the West breeding a burning contempt.

What did he want with the equipment? Spetters had an inkling, but his duty was to Germany. The People's Republic, those socialist fools, they would have to solve their own problems. Allies, but not when push came to shove, and it had come to shove. Germany should had stood with the United States after America split apart over a decade before, he reflected. But its militancy and its rejection of European sensitivities had caused the European elite to bet on the weak horse instead.

He would do what he must for Germany. Still, the impertinence of this dirty foreigner gnawed at Spetters, and the secret policeman inside him wanted to see what more he could drag out of his opponent. It was time to provoke the Arab, and see what happened.

"Your brother Khalid – the Americans killed him in Baghdad, didn't they?" Spetters said conversationally.

It was Hamid's turn to go silent and cold.

"They called him 'The Accountant,' did they not?"

"Don't talk about my brother."

"Yes, I understand an American blew him apart with a shotgun during a raid. That is what happened, isn't it?"

"Don't talk about him!" Hamid pounded the table, then regained control.

"I did not mean to upset you. It's just that I came into some intelligence related to your family that you might be interested in."

Hamid stared coldly, forcing his anger down inside him. Of course, Spetters was studying him. If there was one thing Germans were, it was efficient secret policemen.

"I recently read the American after-action report on the raid." Spetters had gotten it from the People's Intelligence Agency's archives of old United States documents as part of his research into the man across the table.

Hamid said nothing.

"I thought you might be interested."

"Does it say who killed my brother?"

"Oh yes. Apparently, he's killed a lot of your people over the years."

"Tell me."

"I can't just tell you, Herr al-Afridi. That is not how our arrangement works. You give, I give."

"What do you want to know?"

"If I thought you were involved with the disappearances of the addicts and the vagrants, I would ask you about them. But that does not seem your style. So, I will take some information on some of your co-religionists."

Hamid pondered for a moment. "There is a cell near Stuttgart, in a town called Reutlingen. Not my people. But they are talking about taking to the streets with machetes."

"And you knew? You would have let that happen."

"You give, I give, Herr Spetters."

"Give me their names and addresses."

"You will have them tonight. Now give me what I want, Herr Spetters."

"All right," said the Department 6 chief. "He's American, and I am not sure which country because he is what they call 'off the grid,' but I know his name."

"And what is his name?"

"Kelly Turnbull."

4.

"No labels?"

Clay Deeds shook his head. Kelly Turnbull let the dark suit jacket fall closed. It draped perfectly over the Wilson X-TAC .45 automatic he carried on his brand-new belt.

"Sterile suit, and exactly my size. How did you know my size anyway?"

Deeds smiled. "I know all."

"Uh huh." Turnbull sat in the leather seat across the table from his handler. The twin engines of the Cessna Citation XII hummed. They'd been in the air for two hours.

The suit and the new holster had been waiting for him when he and Deeds had stepped aboard the jet as it idled at the Dallas airport's VIP terminal. Deeds had whisked him there straight from the diner. Turnbull had left Jeff the dog with Lorna the waitress. The ungrateful dog barely noticed he left.

The spymaster was not saying much as they flew south; he was nursing a sparkling water with a lime. Turnbull considered his situation. Since Deeds was giving him an untraceable suit and a holster, he figured whatever was going on, there was some non-insignificant chance that he would not be coming back.

"So, are you going to let me in on why we are heading to Mexico City?"

"You'll see."

"You know, there are probably still some people there holding a grudge."

"Not many," Deeds replied. "You guys saw to that."

Turnbull shrugged. After the Split, some foreigners did not fully grasp that the new United States was a considerably different animal than the old one after having shed the influence of the progressive blue states. Sort of like a kitten is different than a tiger.

When it became clear the new USA was serious about border protection and stopping drug trafficking, the cartels started getting desperate. One up-and-coming mob, *Los Matadores*, had been making its reputation by surpassing even its brutal competitors in their level of violence. Their initial debut had been slaughtering a busload of schoolchildren to ensure they got the daughter of one rare honest Mexican prosecutor. And they did it on videotape.

In 2026, they decided to grab a US DEA agent off the streets of Mexico City and videotaped themselves torturing him to death, then released it on the internet as a message about who was boss. But red America decided to send a message of its own.

The USA decided to very publicly eliminate every identified member of *Los Matadores* within one 24-hour period, and it did. All 77 of them. Some got droned. Some found a surprise, ticking package in their daily FedEx delivery. In one case, a B-2 dropped 20 Joint Direct Attack Munitions – Mark 82 500-pound bombs – on the ranch that was their main headquarters. It was flattened. And a number of the head honchos who lived in luxury in Mexico City ended their time in this mortal coil looking down the barrel of Kelly Turnbull's or one of his team's modified M4s.

The cartels got *that* message. The Mexican government was outraged, but nobody targeted red America's cops again.

The pilot's voice came over the intercom. "We'll be landing at Benito Juarez International in under an hour."

"From this suit, I'm guessing I'm your close security," Turnbull said.

"Oh no," Deeds said. "We've got plenty of security. You, Kelly, are the guest of honor."

Kelly paused, awaiting elaboration. Nothing. He shrugged. Deeds just smiled.

"Well, since you aren't going to tell me anything, I'm going to sleep." Turnbull said. He shut his eyes.

"We're almost there," Deeds replied.

Turnbull did not open his eyes. "Like they taught me in Ranger School, if you aren't eating or shooting or shitting, you should be sleeping."

Bright sunlight and hot air flooded the cabin as the door opened. There were three black SUVs waiting for them at the foot of the stairs. What was it with spooks and their black SUVs?

Turnbull's left hand felt for the magazine holders on his waist. He had three holding extended eight-round mags, plus one magazine in the gun and one round in the pipe. Thirty-three rounds. For most people, that would be plenty, he thought. Then he noted, glumly, that history had demonstrated that he was not most people.

They came down the stairs and were greeted by an agent in a dark suit. Turnbull recognized him as Jason Clarke – a good, solid guy. They shook hands. Turnbull noted that under his jacket was hanging a small Heckler & Koch MP7A3 submachine gun with a close combat optic. The other half-dozen guys were probably packing the same.

It was highly illegal to do that in Mexico – his own M1911A1 could probably get him half-a decade in some Mexican jail. But these guys did not seem concerned. Such was the heat that Clay Deeds wielded.

Turnbull also noted who was not there to greet them – Mexican customs.

Clarke took charge. "We got a straight shot into town and the meet location is secure," Clarke said as they entered the back seat of the middle vehicle. Turnbull scooted over to behind the driver and began running through his actions on an ambush. Deeds was in the middle, and Clarke behind the front passenger.

The SUV started moving the instant Clarke pulled the door shut.

"Are they on the ground yet?" Deeds asked.

"That one. Unmarked." Clarke nodded to the right; outside the window was a white jet – probably some model of Bombardier. There was security around it. It disappeared behind them as the small convoy drove past, left the tarmac and pulled onto the road into Mexico City.

The air was cleaner than Turnbull remembered it. Eight years ago, the sky had been a dense brown soup that hung over the city and gave it a weird, yellowish glow. But it was clear today. The clouds were a puffy white and the sun was still up as it neared 6 p.m. Perhaps the winds had just driven the smog away, or perhaps the pollution control campaign was working. Mexico City was determined to become a truly world class city, especially since Los Angeles and the whole People's Republic of North America were in decline.

"A lot more signs in English than I remember," Turnbull observed.

"We're passing through *LA Sur*," Clarke said. "Los Angeles South. It's where the illegals live. They get smugglers to get them over or under *la Pared Grande*, the Big Wall, and they end up here, if they aren't out in the country picking crops. There are at least a million PR illegals here, maybe two. The People's Republic doesn't cooperate with the Mexican government on immigration by accepting deportees back – it likes having a safety valve to the south – and the Mexicans are pretty pissed off about it."

"Someone has to do the jobs Mexicans won't do," Deeds observed. "I guess President Trump was right. There's a big, beautiful wall, and the Mexicans paid for it."

They left the slums and headed into the more fashionable part of town. Many of the buildings were new, and there was less of the grime than he remembered. People were well-dressed and most of the cars were relatively new. The city was quite a contrast to the Los Angeles Turnbull had barely escaped from months before.

It was about seven, still early for the locals, when they pulled onto a street of low two and three-story buildings in what was clearly an entertainment district, and then came to a stop in front of a restaurant with a bright neon sign.

"Lou's All-American Café?" asked Turnbull. "We flew to Mexico City for American food?"

"Fanciest American food in town," Clarke said. "Got four stars. The chef is kind of a celebrity. He's from Austin…"

"Okay," said Turnbull. "I get it. But isn't this a little…public?"

"Public means less chance of trouble," Deeds said. "You'll understand."

"Right," Turnbull replied, giving up.

Clarke was out the door and on the sidewalk. Turnbull could see some of the other security guys fanning out and heading inside.

Deeds stepped out onto the sidewalk then turned around to face Turnbull. "I need to ask you to do something," he said.

Turnbull shrugged.

"I need you to promise not to shoot anyone."

Turnbull paused. "I can't make that promise."

"No, really. Don't start anything. Can you not start anything?"

"Well, if someone else starts something, can I finish it?"

"Oh, I insist you do," replied Deeds.

"Okay, then I won't *start* the shooting."

"Come on."

Clarke, Deeds, and Turnbull entered the restaurant and the *maître de*, clearly American, greeted them effusively and led them to the back. It was early and there were few diners yet, so perhaps a quarter of the tables were full. It was mostly Mexicans on dates being served by a wait staff that consisted largely of blonde-haired surfer dudes and dudettes of the kind that one might have found hanging around the Hermosa Beach Pier back before the Split.

There were three others though, harder men, sitting alone and eyeing the trio. Security for someone. Was that a MAC-10 under one of their coats? Old school.

The room was rectangular straight back – he would have a good view of the whole place up to the front door, which he liked. The back wall on the left was a swinging kitchen double door and on the right a stairway heading upstairs, dark, so that was probably a storage or office space, and at the table to their front...

Turnbull stopped, and his hand went to his .45.

"You," he said to the man at the table in front of them.

Deeds made the unnecessary introduction. "Kelly Turnbull, I believe you have met the new Director of the People's Bureau of Investigation, Martin Rios-Parkinson."

The three were sitting at the table with Rios-Parkinson and his head of security, Rollins. Turnbull was staring, silent, as Deeds made small talk. Rios-Parkinson was smirking.

"I obtained Kelly's promise not to shoot you before we came in," Deeds said. "So perhaps we can all relax."

"The last occasion we interacted, your man there was attempting to shoot me in the back," Rios-Parkinson said, taking a sip of red wine.

"That's because you were running away," Turnbull said.

A blonde man in his twenties approached nervously. "Are you ready to order?" he asked.

"Are you from the People's Republic?" Turnbull asked. "Like from Manhattan Beach or a place like that?"

"Uh, no," said the waiter, visibly uncomfortable. "*Yo soy de Mexico.*" He pronounced the "x" as "x."

"Great country you have there, Director. People can't wait to get out of it," Turnbull said.

"Give us a moment," Deeds said to the relieved waiter. He left, grateful.

"Gentlemen, there is no sense in refighting old battles," Deeds said. "We have a bigger battle ahead of us, and we need to fight it together. And if we lose, we all die."

"As long as he dies," Turnbull said, still staring.

"You want to try..." began Rollins, but Rios-Parkinson interrupted.

"It is all right, Inspector Rollins. The man is an animal."

"Should Rollins be here?" asked Deeds.

"He knows the situation. And he knows that I have been forced by circumstances to work with you…informally…over the last several months. He is loyal to me."

"But not everyone is loyal to you in the People's Republic government, are they?" asked Deeds. "Someone alerted them that we were coming to take Dr. Maksimov away. They whisked him off and left an ambush behind. Someone on your end is working with them."

"So, three of my men are dead thanks to your screw-up?" Turnbull said.

"Yet you survived. How fortunate for us all," Rios-Parkinson said, taking another sip.

"I really want to shoot this guy, Clay."

"No shooting, Kelly. You see, whoever is working with the terrorists is the key to finding the terrorists. And that means we need to work with Director Rios-Parkinson. The answer is somewhere inside the People's Republic."

"Then the Director maybe ought to direct his people to go find the traitor," Turnbull said.

"Unfortunately," said Rios-Parkinson. "Except for Rollins, there is not a single person I can trust in my government. And there are things happening that take precedence."

"Over Marburg X?" Turnbull asked.

"Yes," said Rios-Parkinson.

"Do you know what it does? Because I do. I saw it. I *had* it."

Rios-Parkinson looked to Deeds skeptically. Deeds nodded.

"He barely survived."

"Is he immune?" Rios-Parkinson asked.

"We don't know for sure," Deeds said.

"Well, then he really is the perfect candidate, as much as I dislike the idea."

Turnbull looked from one to the other. "Candidate for what?'

"Kelly, I need you to go back. I need you to go with Director Rios-Parkinson and help him locate these terrorists and stop them."

"You see…," began Rios-Parkinson.

"Shut up," snapped Turnbull. He turned back to Deeds. "You want me to go back in and help this guy?"

"Yes," Deeds said. "Ironically, you are the only one he can trust. Rollins excluded."

"Well, the hell with that."

"You see, I told you he was an animal," Rios-Parkinson said. But Turnbull ignored him. He was focused on something much more pressing than petty jibes.

There were eight salty-looking Mexican men coming into the restaurant, and they were not dressed for dinner.

"Clay, get on the floor," Turnbull said, reaching to his side and gripping his pistol. To his right, Clarke was drawing out his MP7A1.

Rollins reached into his coat.

The men were running now, reaching into their trench coats.

The other security men, both from the People's Republic and the United States were rising and drawing.

Turnbull saw the AK first.

"Gun!" he shouted as he drew his Wilson X-TAC .45.

Two PBI security men barely got their MAC-10s out before they were cut down by AK-47 fire from the attackers. Another American security man was hit and fell back over the table.

Turnbull marked his target, the one at the front of the pack, and fired twice fast into his chest. The guy staggered – there was probably body armor under his coat. Turnbull lifted the barrel slightly and shot the man in the face.

The .45 hollow point ruined his dental work and his day.

All the security men were firing now. Clarke was firing to his right, but to his left, nothing. No firing. Turnbull turned his head to see if Rollins was dead.

No, he was very much alive.

Rollins shot Clay Deeds, then turned and pointed his Beretta at a terrified Rios-Parkinson, who had gone to the floor.

Turnbull fired first and kept shooting. Rollins had no vest. The six hollow point rounds started by wrecking his solar plexus and worked their way up. The last one took off the back of his head.

"Clay!" Turnbull said, dropping the mag and slamming another home. Clarke was firing another burst to his right.

"I'm okay," Deeds said. Abdominal wound. The spymaster fell to the floor, breathing hard.

Turnbull took aim at another shooter, who had dropped behind a table for concealment. But concealment only works if no one knows you are behind it, and the thin wood was not enough to stop three .45 rounds. The dead killer fell into the aisle, where terrified, fleeing diners tried to avoid stepping in the expanding pool of his blood.

Clarke and the other guards were shooting it out with the surviving gunmen, but it was looking bad. Four more entered the restaurant through the front door.

"Get him out," Deeds said, gasping.

"I'm getting *you* out, Clay."

"No!" Deeds said. "You have to get him out. You have to go with him."

Turnbull looked over at the petrified Rios-Parkinson, cowering on the floor.

"Go," Deeds said, blood between his teeth. "Clarke can take care of me. But you have to do this. You are the only one who can do this." He half-smiled. "Go on, Broadsword."

"Shit," hissed Turnbull. Another gunman was advancing at ten o'clock, spraying with an AK. The rounds shredded the table and the glassware. Then the gun ran dry. Turnbull stood up and casually shot him in the forehead, then looked down at Rios-Parkinson.

"Get up."

Rios-Parkinson, panicked, did nothing.

"Get your ass up!" Turnbull shouted, reaching down and pulling the man to his feet.

"Go!" Deeds moaned. Clarke was still firing controlled bursts at the attackers.

Turnbull dragged the director toward the kitchen doors, weapon up and ahead, but the doors swung outward and revealed two more gunmen, *sicarios* in their mid-twenties, one with an AK-47 and another with a Remington 870 pump. Turnbull saw them first and opened up. Both went down with holes in their faces. The slide locked back and Turnbull dropped the empty mag as several rifle rounds tore into the wood of the back wall behind them.

"The stairs!" Turnbull shouted as he pushed Rios-Parkinson ahead of him toward the dark stairwell and up toward the second floor. The plaster wall on the far side erupted in little explosions as bullet strikes followed them up.

At the top, Turnbull pushed Rios-Parkinson down the hall and took a position at the top of the stairway, back against the wall. There was no exit, except for a roof access hatch in the ceiling with a padlock on it and an ancient metal ladder bolted to the wall.

"We are outgunned! What are you going to do with just a pistol?" The Director whimpered.

"What you're supposed to do with a pistol. I'm going to use it to fight my way to a long gun." He slipped in a mag, snapped the slide closed and took aim at the top of the stairs at head level.

There were footsteps on the stairs coming fast, multiple targets. The first thug – he had an AK – turned the corner and Turnbull grabbed him by the collar and held on. The second one had a Mossberg 500 with a pistol grip, and the confusion ahead of him led him to empty a shell of double-aught into his buddy's back. Turnbull pushed the dying man back onto his frenemy then shot the shotgunner in the throat.

They collapsed in a heap, and Turnbull knelt to pick up both the AK and the shotgun.

"Hold this," he said, tossing the 12-gauge to Rios-Parkinson and holstering his .45. Then he checked to ensure the AK was on auto fire, swung it around the corner, and blindly emptied the entire mag of 7.62 mm rounds down the stairwell. The howls and moans that followed indicated that he had scored.

Turnbull dropped the rifle, turned back, and said "Give me the…"

Rios-Parkinson was pointing the shotgun at his face, shaking.

"Are you going to shoot me, or what?" Turnbull shouted. They stood like that for a breath or two. Then he grabbed the weapon out of Rios-Parkinson's hand, pumped it, and aimed it upwards.

The roar made Rios-Parkinson cringe. Not quite there, Turnbull noted through the debris. He fired again. This time, the padlock holding the roof access hatch closed was gone.

"Up!" Turnbull shouted, and Rios-Parkinson began to climb the rickety metal ladder. He got to the top and pushed it open. It was night; you could see stars. Turnbull began to climb. He saw movement at the top of the stairs and let loose a blast of buckshot. That wrecked someone's evening.

On the roof, he pumped the shotgun and they began to run, crossing from building to building until they reached the end of the block. Sirens were wailing now, and the gunfire had stopped. What that meant for Deeds and Clarke he could not know, and there was no time to think about it.

"Down," he ordered, pointing to a ladder. They had to drop the last 10 feet to the sidewalk, and it was a wonder neither shattered his ankle.

They were in an alley next to a relatively busy street. The *federales* had not yet set up a perimeter. Turnbull tossed the shotgun into a dumpster and they stepped out onto the street.

"Taxi!" he shouted, and it pulled over. A lucky break – between Uber, Lyft, AutoCar, GoogleCar, WeDriveU, CarFetish and a dozen other ride sharing apps, traditional taxis were almost an anachronism.

"*Aeropuerto, por favor*," Turnbull said, pulling the door shut behind him.

"So, like, you guys want to go to the airport, right?" asked the driver, a young blonde woman with a Valley Girl accent.

"*Sí*, take us to *el airport*."

Rios-Parkinson mixed his Manhattan at the bar of the Director's jet himself, since all his minions were lying under white sheets at Lou's All-American Café. He turned to return to his seat but Turnbull was there and Turnbull's fist was headed toward his jaw.

He landed on his ass, his drink going everywhere.

"What the hell was that for?" Rios-Parkinson shouted.

"I'm not sure," Turnbull said. "Maybe for getting my friend shot. Maybe just because you're an asshole. Or maybe because you pointed a gun at me."

Rios-Parkinson rubbed his jaw.

"I did not shoot you," he said.

"Thanks," Turnbull said. "But we both know you wanted to. See, you don't know if Clay is dead or not. If he isn't dead, and finds out I'm dead and thinks you had a hand in it, then maybe he tells your people you've been a US spy and that won't end well, will it?"

Rios-Parkinson laughed a strange, sick laugh that one could just barely hear over the roar of the engines.

"But then, the converse applies too, Turnbull," he said. "I figure he kept an intelligence coup like me his own personal secret. So, if I find out Clay Deeds *is* dead, then I am free to put you out of my misery."

He kept laughing, pleased with himself, until Turnbull squatted down in front of him.

"Maybe," Turnbull said. "But one thing is absolutely certain. If you ever point a gun at me again, I'm going to blow your head off."

Then Turnbull went back to his seat and tried to fall asleep.

5.

It certainly was not Reagan-National Airport anymore. In fact, it was barely even an airport anymore.

The jet had come in low from the south, descending over the brown, choppy Potomac. Their flight time was almost nine hours instead of the six it would have been if they had flown directly from Mexico City – the plane had to avoid United States airspace and took a wide swing around the tip of Florida, then north up over the Atlantic until it could cut inland above the international border that now ran along the old Virginia-North Carolina state line.

Turnbull, peering out through the porthole during the descent, had expected to see more farms, but southern Virginia looked almost deserted. Then he remembered a mission briefing where the briefer mentioned how the region had been forcibly depopulated of "unreliables" years before. The People's Republic did not want another Indian Country problem arising in the old Confederacy.

Unfortunately, it was the politically unreliable type of people who were willing to do the kind of work that made the land productive. The people the new government had moved into the confiscated farms tired of agriculture after about an hour of labor, and now they mostly just sat in decaying farmhouses collecting their welfare payments and watching government television while the fields lay fallow.

The jet made its final approach over the northern Virginia region south of the old capital – no one called it "Washington" anymore because the Father of the Former Country both owned slaves and had a penis, and these disqualified him from being remembered. And "District of Columbia" was obviously a non-starter. So, since all the suggested alternatives were likewise disqualified, the People's Republic of North America government re-named it "Capital City." Then it moved the capital to New York City.

Capital City looked tired and dirty even from 5,000 feet.

Turnbull was groggy, the adrenaline from the firefight having dissipated and been replaced with an all-encompassing fatigue. He had only slept a little, though he tried his best to get some rest. Rios-Parkinson had solved the problem by gobbling some pills and washing them down with a tumbler of Glenlivet. The label said it was bottled in 2008; nothing but the best for him. The People's Bureau of Investigation's director passed out over the Gulf of Mexico and Turnbull had to kick his seat to wake him up after the pilot announced their descent. Rios-Parkinson just snored.

The runway came into view as the plane descended further. Along the east side of the airport, now named for the People's Republic's first "Minister of Restorative Justice," Maxine Waters, were several large, grassy expanses that abutted the river. These were junkyards packed with several dozen rusting aircraft, mostly old 737s and 777s in government airline livery that had stopped working and that no one had bothered to either fix or haul away.

Turnbull remembered the statue of a jolly Ronald Reagan that used to greet people driving in toward the passenger terminals. It had lasted about a month after the Split. The ink had not even dried on the Treaty of St. Louis dividing the old United States in two when a mob appeared to spontaneously pull down the now-hated symbol of "oppression, cisnormativity, and racism." That the two government news networks, CNN and MSNBC, happened to be there with cameras set up to broadcast this unplanned event was pure chance.

The jet touched down and rocked viciously enough to finally jolt Rios-Parkinson out of his slumber. It was not the pilot's fault –

even from the small porthole Turnbull could see that the runway was deteriorating from lack of maintenance. The terminal buildings in the distance were falling apart, and about one glass window pane in three had been replaced with black plastic sheeting. A faded banner hung limply across the wall facing the runway: "The Peoples Republic Welcomes You To Justice. Tolerating Intolerance Is A Crime."

But then, no one really used the terminals anymore. Commercial traffic, for those with the juice to secure permission to fly, now all departed out of what used to be Dulles International. Dulles had a new name too – Diversity International, which also had the benefit of not making everyone change its International Air Transport Association code, "IAD."

Waters Airport was reserved for the use of government officials and select individuals. As head of the People's Bureau of Investigation for the People's Republic of North America, Martin Rios-Parkinson qualified.

They stepped down the ladder onto the tarmac, Turnbull eyeing the three older-model black Toyota SUVs waiting to pick up their boss. Several plainclothes goons provided security. Others were getting luggage. A man in a suit wearing too much black eyeliner approached, gave Turnbull the once over, and then faced Rios-Parkinson.

"Director, we have what you asked for in the vehicle," he said. "Are you all right?" The agent looked around for the rest of the team.

"I am fine, Inspector Cooley. The others are dead. We will find out who tried to assassinate me."

"We will," Cooley replied. Then he looked again at Turnbull.

"Xe is now assigned to me," Rios-Parkinson said. "Xe is my special assistant. You do what xe asks. Do you understand, Inspector Cooley?"

It took Turnbull a second to realize that he was "xe."

The man nodded, turned and led them to the middle SUV. Rios-Parkinson and Turnbull climbed into the back and Cooley leaned his head inside.

"We cannot go directly. The route is insecure. Looters and malcontents. We are calling in military support to suppress it."

"Harshness, Inspector. These are traitors. Treat them accordingly."

Cooley nodded and closed the door behind them. Rios-Parkinson reached forward and toggled the switch raising the black privacy glass between the front and rear seats.

"Xe?" asked Turnbull.

Rios-Parkinson reached forward and plucked a manila envelope out of the seat pocket in front of him, then passed it to Turnbull.

"Your pronouns are "xe," "xis" and…I forget. "Xoot," maybe." The Director smiled. "It's all in there."

The SUV started moving. The engine made a weird noise, like the alternator belt was too loose, and the leather seats were cracked. It smelled moldy. This was the PBI Director's ride? This was the best they had?

Turnbull opened the sealed envelope and sorted through his new documents – ID card, passport, ration cards, and a write-up of his background story.

"Our perhaps deceased mutual friend Clay Deeds expected that you would be coming along, though likely not under these conditions. He forwarded me your biometric data and I had a new identity created for you. You are now PBI Inspector Oliver Arnold Warren, originally from Los Angeles, since you know that location so well, and you identify as 'non-binary.'"

"Non-binary?"

"Non-binary. You have no gender identity. Or maybe all of them. I am not sure." Rios-Parkinson smiled again, and the smile grew larger as he saw Turnbull's scowl. "I could not very well list you as a cis-het. A heterosexual male would draw too much unwanted attention, and you will have enough coming out of nowhere to be my special assistant."

Turnbull examined the identification card. It was his picture, and his new name. The birthdate was a month off. There was a long list of digits, his Individual Identity Number. He'd have to memorize that. And, sure enough, his "Identity" category read, "Non-Binary (Versatile)."

"Look on the bright side, Oliver," Rios-Parkinson said. "'Versatile' means you have unlimited options."

"I'm not happy about 'Oliver' either. Only assholes are named 'Oliver.'"

"I know," Rios-Parkinson replied.

Turnbull noted that his ID card also listed his Privilege Level, 9. That was very privileged indeed. Rios-Parkinson saw what he was contemplating and spoke.

"If asked, attribute it partly to your gender identity and partly to your Native American heritage."

"That explains my new last name." Elizabeth Warren had been the PRNA's first American Indian president.

"And you are Muslim and differently abled for good measure."

"Oh. I assume non-practicing."

"Think of it not as a faith but as a useful affectation."

"So, what's my handicap?"

"We do not say 'handicap' here," said Rios-Parkinson. "I believe the term is now 'challenge overcome.' I think."

"Okay, what challenge did I overcome?"

"I did not select one for you. Make one up, but it should be mental and not physical. That gives you more flexibility to tailor it to your advantage."

Turnbull examined the cell phone. He did not recognize the brand.

"My number is loaded," said Rios-Parkinson.

"And you can track me with it," replied Turnbull.

"Of course," Rios-Parkinson said. "Every minute. Oh, and don't forget your social media profiles. The accounts are in your phone already."

"Social media?"

"Caring Community, which used to be called 'Facebook,' except that term was replaced because 'book' insults the alternatively literate and because not everyone has a face. Also, Twitter."

"Twitter is for idiots," hissed Turnbull.

"Twitter is *mandatory*. Just retweet whatever my assistant tweets on my behalf. The key to your apartment is there too. It is near the headquarters. The area is inside the Control Zone with a wall. It is mostly secure. Do not wander."

The SUV jolted as it hit a pothole near the airport exit. There was tight security around the perimeter and the little convoy was waved out of the gate and onto the road. They went fast because the Washington metro traffic Turnbull remembered from visiting before the Split was entirely absent. It was now all smoky buses for the masses and a few black cars for the elite.

"I have a mag plus change left. I'll need bullets," Turnbull said as they blew through a red light. They had not slowed at any other intersection either, but with those the lights were mostly out.

"I am sure you will," Rios-Parkinson replied. "You can go to the armory and get what you want once we get to headquarters. No one will challenge you if you are acting as my assistant. But you still need to be careful."

"You think they will try to kill you again?"

"Besides the obvious," Rios-Parkinson replied, frustrated. "I mean with how you behave. You need to not draw attention to yourself. You need to watch what you say. You need to watch what you do. And if I thought it might ever happen, I would say that you would need to watch what you think. Your racism, sexism, fatphobia, and your general hate criminality make you vulnerable."

"So, you want me to play along with your politically correct bullshit?"

"It is not bullshit. You may consider it all a joke in your racist country, but here it is literally life and death. Intersectionality and social justice are how power is accumulated and exercised here, regardless of what you think of it. I can surround myself with thugs like you to protect myself from bullets, but if someone were to make an accusation against me of bias or a hate crime or adherence to the patriarchal power paradigm, that becomes a weapon in the hands of my enemies that I might not be able to defend against."

"I think it's stupid and fascist."

"And what you think is irrelevant. In this world, it is the currency of power. It is how I got here."

"So, get woke or get killed?"

"No one says 'woke' anymore, but yes."

The convoy was heading past Alexandria, which had a decade before been fashionable but was now overrun with derelicts and bitter, bored residents. One tossed a rock that bounced off the lead vehicle.

"You guys are sure popular with the folks," Turnbull observed. He peered out the window at a wall where someone had spray-painted a thin, sharp-featured face and the words "Larry O'Connor Lives!"

"The Peoples Security Forces are getting lax – the PSF Hate Speech unit should have covered that over immediately," snarled Rios-Parkinson, staring at the graffiti. O'Connor had once been the top drive time host in the DC area, until the Split happened and he soon after had to flee to Texas one step ahead of the not-so-secret police. He continued to do his show in Dallas, and the US government helpfully broadcast it into the blue as part of the daily line-up on Radio Free America. You could get five years in a reeducation camp if you were caught listening.

The convoy turned down a side street to avoid a sullen crowd that had gathered around a community feeding site, and it slowed to a crawl, then stopped. The faces lining the sidewalk were distinctly unfriendly, and Turnbull's adrenaline kicked in again. He put his black Wilson.45 on his lap and Rios-Parkinson pounded on the glass divider and shouted, "Get moving!" to the driver.

More faces lining the street, thin and drawn. Angry Faces. Hanging back, for now.

The SUV ahead of them was stopped. No brake lights either. Just stopped.

"Fifteen rounds," Turnbull thought, looking at his pistol. A crash echoed from their front. Someone threw a tire iron at the windshield.

"Go!" shrieked Rios-Parkinson, pounding again on the glass. "Why are they not going?"

The crowd was growing. The original half-dozen had swollen to at least two dozen in under a minute.

"Your boys need to hit the gas," Turnbull said.

Rios-Parkinson pounded on the glass partition again. Through the panel, Turnbull could see the security man in the passenger seat talking into the radio microphone.

The convoy did not move.

"Stay here," Turnbull said.

"Wait!" Rios-Parkinson began.

"If we don't get moving they are going to tear us apart. I'm going to apply some boot to ass."

Turnbull opened the door and stepped out into the street, handgun hanging low in his right hand. The crowd was mostly young, very thin, and all angry. They were bored and hungry men and women in dirty clothes and apparently with not much to lose.

"Hey bitch, this is my street!" shouted one in a faded T-shirt celebrating the 2027 People's Republic Best Picture winner *Titanic 2*. It depicted a gender indeterminate person on the bow of a ship, fist pumping, and read "I'm the Queen of the World!"

Turnbull ignored him and walked forward to the stalled lead SUV. T-shirt Man sputtered in fury at being disrespected like that, and took a few steps forward, then halted three feet away from his quarry. Turnbull's .45 loomed in his face.

"Sir, you need to step back," Turnbull said politely. The crowd went silent. T-shirt Man swallowed and complied. That hand cannon was not like anything he had seen in the paws of the few People's Security Force cops who occasionally ventured around there.

"Thank you," Turnbull said, lowering the pistol and turning toward the passenger door of the first vehicle.

He tapped on the glass and Cooley, his eyeliner smudged, opened it a crack.

"Why are you stopped?"

"Gas," Cooley said.

"Gas what?"

"We're out."

"You're kidding." It was clear Cooley wasn't. "Okay, get your men out –"

"They aren't all men –"

"Get your men out of that vehicle! I want two each in the other SUVs. Bring your weapons but you tell them that no one shoots unless I do. Do it now!"

Turnbull turned back to the crowd, grateful no one had tried to clobber him while his back was turned. The crowd was still trying to figure him out, but eventually one of these guys was going to test him again. That was the nature of mobs.

The four doors of the SUV flew open and four agents in suits spilled out, their AKs in hand. They were terrified, and if Turnbull could smell their fear then the mob could too.

"Move!" hissed Turnbull, pushing Cooley toward the remaining vehicles. The agents broke into a run, a bad move. The crowd surged, and Cooley tripped and fell, his AK slipping out of his grasp and sliding along the sidewalk.

"Get up!" Turnbull shouted, pulling Cooley to his feet then leaping forward.

The weapon slid to a stop right in front of T-shirt Man. The crowd shouted and cheered.

His eyes met Turnbull's and they locked.

Turnbull knew there was no way in hell this guy could not pick it up with all the attention, but Turnbull tried anyway.

"Don't."

The .45 looked smaller ten feet away, small enough that T-shirt man could rationalize that it was a good idea to pick up the gun.

He got his hand on the barrel when his kneecap exploded in a pink and white spray out the back. He fell over, clutching the shattered joint and screaming. The crowd pulled back and Turnbull stepped forward and picked up the rifle by the sling. It was old and beaten-up – it had obviously not been cleaned in a while – but it could have still ruined their day in the hands of this mob.

The agents were piling into the SUVs as Turnbull walked backwards, the assault rifle up, the selector switch toggled to full auto. T-shirt Man was rolling around on the sidewalk howling. The crowd was debating what to do, so as Turnbull slid inside the vehicle he gave them something to think about. He fired a long automatic burst over their heads, causing the mob to hit the cement.

"Go around! Punch it!" he shouted, slamming the door and pressing in close with Rios-Parkinson, Cooley, and another security man, who was actually a woman – or appeared to be. Evidently Turnbull's voice was loud enough to be heard through the partition because the SUV roared to life and the crowd scattered as the convoy tore past.

Cooley was nursing a scraped knee – there was a chunk missing from his slacks. Turnbull removed the mag, ejected the chambered round, and handed him the rifle.

"Inspector Warren is my head of security now," Rios-Parkinson said. Cooley said nothing.

"It's about to explode out there," Turnbull said, ignoring the two new guests.

"It is under control," Rios-Parkinson said.

"What happens when you add Wildfire to that?" Turnbull said. Cooley looked confused, and Rios-Parkinson glared.

The two SUVs were hauling now. There would be no question of stopping. They got on the freeway, which was nearly empty except for a few PSF patrol cars keeping watch, and Turnbull stared out to the left.

"The Pentagon?" he said, but he was not quite sure.

"It's now people's free housing," Rios-Parkinson said. For the benefit of the new passengers, he explained: "Inspector Warren is from Los Angeles."

The huge building was covered top to bottom with graffiti. Even from the road it was clear most of the windows were broken, and smoke from what were probably cooking fires wafted out of many of them. The massive parking lots surrounding it were now shantytowns.

"No one goes in there," Cooley said. "It's not safe. I worked it before we stopped patrolling it. The gangs run it."

"Gangs?" Rios-Parkinson said. "Inspector Cooley, 'gangs' is a racist term applied to organic collections of oppressed individuals banding together to defend their rights against a heteronormative white supremacy paradigm."

Cooley swallowed. "Sorry, Director. I am still fighting residual racist programming from my upbringing. It is a constant struggle to validate my allyship."

"This guy forgets to fill his tank before he picks you up and you're pissed off that he called gangs 'gangs'?" said Turnbull.

Cooley's black-lined eyes were wide with horror. No one spoke to the Director that way.

"Inspector Warren," Rios-Parkinson said. "We will discuss this issue once we reach headquarters."

The tiny convoy drove on. The Pentagon receded and a large pile of steaming garbage came into view. It was the new city dump; shapes crawled over the piles, foraging for what could be salvaged. At the summit of the hill beyond it were some abandoned ruins. Turnbull knew it immediately – Arlington. He took a deep breath and held his tongue.

They headed into the city, passing the checkpoints at the bridge and into the Control Zone. This was the walled off area of the city containing the Mall and the many governmental buildings that still remained in DC simply because there was no room for all the agencies, departments, and ministries to fit in Manhattan after President DeBlasio moved the capital to New York City several years before.

The old Hoover Building had housed the Federal Bureau of Investigation before the Split, but the FBI was long gone. The People's Bureau of Investigation now occupied that building and several others in the area, forming a huge complex dedicated to the dark work of internal security. The name "Hoover" had been scrubbed from the building and whitewashed from history when the People's Republic had first arisen, but later came back when J. Edgar had been embraced as a pioneering example of resistance and the face of the toll oppression had taken upon gender-fluid individuals in the hateful old United States. His statue, in a flattering cocktail dress and a pair of strappy heels, graced the central foyer of the recently added annex.

The PBI complex was itself further isolated by another perimeter wall within the Control Zone wall that blocked off much of the old capital. The guards, all with AK-47s, waved the convoy through, and the vehicles pulled into the underground garage and up to a bank of elevators. Two of the three had handwritten signs that read "Out of Order" or "Brokin."

As Turnbull stepped out, Cooley reached for his shoulder. Turnbull overcame his instinct to strike – this was not an attack.

"Thank you for helping me," he said.

Turnbull grunted.

"The gas gauge was broken. I told the driver to make sure it was full. She probably just forgot to. But then she's Privilege 8 and what the hell can I do, right?"

Turnbull shrugged.

"What were your pronouns again, Inspector Warren?"

Turnbull just walked toward the elevator.

6.

The Director's office was on the seventh floor; the entire sixth floor, which had been devoted to operations in the past, was devoted entirely to the various departments and sections devoted to stamping out the hatred and oppression that festered within the People's Bureau of Investigation itself. The other floors were devoted to stamping out the hatred and oppression that festered within the People's Republic of North America as a whole.

"Do you do actual crime crime anymore?" Kelly Turnbull asked as they approached Martin Rios-Parkinson's expansive and walnut-lined office.

The Director ignored him and turned to his assistant, who sat at a desk in the antechamber outside the double doors. A young woman sat in one of the chairs set against the wall.

"Swept?" he demanded.

The assistant had Blue Hair and a large metallic nose ring. "Yes, Director, fifteen minutes ago."

Rios-Parkinson went inside, with Turnbull following. Blue Hair eyeballed him hard.

"Shut the door," the Director directed.

"So, what do I do?" Turnbull said, pulling the heavy wooden doors closed behind him. "I assume you and Clay had a plan for what I was actually going to do when I got here."

"You are going to follow leads for me. Things I cannot have my own people do."

"Your own people set you up. You might want to do a personal inventory on your leadership style, Niedermeyer."

The reference went over Rios-Parkinson's head.

"You need assistance," the Director said. He walked behind his desk and punched the intercom button. "Send Carter in here."

"Doing what?"

"Navigating this building and this city. I know you have been in the People's Republic many times. I know you can neutralize physical threats. But this is different. You need to avoid drawing unnecessary attention to yourself because it will draw unnecessary attention to *me.*"

There was a faint knock on the doors.

"Enter!" shouted the Director.

It was the woman who had been sitting outside. She was in her mid-twenties, in a suit, though like the clothes of most of the agents he had seen it looked like it was a grade below off the rack – perhaps off the linoleum beneath the rack. She was pretty, but she was trying to downplay it by pulling her hair back. Her face was fixed with a stern expression, like she had bit into a lemon. Turnbull assessed her as very nervous, but also very excited to be called up to see the director. Ambitious? A striver?

She ignored Turnbull, who stood off to her right, and stopped in front of the desk, coming to something like the position of attention.

"Inspector Junior Grade Kristina Carter," she announced a bit too loudly. "My pronouns are 'she' and 'her'."

"Inspector Carter, you graduated from Princeton, majoring in the literature of colonial dismantlement, and joined the Bureau a year ago. You have an excellent record in Social Media Operations and Internet Oversight."

"Thank you, Director."

"You located those Christian extremists we rounded up in Philadelphia."

"I followed their trail online. They were spreading their hate speech, but we shut them down and arrested a dozen of them last week."

"Busted them for felony Jesusing, huh," Turnbull said. Carter turned to him, shocked, not sure what to say.

"This is Inspector Oliver Warren. He arrived today from the West Coast, and he is my new head of security. He can be...abrasive. He spent considerable time undercover among hate criminals, and you can understand that he suffers from post-trauma stress that sometimes can be confused with insensitivity."

"I respect and validate your challenge overcome," she said to Turnbull stiffly. "What are your pronouns?"

"Guess," Turnbull said. Rios-Parkinson answered for him.

"'Xe' and 'xis'. The inspector identifies as a non-binary Muslim of indigenousnessness. You can imagine the struggle xe has endured."

"Yes, Director," Carter replied, but her voice was unsure. "The patriarchy does violence to us all."

"I need you, Inspector Carter, to assist Inspector Warren. It is a matter of the utmost delicacy and urgency. You know what happened in Mexico City, and you read the file on Marburg X. You know the seriousness of this operation. It has the highest security classification. At times, you may not understand exactly what is happening. You will ignore that. At times, Inspector Warren may need to act in a manner that appears offensive, or even micro- or macro-aggressive. I assure you, it is part of the mission. Inspector Warren hates all systems of oppression as much as you or I. The question is whether you can accept this burden in order to achieve a greater objective?"

She still looked unsure, but she said, "Yes, Director. I think I can."

"Have you ever been in the field?" Turnbull asked.

"Are you asking because I am a woman?" she shot back, then caught herself.

"No, I'm asking because I don't want to get killed because you don't know what you're doing."

"Inspector Warren," Rios-Parkinson said, irritation apparent though he kept his tone steady, "Inspector Carter was fully trained at the Academy. And her assignment is not intended to place her in the midst of a firefight."

"Well, the problem is that I always seem to find myself in the midst of firefights. I'd prefer I be there with someone competent."

"Inspector Carter, wait outside." She turned and left, closing the doors behind her. "Turnbull," Rios-Parkinson began.

"She'll get me killed," Turnbull said. "Give me someone who's not twenty years old. Anyone. Give me freaking Cooley."

"She is twenty-five. And Cooley, like everyone else on the top three floors, is potentially compromised. Inspector Carter is perfect. She is so lowly and so far from power that she cannot possibly be corrupted. And she is also perfect because having a woman with you will help dilute your cis-het, patriarchal modes of interaction."

"So, she's so unimportant no one would have bothered turning her against you," Turnbull said. "And she can help me navigate this 'ed up system of yours?"

"That is correct. Now I suggest you begin identifying who is behind this by interviewing the life partner of Inspector Rollins. You recall Rollins? I believe you shot him several times yesterday."

Turnbull walked toward the doors, but Rios-Parkinson called out from behind him. Turnbull stopped and about-faced.

"Do not push Inspector Carter too far. A complaint about your behavior could complicate matters," he said. "And obtain formal consent upon attaining each level of intimacy before you have sex with her. Consult one of the posters on 'Affirmative, Enthusiastic, and Validated Consent' hanging in the hallway."

"Shit," hissed Turnbull as he turned away and went out the door.

Carter was back, sitting in one of the chairs lining the walls across from Blue Hair. Blue Hair clearly disapproved of both new additions to the Director's entourage, but Turnbull was tired and largely beyond caring.

Carter stood up as Turnbull approached her.

"Here," he said, handing her the cell phone Rios-Parkinson had given him. She looked at it doubtfully.

"I don't need an electronic leash," he explained.

She pocketed it. "What do we do first?" she asked.

"Come on," Turnbull said. He headed toward the door out of the antechamber and into the seventh floor's main corridor. Blue Hair pursed her lips in disapproval. Carter followed him, unsure.

"Where are we going?" she asked.

"The armory."

"The armory?"

"The armory. You know, where they keep the guns?"

"I know what an armory is," she snapped, hustling to keep up. "I am not clear why."

"Well, it probably has something to do with guns. Take me there."

They took the one good elevator down. It stopped at the third floor, opening up to a vast room full of PBI agents staring at computer screens and wearing headphones.

"Those are nice computers," Turnbull observed. It was the first gear, outside the Director's office, that had not looked like it was secondhand in 2024.

"Monitoring is our most important duty," Carter said, with some level of pride. "We've just brought online brand-new servers that can scan a million communications a second for hate criminality with our new algorithms."

"We have new servers to watch people, but not enough food for them?" Turnbull said.

Carter looked genuinely puzzled. "What good is food if racists are committing hate crimes without accountability?"

Turnbull decided to treat that question as rhetorical. The doors slid shut and the elevator descended.

They opened again in the basement, and Carter led him through a meandering series of hallways lit by flashing fluorescent lights. Turnbull paused for a moment – it reminded him of the bioweapons institute – but then he followed.

On the right side of the hall was a metal double door with a sign that read "ARMORY." There was a shooting range on the left, but no one was using it.

"You do carry a gun, right?" Turnbull asked.

"I have an assigned Beretta," Carter said. "But I haven't signed it out before."

"Well, let's sign you out something now."

Turnbull pushed open the doors and was confronted by a counter stretching across the room. Behind it were long racks of weapons, pistols, rifles, shotguns, reaching back into the dark. A tall, thin man with a shaved head was sitting on a stool, cleaning a Remington 870. He looked up at the visitors and seemed almost surprised to have guests.

"Hi," Turnbull said pleasantly, despite his sour mood and fatigue. "How are you doing today?" His years in the Army had taught him an important lesson about how you treated the people who ran their own little fiefdoms, like a supply room or a chow hall, or an armory. A bit of courtesy went a long way to making problems disappear.

"Fine, fine," said the armorer, a little surprised at the greeting. The man put down the scattergun, got off the stool, and stepped over to the counter.

"I'm Oliver Warren. I'm new here. Just started as the Director's head of security." Turnbull extended his hand across the counter, and the man shook it.

"Working for the Director, huh?" he said, still uncertain. "I'm Ernie Smith." There was a tattoo on the man's right forearm that peeked out from under his rolled-up sleeves. The lower hemisphere of a globe, and the bottom of an anchor.

"Old US Marine Corps, huh?" Turnbull said pleasantly.

"Yeah," Smith said, suspicious. "From the bad old days. Before."

"Well, say what you will about the old USA, those Marines could fight."

"That we could," Smith said, smiling a little.

"Look, I need some ammo and mags. Can you square me away, Sarge?"

Smith laughed a little. "Nobody's called me 'Sarge' since I was discharged."

"This place is squared away. You had to have been an NCO."

Smith smiled. "Well, Inspector Warren, I have a lot of choices when it comes to ammo. What's your pleasure?"

".45. Got any Federal Hydra-Shok?"

"Damn, you are particular. Of course, they don't make that anymore. Not here anyway. But I might have some left over. What kind of mags?"

Turnbull pulled open his jacket, exposing the Wilson X-TAC Elite M1911 .45 on his hip."

Ernie Smith whistled. "Where the hell did you get that? Wait, I don't want to know. But I can help. You have an extended mag in there, right?"

"Yep. Eight rounds."

"I might have a few in back." He turned and disappeared into the rear.

"That gun's from the red," Carter said, alarmed. "I remember it from my weapons training. The M1911A. It was created to murder indigenous peoples."

"It was designed to drop Moro tribesman during the Philippine Insurrection," Turnbull said. Carter's face was registering horror.

"The old .38 Long just didn't have the stopping power," Ernie said, coming back with his hands full. He dumped a box of hollow point ammo and a half-dozen magazines on the counter. "A .45 hollow point does."

Turnbull smiled and broke open the box to start loading mags. "This gun has served for a century and a third and never let us down. You know Ernie, I gotta come down here at lunch sometime and talk guns with you."

"Anytime, Inspector Warren. Now, is there something I can do for the...?" he paused, trying to navigate the obstacle facing him.

"Woman," Carter said helpfully.

"Thank you," Smith said.

"She needs to sign out a service weapon. She says she's assigned a M9, but I'm thinking she needs something a step up."

"Have you shot much, Inspector?" Smith asked her.

"I qualified at the Academy and then six months ago."

"So that's 'no,'" Turnbull said. "You thinking what I'm thinking?"

"Glock 19, nine-millimeter?"

"You are," Turnbull said.

"You can dip it in a puddle of mud and it will still shoot," the armorer said. Smith disappeared again.

"I've never shot one of those," Carter said.

"That's why we're going across the hall and getting you a block of instruction."

Ernie had clearly foreseen that. He brought out a black pistol, five mags and a box of hollow point +P rounds and a box of ball rounds for practice. "Let me get you some eye and hearing pro too." He reached under the counter for them and handed them over.

"Thanks, Ernie," Turnbull said. "We'll be about an hour."

They signed out a blue 2022 Chevrolet and headed north out of the secure sector toward Maryland and Larry Rollins's home. They were waved through the gate in the wall surrounding the Control Zone where those supporting the remaining federal operations in Capital City mostly lived. Getting out was no issue; the guards were concerned about those without business or menial jobs getting in.

Once through, they headed north through the largely car-free streets. They passed through a part of DC that had been largely burned out and looted during the food riots several months before, and the few people on the streets watched them pass by with thinly veiled hate. If someone had gas, he had food too. Turnbull kept up his speed in case some enterprising local decided to act on his envy.

"But why would Rollins try to kill the Director?" Carter asked, shocked, after Turnbull filled her in on more about what happened in Mexico City – leaving out the details about Clay Deeds and Rios-Parkinson's treason.

"Maybe his wife will know," he replied, accelerating through an empty traffic circle.

Carter laughed. "Where are you from? *His* wife. Even if his life partner is a woman, how is she *his*?"

"Through English?" suggested Turnbull. "Out in the field offices, we have a different attitude than you headquarters hobbits."

"What's a hobbit?"

"Something from books that are probably illegal for being phallocentric or something."

She glared at him from the passenger seat. "You don't seem to take inequitable power paradigms very seriously, Oliver."

"Probably true, Kristina."

She shook her head. "You spent too much time undercover with those racists. I know you are challenge overcome by the trauma but you need to work on your growth and allyship. And I need to confront you about something else."

"You need to confront me?"

"Yes. Because when we were training on the Glock I felt–"

"You *felt?*"

"I *felt* that you were assuming a power position above me and lecturing to me as if my skills and knowledge were unvalued."

"Well, I was, and they were."

Carter blinked at him twice. Turnbull continued.

"See, I am in a superior position, since I both outrank you in the PBI and since I'm enormously more proficient with weapons than you are. And I did not value your weapons skills or knowledge because, until I taught you how to shoot, you effectively had none."

"I cannot believe you just said that."

"Why?"

Carter did not have an answer, at least not for about a minute. Then she spoke again.

"I am trying to validate your experience as a non-binary Muslim individual of First People's heritage who has suffered trauma when forming my reaction to what superficially appears to be a significant macroaggression."

"Can we save this important discussion for after we go roust Rollins's wife?" Turnbull pulled the sedan to a stop along the street in what had been a middle-class neighborhood. Several of the homes were clearly abandoned. Others were a mess, with debris and overgrown yards, but still occupied. A few seemed to be moderately well-kept, but even some of the nicer ones had boarded windows. Glass was hard to find.

There were no people out and about.

Rollins's house was a low, single-story ranch. They exited the car and walked up toward the front door. It was ajar, and Turnbull drew. Carter stood there, uncertain.

"Take out your gun," Turnbull said. The lock was broken in. He pushed the front door open with his foot, and it revealed a dirty carpeted hallway heading back into the dark rear of the house. Turnbull listened – nothing – then stepped inside, .45 up. Carter followed.

"Don't sweep me with the Glock," Turnbull whispered.

She blinked, her black pistol in a two-hand grip.

"Don't point your gun at me," he said.

Turnbull reached out for the light switches on the hallway wall and flipped them. Nothing.

"It's Earth Rescue Time," Carter said. Turnbull remembered – three hours of daily blackouts designed to fight global warming. He would make due with what light there was.

They went down the hall toward the kitchen. It was at the back of the building, and light was coming in through the rear windows. There was a body on the floor, a large woman.

"I guess someone thought Mrs. Rollins was a loose end," Turnbull said. "Two in the chest, one in the forehead. Professional."

Carter was pale. Turnbull holstered his Wilson X-TAC.

"You okay? Is it seeing a body, or that I said 'Mrs.'?"

"We need to call someone."

"Not yet. They are long gone. Go check the bedrooms anyway. My guess is that the place has been tossed and all the electronics taken, but look around for anything interesting."

Carter nodded and disappeared toward the bedrooms.

Turnbull walked to the door leading to the rear patio. There was an ancient plastic patio set, a couple of rickety chairs and a table covered with empty beer cans and plates. There was a grill too, with a sheet of cardboard Rollins likely used to disperse the smoke so no one saw evidence of his envirocrime. Turnbull looked back at the dead woman as Carter returned.

"No computers or phones, and someone went through the drawers and closets," she said, staring at the dead woman.

"You get used to it," Turnbull said.

"No, I – I'm okay. It's just…"

"What?"

"She's…fat."

Turnbull looked down. Come to think of it, she wasn't huge but she was still one of the larger women he had seen in the People's Republic.

Carter opened the refrigerator door. There was food inside, a lot of it. Meat, vegetables, milk. She marveled at the bounty, then from habit quickly shut the door to retain the cold while the power was off.

"You can't get all that on PBI rat cards," she said.

Turnbull looked out at the patio set again.

"You think she could have sat out there with Rollins in one of those chairs?" he asked.

"I think it would have collapsed," Carter said.

"Then Rollins sat out there drinking and eating with someone else. Do you want to bet that the subject of where all the food came from came up?"

"I would take that bet," Carter said. "He had an illegal food cooker –"

"A barbecue grill," Turnbull said. "Looks like an old school Weber."

"Is that what those are called? Anyway, it's got to be a neighbor because I bet they could smell it and Rollins had to give them a reason not to report him."

"Okay," Turnbull said, mildly impressed. "Let's talk to the neighbors."

"What about her?" asked Carter.

"She's not going anywhere."

It was easy to narrow down the correct residence. The house to the left had been abandoned years before. It was empty, and all the windows had been salvaged. The house to the right looked lived in. Turnbull knocked. There was movement inside. Turnbull knocked again.

"People's Bureau of Investigation," he shouted as he pounded with his fist. "Open up in the name of...the People."

The door cracked open.

"I have a bat in here," said the middle-aged man on the other side. Turnbull and Carter flashed their credentials.

"We just want to talk. You don't need your bat," Carter said. He hesitated, then pulled the door open.

The guy was about 50, unshaven, thin, and wearing a threadbare pair of People's Pants, the PR's government brand of dungarees. He also wore a black T-shirt with red lettering commemorating his attendance at "Shed Your Cis-Paradigm Day" at the Metropolitan Transit District.

They followed him back to his kitchen and sat down at his table. He went to the gas stove, where a kettle was heating on a portable propane stove. He was shaking.

"Eric Tolson, works at Metro Transit, age 48, priv level 2, cis-het," Carter said, reading off his ID card. Tolson's head hung a little, as if a secret sin had been revealed.

"Yeah," he said. "You, you want some coffee?"

"Is it responsible?" Turnbull said. Tolson, and Carter too, looked at him as if he was mad.

"Of course," Tolson said.

"Save it."

"It's only the third brew."

"Save it."

Tolson sat at the table. "Look, if this is about my web searches, I can't help who I am. I'm cis. I can't help it." Carter stared at him with distaste.

"It's not about your web searches. You aren't in trouble," Turnbull said. "At least, as long as you answer our questions."

"I'll tell you anything I know. I know a lot of racists and hate criminals at work," he said, leaning in. "A lot."

"I want to know about your neighbor Larry. Larry Rollins."

"Larry? He's a good guy. He's in the PBI. He's not a racist or sexist or anything. He's a good guy."

"He's a dead guy, Larry. So's his wife," Turnbull said.

"Sienna? Dead?"

"Yeah, she's next door on the floor. Somebody came in and put her down today. You see or hear anything unusual today?"

"Dead?"

"Eric, focus," Turnbull said. "Did you see anyone unusual around here today?"

"No. I did a night shift and woke up a couple hours ago when the march came through."

"March?"

"College kids. I think they were chanting about Palestine today. I don't remember. I mean, I share solidarity with the Palestinian people –"

"I don't care about your solidarity, Larry," Turnbull said.

"You used to sit out back with Larry Rollins and eat and drink with him, right?" asked Carter.

"Is this about the grill? I told him. I told Larry he was killing the earth with that thing."

Carter leaned in. "We have you as an accessory to his environmental crimes, Eric. But you can do yourself a favor by telling us what Larry Rollins told you."

"About what?" Tolson asked, getting desperate.

"About the food. Where did Rollins get the food?"

"He said he was doing something special, that he had a new assignment. He didn't say what."

"Did you ask him?" asked Carter.

"Yeah, I wanted to know. He was getting all sorts of extra rats and of course I was curious how. I know he was in the PBI, but this was something different."

"How was it different?" asked Carter.

"He said he'd be leaving the PBI soon. 'Moving up' he said."

"Where?"

"I don't know. I didn't push him. I mean –"

"You didn't want to take a chance on him not giving you any more food?" asked Turnbull.

"I'm a cis-het priv 2 working fixing buses," Tolson said, his eyes getting watery. "I barely get any rats as it is."

Turnbull stood up. "Thank you, Mr. Tolson. You have done outstanding work for the People's Republic today. Of course, you will keep all of this in complete confidence."

"Yes, of course," Tolson said, relieved.

"And watch what you do on the Internet," Carter said. "We do."

The sullen buildings of the former capital passed by outside the sedan's windows as they headed back downtown to the PBI headquarters. The wall around the central city, higher than the one around West Los Angeles and actively patrolled, was controlled by a massive gate. But there was no long line of autos waiting to get back inside the Control Zone – most of the people with access to gasoline were already inside and they rarely ventured out.

After they left the house, Carter had called in the murder; a PBI forensic team would clear out the body quickly and quietly. Turnbull expected that Larry Rollins's overflowing refrigerator would be empty before the cleaners got there.

"I don't suppose you found her ration cards," Turnbull said.

"No, they took everything. No rat cards, no ID, no travel papers. Nothing."

"So, what is 'moving up' from the PBI?" asked Turnbull.

"Nothing," Carter said. "The PBI is the premier crimefighting organization in, well, the world."

"How about the FBI in the United States?" asked Turnbull.

"Is that a joke?" she scoffed. "They're just a tool of the oppressive red regime, and they have been ever since they denied Hillary Clinton the election in 2016."

"I remember that election." That was only partially true. He had celebrated Donald Trump's victory with a bottle of Johnny Walker Blue Label one of his pals had liberated from his father's liquor cabinet.

"I was only seven or eight when the Trump coup took place. You were what – thirty?" She was smiling a little.

"Sounds ageist," Turnbull said, and her smile vanished.

"I'm sorry. That was offensive."

"You can make jokes. I won't arrest you," Turnbull said. "I was in high school."

But the rest of the drive was silent. It was starting to rain, and the people who had been outside on the streets of the Control Zone all rushed inside.

They flashed their ID as they entered the headquarters, then took the one working elevator up to the seventh floor. Blue Hair stood up as they entered the antechamber of the Director's office.

"He's busy," Blue Hair announced, happy to be an obstacle. But then the doors opened.

Two men were there, Rios-Parkinson and a tall, handsome man in a fine suit, maybe in his early-thirties. A familiar man. Turnbull stared for a minute, trying to place him. And the man stared back, similarly puzzled.

"This is Inspector Oliver Warren, my personal security chief, and Inspector Kristina Carter," Rios-Parkinson said.

The other man looked Turnbull over.

"Adam Marshall, Deputy Director, People's Intelligence Agency."

There was something familiar about him. "You're a spook," Turnbull said.

"That's offensive," Marshall replied, frowning, and then he walked past Turnbull and Carter and out of the office. The pair entered. Rios-Parkinson shut the door behind them, blocking the view of a scowling Blue Hair.

"And?" the Director said.

"Mrs. Rollins is dead," Turnbull said. Rios-Parkinson stared.

"Mrs.?" he said, disgusted.

"Xe keeps saying that word," Carter said.

"Somebody pulled a Mozambique drill on her, two in the sternum, one between the headlights. Then they tossed the place and took anything they thought was incriminating. Did I get the pronouns right, because I want to make sure my priorities are in the right place?"

"We called in the cleaners," Carter said.

"Rollins was getting paid off in rat cards. He had a fridge full of food and a fat wife," Turnbull said.

"Your fatism and sexism aside, which I only excuse because of your challenge overcome, the question is who bribed him?" Rios-Parkinson said.

"We braced his neighbor, some cis-het priv 2," Carter said. "He told us Rollins said he was 'moving up.'"

"Within the PBI? Rollins was a drone. He had long ago topped out right there in the middle."

"What else would be considered moving up?" asked Carter.

"I bet that Adam Marshall guy thinks the PIA is moving up," Turnbull said.

"The PIA is focused internationally, not domestically," Rios-Parkinson said. "It seems odd that they would kill a bountiful woman in Maryland after trying to kill me in Mexico City. But then... they have motive."

Turnbull caught what Carter missed. The agencies were rivals.

"So, you think it was the PIA?"

"I think it is a possibility," Rios-Parkinson said. "The PIA is the only entity with the foreign capabilities to organize an operation like that. And I think Marshall's visit was an attempt to see whether I assessed them as the perpetrators."

"That's treason," Carter said, stunned.

"Yes, that accurately assesses it."

"That Marshall guy – I can't place him but we've met," Turnbull said.

"His cover in coming here was to report to me on the PIA's activities overseas attempting to track the scientist and the people behind him."

"Let me guess," Turnbull said. "Zip?"

"Deputy Director Marshall had no further information," Rios-Parkinson said.

"So, either they are incompetent, or they are somehow involved," Turnbull said.

"The People's Intelligence Agency is the sword and the shield of the People's Republic," Carter sputtered, shocked. "They cannot be involved."

Turnbull ignored her.

"I do have a lead, but it's in Germany."

"Germany?" repeated Rios-Parkinson.

"Yeah. Feldschall Fabrik Gmbh, in a town called Hebertshausen."

"I do not understand," the Director said.

"That's where the lab equipment came from."

Rios-Parkinson thought for a moment, then walked behind his desk and hit the intercom.

"How do you know that?" Carter said to Turnbull.

"I have my sources."

Rios-Parkinson spoke into the phone. "I require all your information on a Feldschall Fabrik Gmbh. Only in-house – do not request it from any outside agency. And you will obtain the necessary travel papers and carbon credits for Inspectors Warren and Carter to fly to Germany tomorrow. Diplomatic credentials." He hung up.

"We're going to Germany?" asked Carter, astonished.

"Yes," the Director said. "And as diplomats, you'll have a diplomatic bag. For the guns I expect Inspector Warren will insist on taking.

"Damn straight," Turnbull said.

Adam Marshall sat in the back of his black SUV, in a convoy of three vehicles, heading toward Langley. He hated that the PIA helicopter, which he usually took for these jaunts, was going to be down for maintenance for another 24 hours. These parts delays would not have happened back in the United States. He mentally checked himself; he was in the PR now and that kind of talk, that kind of *thought*, was dangerous.

He especially hated the drive out into the Virginia countryside – it was ridiculous that they still used the facilities of the old Central Intelligence Agency. Just as it was ridiculous that he had had to feign respect when he was briefing that jumped-up little secret policeman at PBI headquarters. But for the present, it was necessary. Marshall sighed.

Now, who was that man, that – what was the name? Oliver Warren?

Marshall knew he had met the man before, but it was long ago. He searched his mind for the context, but there was nothing except the certainty they had met before. Obviously, Warren felt it too.

He picked up his secure phone and dialed his assistant.

"I need the complete file on a PBI agent. Warren. Oliver Warren."

7.

"What do you think of our waitress?" Richard Harrington said, using the forbidden term without irony or apology. He lifted his glass of 2024 Krug Grande Cuvée to his thin lips and sipped, watching his companion. Director Rios-Parkinson broke eye contact and looked over at the young woman as she walked away across the deserted dining room on the ground floor of the government-owned Hay-Adams Hotel. She had been intimidated and nearly spilled the champagne as she poured it. She was clearly not used to heels and she walked awkwardly in her short skirt.

"I respect her struggle," Rios-Parkinson responded sourly.

Harrington laughed, just a little.

"Director, for a man who is moving up so quickly you always seem so miserable."

"Why am I here?" Rios-Parkinson said, adding, "Mr. Vice President."

"You answer my question first."

"I think that she is thin." She was, almost to the point of being bony. It marred her appearance only a little, though. She was very pretty – Harrington was always served by pretty young women though he was publicly anything but cis-het. Rios-Parkinson had the surveillance tapes to prove his willingness to do what was necessary. But his public identity – "pansexual (queer butch)" was how his official biography put it – made him just diverse enough to overcome the resistance and move up into the vice-presidency even as a male not-of-color. The prior holder of the position had been found dead in her bed three months before. Natural causes, the media said. But several prominent figures quietly retained food tasters, who all accepted the risk in return for the additional calories.

"Yes, she's thin. Exactly," Harrington said, smiling at Rios-Parkinson's analysis. "You are one of the few who understands what is truly important. She *is* thin. Everyone waiting for us outside this room is thin. Everyone in the country, except people like us and certified victims of fatphobia, are thin. Food is power, and the food crisis has only gotten worse. Everything has gotten worse since we made our arrangement last year. My concern is that it does not get too much worse too fast, before I am ready to move."

"To take power."

"As I have told you before, whoever can feed them just enough to keep them from revolting will rule unchallenged," Harrington said. "And as I promised, you will be my second and my heir. If you do what I need done."

"I must be satisfactory so far. You saw too it that the President appointed me Director of the People's Bureau of Investigation."

"He takes my advice, occasionally."

"I take it your relationship with President De Blasio remains superficially mutually beneficial."

"He's a fool, a doddering buffoon spouting Marxist platitudes and smoking pot inside the penthouse of People's Tower while I am in exile here, working out of that deteriorating shack across the street." After the Split, the name on the side of Trump Tower had been removed and the building confiscated. It now served as the presidential residence in New York City. The old White House was now the office and home of the vice-president.

Harrington continued. "And he's dying. Alzheimer's."

Rios-Parkinson nodded. He had suspected as much during his pre-appointment meeting with the President.

"And here you are, where no one is watching you," said Rios-Parkinson.

"Except you. And so our project continues."

"When do you intend to fill me in on the entirety of your plans?" Rios-Parkinson asked. "I only see pieces of your puzzle."

"Which is how I intend it."

"I am concerned you might be making the same promises to others that you are making to me."

Harrington laughed. "Do you imagine I was behind the attempt on your life?"

"No. I think I am still useful to you. I will, however, begin to worry should you start considering me not useful."

"As you should, Director. The lesson is not to become not useful to me." Harrington took another sip.

Rios-Parkinson considered returning the threat in kind, but rejected that idea. A rich, white male who had reached his level of success in the arena of the People's Republic government would have long ago factored in the potential threat of a Director of the People's Bureau of Investigation and hedged against it somehow. He went another way instead.

"Then how may I be of service, Mr. Vice-President?"

"As I said, the conditions are deteriorating quickly, too quickly. Are you aware of what is happening in Chicago?"

"That is the Army's operation, not mine and not the People's Security Force's. The President's decision, I believe."

"His advisors. Using the iron fist. There are hundreds dead. Oh, our media calls them 'traitors' and 'criminals,' but they are just hungry proles, ruled by their stomachs. It will get worse. I've seen the crop estimates, the real ones."

"As have I."

"This country is on the edge. Any new crisis can tip it over into chaos. And if something does, your secret police force, even with the Army, can't stop it."

"I never represented that it could," said Rios-Parkinson. "The old United States ruled by consent. We rule by fear, fear on the part of individuals who know that anyone who rebels will be punished. But if *everyone* rebels, then we are effectively helpless."

"I need time, Director. I need time to put the pieces in place so I can be the savior who can feed our people. And I need you to stick your fingers in the dike until I can put all the pieces in place to act and bring this game to its climax." Harrington grinned, amused at his double entendre. Then he stopped grinning. "Tell me about Marburg X."

"I am still investigating."

"Who is behind it?"

"I am still investigating."

"Is it *here*?"

"I am still investigating," Rios-Parkinson repeated.

"My other friends tell me that if it gets loose, it will be a catastrophe," Harrington said. "The tipping point."

"The same friends who told you about the facility in Siberia?" The information had come to him from the Vice-President. Where he got it, Rios-Parkinson had no clue, but the Director had his suspicions. "The Chameleon?"

"You do not need to know, Director. What matters is that your attempt to destroy it in Russia failed. Should I ask how you convinced our enemies to do our dirty work for us?"

"I have sources and resources you are unaware of too, Mr. Vice-President."

"Yes, you do, Director. And they make you dangerous, but they also keep you useful.

Now Rios-Parkinson took a sip of his champagne, then spoke.

"I very much want to remain useful."

"Then stop failing like you did in Siberia."

Rios-Parkinson sat silent, chastened.

"I will not fail."

There were footsteps and the waitress returned, a plate holding a filet mignon in each hand. They fell silent, and she placed one before each of the men, then stood there, waiting and gazing at the food.

"It looks delicious," said Harrington. "Truly delicious."

The young woman stared down. "Yes, Mr. Vice-President," she said uncertainly.

"Would you like some?" he asked. She said nothing, her mouth moving silently. "Come join me after my companion leaves and perhaps I may have something for you. Now go." She nodded, turned, and walked away.

"Food," Harrington said, "is power."

Rios-Parkinson picked up his knife and fork and began to cut into the delicious flesh.

The power never went off in the walled Langley complex that housed the People's Intelligence Service. It had its own dedicated generators and fueling them was a priority. While the rest of the country went dark several hours a day for the sake of Gaia, the lights in the headquarters never went off and the air conditioners never stopped. Unless they broke down.

"Get them fixed," Adam Marshall said to the technician. The worker was clad in overalls, Marshall in a suit that probably cost a year of his wages. Both were sweating.

"I'm feeling –" began the HVAC tech, but Marshall cut him off.

"I am feeling like declaring you an enemy of the state," Marshall said. "Get the air conditioning working."

Marshall continued down the hall, waved through the checkpoints that guarded the suite that housed the Director of the PIA. He stepped inside the Director's office, and shut the door behind him.

"How was your visit?" asked the Director, standing up at her ornate desk. She was short, with a severe haircut and tiny green eyes. She never saw the sun, or so it seemed. Her skin was very pale. The files said she was almost 60 years old but it was hard to tell. She had been working out of the building for at least 35 years, though her official biography and the public records ignored her time at the old CIA prior to the Split.

Her name was Louise Stenz, but people called her "the Chameleon" because she always blended in, never drawing the attention of the predators. But they never called her that to her face. Chameleons are themselves predators.

This predator had a tear of sweat running down the side of her head.

"I told the head HVAC tech to get the air conditioning up," Marshall said. "He tried to tell me how he felt."

The Chameleon sighed. "Adam, your intelligence skills and general ruthlessness make you very useful, but you still have the same weakness you have had since I brought you in a decade ago. You have never quite purged the red out of you."

"I am as loyal to the People's Republic as anyone," he replied, hurt. Since he had defected, doubts had always hung over him like a dark cloud. But never in the eyes of Director Stenz.

"That's not what I mean. I mean that you still maintain some of the bad habits you learned while you were there. You are not sensitive to the intersectional paradigms of oppression at play here."

"I am," he said. "Sensitive."

"No," the PIA Director said, smiling a little. "You say it, but you don't internalize it. You don't live it. It is not part of your essence."

"I believe in our principles," he said.

"Our principles," she sighed. "Adam, I know they call me the Chameleon. I take it as a compliment. Do you know why a predator cannot see a chameleon in the wild when it blends into a green leaf? Because the chameleon actually *becomes* green. You never actually *became* blue. That is your weakness."

"I will try to do better," Marshall said. Stenz nodded. She preferred refugees from the red states. There weren't many, but those that crossed over were positively evangelical in their dedication to the cause, as if through their fervor for the promise of the People's Republic they could ignore the reality.

"Now, your meeting with Rios-Parkinson. What happened?"

"He gave no indication that he suspected us."

"He wouldn't," said Director Stenz. "And about what he knows of our project?"

"He hinted at it, obliquely."

"What did he say, exactly?"

"He indicated he was seeking information we might have on Doctor Maksimov. He said it was for a drug investigation."

"As if those secret policemen still conduct drug investigations. He thinks we are fools."

"I told him we would query our sources, but that our Eurasian operations were limited. That the United States remains our primary focus."

The Chameleon sat back down in her chair. There was nothing on her desk but a monitor, keyboard and a few papers. There was nothing related or referring to any kind of life outside the PIA – not a photo, not a book, not a pen set given to her by her kids on her birthday. She had had a husband, once. He was gone. And children too – they were also gone. There was simply her and her office now, and nothing else.

"Do not underestimate Rios-Parkinson, Adam. We've certainly learned that about him. He's dangerous. The question remains, why was he in Mexico City? Who was he meeting?"

"Still unsure. The only bodies recovered by the Mexican authorities were his security team and the *sicarios*. And Rollins."

"It was a chance worth taking, but that kind of opportunity will not likely present itself again anytime soon. He has no doubt increased his personal security."

"I met his new security chief. Except, not for the first time. We have met before."

"Who is he?" the PIA Director asked.

"I don't know, but I intend to find out. In any case, I have arranged for something today to keep him off balance. To refocus his attention on securing his own position internally."

"Remember your priorities. Make sure you prepare the way for our guests so that there are no surprises and no obstacles. This must all go as we have planned it. The stakes are very high. But if we succeed..."

"If we succeed, no one will ever call you 'the Chameleon' again," Marshall said.

Adam Marshall sat at his desk and activated his Lenovo monitor. The PIA system was slow – it was out of date and there was no funding to replace it. What money was available for information technology mostly flowed to the surveillance departments of the PBI – that was one expense the rulers of the PR never spared. He waited for it to load the internal mail utility. The delay was maddening – his civilian desktop back in Texas a decade before was faster. For just a moment, he imagined his life if he had completed his military service and become a citizen there. But the success he might have had there if he had not left for the blue would pale in comparison to what he might achieve beside the Chameleon here. What was the saying – better to rule in hell?

The email app finished loading; he had several dozen messages of various classifications. Skimming the subject lines, he settled on the one reading "WARREN, OLIVER" and opened it.

It was a basic individual record. High priv level, probably based on his non-binary gender identity, Islamic identification, and handicap. Marshall caught himself – different ability? Was that the term now?

No family – only child and his parents were dead. No life partner. Education was standard, and he was a member of all the right student groups. He had been PBI for a decade, but the specific assignments were missing – it just read "SPECIAL." Maybe that meant undercover breaking up racist groups or anti-red counterintelligence. Nothing on family or friends. No negative social media findings. Nothing that drew one's attention.

Adam Marshall exhaled. This record was exactly how it would look if someone had given this "Oliver Warren" person a new identity.

The PIA was a foreign-directed organization and was prohibited from operating in the People's Republic, but the PIA still had secret networks within the People's Republic. Marshall gave serious thought to using them to dig deeper into Warren's background, but why risk his agency's assets when he knew what the result would be? Oliver Warren was not Oliver Warren. There was no Oliver Warren.

Rios-Parkinson might have any number of reasons for giving a new identity to his security chief, especially after the last one had tried to murder him. But none of them seemed important enough to risk exposing internal PIA assets by trying to dig through his background.

Marshall just wished he could remember who the hell this guy was.

There was howling, always howling, and though he would not show it, the howling unnerved even Hamid al-Afridi. He was used to screaming – he and his people enjoyed that. But the howling of the men and women locked in the cages was something else. You could hear it even through the locked door, echoing through the basement laboratory.

Dr. Maksimov's hands shook. Probably the howling, and probably his body's anticipation of the limited vodka they allowed him every evening after his work was done.

"We will need fresh carriers for the flight," the professor said in broken English. That was the common language between the Iraqi and the Russian, and they had used it since the beginning of the project.

"Has not Azzam been bringing you enough of them?" asked Hamid. Azzam seemed offended. It had been his task to take to the streets at night, to find the healthiest looking German derelicts available, and drag them here. In incubating the Marburg X, they would finally serve Allah's purpose.

"They are only good for three days, maybe four, maximum. If the carriers die before transmission, it will be months for me to recreate the virus, assuming you even have the proper equipment available to me."

"You will have your carriers. Where we are going, there will be an ample supply. And you will have your equipment."

Maksimov mumbled something. In the other room, the caged carriers howled.

Hamid left the basement, climbing up the stairs to the ground floor of what had been an office building in downtown Munich. They had moved the project here after the warning had come that the enemy knew about Siberia. He hoped his uninvited visitors had been pleased by the little surprise he had left for them. He had monitored the media closely, but there was nothing indicating an outbreak. It had clearly been contained, *insha'Allah* with some casualties among the infidels.

This was a lesson that validated his plan – a single, easily accessible location with a few mindless vectors could be easily quarantined and the epidemic stopped. But an inaccessible location, with many carriers – that would be unstoppable. It was a matter of getting them into position in the heart of the enemy.

But to do it, he needed new equipment. That meant dealing with the infidels.

"The money will be in your Swiss account tonight," Hamid al-Afridi told the German businessman later that day at the factory. Hans Teuffelmann seemed grim, much grimmer than he should in light of the amount of money his company was being paid for the equipment. And this was the third time al-Afridi had bought the complete package from Feldschall Fabrik Gmbh. The German should have been positively jolly.

The noises down below on the factory floor made it difficult to hear him, but al-Afridi made out a grunt that sounded like "*Ja*."

The acknowledgement was sufficient. The Arab had no desire to spend any more time with this red-faced *kaffir* than he must, and he sensed the feeling was mutual. Tueffelmann's two slabs of Teutonic beef stood by, watching him, earpieces in, bulges under their jackets. But al-Afridi was unimpressed. The Germans had their thugs and their guns, but he had Allah.

And thugs. And guns.

Hamid reclined in the backseat of his Mercedes as the little town of Hebertshausen passed by outside the window. Luckily, the windows were tinted. His kind was not particularly welcome here, though the hostility he would face as an Arab out in this Munich suburb would be nothing like what he might face out in the Bavarian countryside.

But that was a problem for another day. The *ummah* would deal with the Great Satans of North America first before returning to mop up the infidels in Europe. Of course, after they saw the wrath Allah was poised to bring down upon his enemies across the ocean, perhaps most of these decadent creatures would choose submission and mercy over defiance and slaughter.

It was a pleasing thought, but one interrupted by his phone's buzz. He looked at the screen. It read "*Nadhil,*" which translated as "bastard."

"Yes, Herr Spetters."

"Herr al-Afridi, have you something very valuable to give me?"

He flashed with anger. "Herr Spetters, we have an agreement that my shipment is to be unmolested."

"Not your shipment. Something else. Something you will be willing to pay a very high price for."

"Enough riddles, Herr Spetters. Speak plainly."

"*Jawhol.* The American we spoke of is here. Kelly Turnbull has landed in Germany."

8.

"What's wrong with the food?" Kristina Carter asked. They were seated in the back corner of the PBI cafeteria, off alone at a long metal table, trays in front of them. The place was crowded – PBI agents did not need to use their rat cards to eat on site. No one browned bagged it. But the quality of the food left something to be desired.

Quality.

"This meat tastes like ass," Turnbull said, dropping his fork into the gooey pile on his tray.

Carter seemed puzzled, so Turnbull clarified.

"Not the donkey kind. I've eaten that. It tastes better. I mean the other kind."

Carter looked down at her own tray, then back up. She had been scarfing it down eagerly.

"You know, a lot of people in the racist states would love to have food like this," she said.

"No, that's not so," Turnbull replied. "That's entirely wrong."

"What, have you been there?"

"Kristina, you have a very narrow worldview because you have very little experience and –"

He stopped talking, and stared over her shoulder.

"What? What is –" she said, confused. She turned around and saw what had caught Turnbull's eye.

"Where is everyone going?" Turnbull said.

"It seems like out to the foyer. That's where they have protests."

"Protests?"

"Yes," she said. "Don't they protest in the field offices?"

Turnbull didn't answer. Instead, he listened hard to a growing noise coming from outside the emptying cafeteria. It sounded like a chant.

Faint, but he could make it out.

"*We won't buy the lie! Racist! Sexist! PBI!*"

"Our own people are protesting...us?" asked Turnbull.

"We need to go," Carter said.

"I've seen dipshits protesting before."

But Carter was obviously afraid. "You don't understand. If we don't go, they may protest *us.*"

They trotted out of the cafeteria behind the rest of the diners, most of whom carefully wrapped up and took with them whatever food they had not eaten. Turnbull and Carter made their way through the various halls and corridors until they found themselves at the edge of a crowd on the ground floor of the central foyer.

The foyer of the complex was inside the poorly constructed expansion to the original Hoover building. It was a cement monstrosity, with a ceiling that went up five or six stories and a barely finished asphalt floor that was supposed to look modern and industrial but really only looked cheap and incomplete. The big space was packed with people – it must have been nearly everyone in the complex. Many were on the various balconies lining the sides of the space, but most of the people – over a thousand PBI employees with more flowing in every second – were standing on the floor in a circle around the Hoover statue. There, at the foot of the monument at the center of the mass, surrounded by co-workers, were maybe a dozen agitated-looking individuals of various genders and non-genders, leading the chants and holding signs.

There were a lot of both, but they basically came to one conclusion – Director Rios-Parkinson was a hate criminal who devalued the contributions of womyn, non-binary beings, and pretty much every racial and ethnic group except Jews. Anti-Semitism would not have been an issue.

One had a bullhorn.

"Our spontaneous uprising shows that other-gendered people of oppressed races and identities will no longer tolerate the climate of hate perpetuated by Director Rios-Parkinson!" shrieked the lead protestor. Xe had pink hair and a nose ring. Behind Nosering stood a tremendously obese man – he was issued triple rations to maintain his size as a blow against fatphobia – clad in cargo shorts holding a sign that read "DEVALUED FOR MY GIRTH BY THE DIREKTOR." He was weeping.

There was some finger snapping from the audience. Turnbull recalled that applauding was disfavored because slapping the palms together demonstrated hostility and re-traumatized victims of abuse. Of course, there was some grumbling about the snapping – someone complained that "It reeks of thumb privilege." After all, some people did not have thumbs. The dissenters raised their hands up and wiggled their fingers, a move called "up-twinkles."

"Everything the PBI has become today, with its rape culture and hegemony of macro-oppressions, betrays the legacy of J. Edgar Hoover and his resistance to cisgender normative internal security work!" Nosering screeched, the bullhorn in xir right hand, xir left gesturing toward the statue of Hoover in a dress looming above them.

More snapping. Scattered up-twinkling.

"Spontaneous, huh?" Turnbull said. "With preprinted signage and a bullhorn?'

Someone shushed him. Turnbull turned and saw a man dressed as a blue fox wagging a finger – a paw, really – at him.

"Respect their rejection of oppression," said a high-pitched voice from inside the plastic fox head.

Turnbull started to laugh but Carter dragged him away before he lost his composure.

"It's not funny," she said. Her face showed real fear, and Turnbull pulled himself together.

"I just got shushed by a grown man in a cartoon fox suit," he said. "How am I supposed to take this seriously?"

"They could turn on Director Rios-Parkinson," Carter said. "Don't you understand?"

"No one is more woke than Rios-Parkinson," Turnbull said.

"Who says 'woke'? Look, you don't get it. None of that matters. If this gets out of hand and they turn on him, it's over. I saw it happen to some of my professors. It doesn't matter who you are. It doesn't matter what you did or didn't do. If you get labeled a hate criminal and it sticks, it's over."

"Shit," said Turnbull.

"We call on the racist Rios-Parkinson to answer these charges and we demand his resignation and discipline for his litany of hate crimes against marginalized peoples and otherkin!" Nosering screamed.

The crowd was murmuring and muttering. A few were snapping their fingers. Some twinkled tentatively. Turnbull could feel something happening.

The protestors were winning.

Turnbull glanced around – no sign of the Director.

"End the otherization of otherkins of color!" shouted the fox from behind them. Turnbull glanced back and saw that his brushy tail was somehow wagging. Several people around him nodded.

In agreement.

This was getting out of hand.

Something else was wrong. It hit him.

Kristina Carter was gone.

Turnbull looked around, pushing aside the crowd as he moved forward deeper into the audience. He caught a glimpse of her head to his front, bobbing up and down as she pushed to the front of the mass.

"Shit," he hissed again. Carter was heading toward the protestors.

Turnbull pushed forward, even less gently. One thin man with a scraggly beard grabbed his arm as he pushed past, but Turnbull grabbed him by the wrist and twisted. Grabby Boy was jerked off his feet and dumped to the ground, and Turnbull pushed past.

Carter broke out of the crowd and stumbled into the center area where the protestors stood. Surprised, Nosering stopped shouting to see what was happening. People quieted. The finger snapping died down, the twinkling faded. Carter faced the crowd.

"I reject the accusation that Director Rios-Parkinson has failed to show allyship with marginalized peoples!" Carter shouted.

The crowd was silent, shocked. Then more murmurs, a few fingersnaps of approval. Some twinkled.

But Nosering was not giving up xir crowd so easily.

"This cis-het bitch is invalidating our resistance!" xe screamed, the bullhorn-powered shout echoing through the huge space. "Shame! Shame!"

Carter looked around. The finger snapping increased – angry finger snaps, along with harsh twinkles.

"My truth is that Rios-Parkinson is a valued friend of otherized persons!" Carter screamed, but her voice was swallowed up by the size of the foyer and the howls of the protestors.

Turnbull got to the edge of the circle. Inside, Carter seemed horrified as Nosering accused her of being a willing agent of the patriarchy. The vicious finger snapping was reaching a crescendo, the twinkling was coming fast and intense.

So much for low-profile.

Turnbull burst out of the crowd and leapt forward to a stunned Nosering, grabbing xir loudspeaker. Xe tugged back and Turnbull pulled xir in close to his face and whispered, "If you don't let go of it, I'm ripping that ring out of your nose and shoving it down your throat!"

Xe was stunned and let go. Turnbull swung it to his mouth.

"Uh," he said, the bullhorn exploding with a burst of ear-piercing feedback. Nosering covered xir ears. Turnbull tried again.

"I demand, as a person of binary...ness," he said. "I demand to be heard and validated. Also, I am a traumatized individual of trauma and I will not let my voice be silenced by...uh, patriarchy."

He guessed right. The echoes died; a few fingers snapped. One nodding guy with red hair twinkled in solidarity.

"This one," he said, pointing to Nosering, "has marginalized my voice as a person of binaryness and totally denied my experience with

Director Rios-Parkinson, which is an experience of allyship and caring, and…"

More snaps, twinkles, and murmurs.

"Hey asshole, give me back my bullhorn!" xe shouted.

"Hate crime!" howled Turnbull into the speaker, his other hand pointing. "You heard it! You all heard it!"

More snapping. The twinkling was growing. Carter stared, stunned. Nosering looked around at the faces surrounding xir; now xe was panicking.

"And this one is racist!" yelled Turnbull. "The other day, this one was totally talking about hating nonbinary people like me and…furries. This one hates furries too!"

In the rear of the audience, the blue fox gasped. Someone put her hand on his sagging shoulder.

Turnbull continued. "Are we going to deny the allyship of Director Rios-Parkinson on the basis of lies from a proven liar? A proven hate criminal? What is this one's oppression? This one is privileged! Are any of you going to deny my experience as a nonbinary Muslim individual of color with a challenge overcome?"

There were more snaps now, many more. The crowd rippled with twinkling.

Turnbull turned to the sobbing fat guy and said, "Join the struggle, my hefty friend, along with Director Rios-Parkinson, against the kind of hate this one spreads that denies your humanity."

The obese man nodded, his eyes moist, his several chins jiggling as he did. He dropped his sign.

"Rios-Parkinson! Rios-Parkinson for the marginalized people!" Turnbull shouted. The growing tsunami of finger snapping and up-twinkling gave way to people picking up the chant, after assuring themselves that their neighbor was doing so too.

"Rios-Parkinson! Rios-Parkinson!"

The volume grew as the people in the audience raced to join in, to not be the last one to start chanting "Rios-Parkinson, Rios-Parkinson!"

Nosering stood there, alone, pale and breathing shallowly.

The crowd's eyes as one went to the balcony on the fifth level, where a figure stretched out his hands for silence.

The chanting stopped. Silence.

On the balcony, Rios-Parkinson surveyed his thousand plus subordinates on the floor far below him. They did not see the Walther PPK pistol he had in his front pocket.

"I will always show solidarity with the oppressed peoples and otherkins of the People's Bureau of Investigation!" he said. "My faith in the wisdom of your social justice is total. Long live people's justice!"

Then he turned and walked past the thirty security officers with AK-47s that stood out of sight behind him and got into the one operating elevator.

The crowd roared its approval. Turnbull watched three security officers appear and drag off Nosering. The rest of the dozen protestors quickly faded into the crowd, hoping no one had caught their faces on video.

They were hoping in vain.

"We have them all in custody," Rios-Parkinson said to Turnbull and Carter as they stood in his office. On a monitor on the wall behind them, the fat guy was sitting naked in a cramped cell in the basement, head in his hands, weeping.

"What are you going to do with them, Director?" asked Carter.

"First, I am going to find out who set them up to do this," answered Rios-Parkinson bloodlessly, which made it more ominous.

"And then he's going to shoot them," said Turnbull.

"We normally do not waste bullets on hate criminals," Rios-Parkinson said, still cold. Normally, he might just send them off to a Reeducation and Reintegration Center out in the wilderness of Maine or Oregon, but he felt kind today. The gentleman in the cage would not appreciate the camp's menu, and examples needed to be made. Then he went on.

"I have to commend you for your loyalty, both of you. Agent Carter, there is going to be a commendation for you."

"But Director, it was Agent Warren who showed the crowd how you're an ally of all oppressed peoples," Carter said.

"I know Agent Warren, Agent Carter, and I am certain Agent Warren would prefer to forgo a commendation from me."

"That's a safe assumption," Turnbull said.

"You are dismissed, Agent Carter." She nodded and departed the office. Turnbull stayed. They were alone.

"I didn't save *you*, Marty," Turnbull said, noting that the Director was annoyed at being called by his first name diminutive. "I saved the mission."

"And your partner. They would have torn her apart."

"I don't know if it's funny or frightening, but she believes all this bullshit."

Rios-Parkinson laughed. "They all do. Or they believe they need to believe it, and so they believe it."

"It's all a joke to you, isn't it? Just a scam."

"I grew up, *Kelly.*"

"You're a real piece of work, Marty."

"I am a tool for you to fulfill your interests, just as you are a tool to fulfill mine."

"You haven't told me if you've found out if Clay Deeds is still alive."

"I still don't know. Mr. Deeds seems not to exist officially. So, I suspect we need to wait until he contacts us."

"Then I guess you and I should focus on Wildfire and save our personal business for later."

"Yes. We will put that resolution in abeyance for now. You leave for Germany in the morning. And you had better pick up the trail of Wildfire or saving me will be completely in vain."

"This is a very nice place," Carter said, looking around the restaurant. It was called "Pirates" – there were lots of multi-ethnic pirate images on the wall, equal numbers of men, women and androgynous pirates. A pirate in a wheel chair had a parrot on his shoulder. Oddly, none had peg-legs.

The few other diners were busy in their own conversations. Turnbull had asked for and received a table in the back, where he sat with his back against the wall facing the front door. The restaurant was the best he could do; he had to play his privilege level and PBI cards. Of course, the really nice establishments were reserved for the people above his station, people who did not bother with privilege levels.

"Yeah, I asked around for a good place since I didn't get to eat all of my ass today at lunch, and this is what everyone told me was the place to be in Washington."

Carter looked at him oddly.

"I mean the District of Columbia. Whatever this town is called now."

She shook her head. "You are very strange. I mean, in the way you talk. I'm not judging your identity."

"I would hate to have my identity judged," Turnbull said, trying the drink called "Pirate's Grog." It tasted like distilled battery acid with orange flavoring.

"This is going to cost a lot of ration cards."

"I have plenty," Turnbull replied. His chicken was cold, but then the dining assistant – that was what Carter had informed him waitresses were called this month – had brought it that way. He knew better than to complain when in the blue. It drew attention. But then, the whole low-profile thing was kind of moot now.

"I've never been to Germany," Carter said. "Have you?"

"Yeah."

"On assignment?"

"Oh, yeah."

"What is it like?" Like most citizens of the People's Republic, Kristina Carter had no realistic chance of ever accumulating the climate credits necessary for a personal flight to Europe.

"Dangerous. The inner cities are hardcore Muslim extremist. Berlin, Frankfurt, Munich – no-go areas. Like a Shariatown."

"You can't say that!" she said, looking about instinctively. "You're Muslim yourself! Show some solidarity." The preferred term was "Majority Muslim urban safety regions."

"Arrest me, but after we get back from Munich. Now pay attention. The government really only holds the suburbs where the rich and middle class live. Out in the country, the Germans have reverted to form. Out there you find the tough country folk and they are pretty belligerent. They don't bother to pretend to like the Muslims and vice versa. They rumble."

"Rumble?"

"You ever read *The Outsiders*? Stay golden, Ponyboy? Probably not. They fight, over turf. Territory. Like gangs."

"That's a racist word," she said. "But Germany is anti-racist, right? They support the PR over the United States."

"Germany is full of Germans. Where do you think Nazis came from?"

"The United States."

"I...," Turnbull began, but he saw Carter was serious.

"Trump, Bush, they were Nazis," she said as if explaining something to a child.

"Is our dining assistant around? I need another Pirate's Grog."

Only one streetlamp was working outside, and the sidewalks and asphalt were dark and wet from a quick shower that came through while they were eating. The restaurant was about the only place still open, though it was not yet eight. Turnbull scanned the street before he stepped out, both directions. The Pirate's Grog wasn't potent enough to deaden his instincts.

Gunfire, off in the distance. Probably someone hungry trying to come in over the wall. Ironic, since it was not that much better there inside the Capital City Control Zone. Turnbull had seen the intel reports on Rios-Parkinson's desk. Riots all over. Soon enough, they would be here too. Hopefully by then he'd be done and gone, back to where they only had two gender identities and knew how to mix a drink.

The pair headed to the car, which was parked on the street north of the restaurant past an alley. Turnbull pegged it as a potential danger area without any conscious thought. He walked fast and moved to the far edge of the sidewalk as he passed the opening, and he looked down it for threats.

A yelp. He stopped. Carter did too, after a couple more steps and seeing her partner had halted.

There were shapes maybe 25 meters down the alley, two of them, and something on the ground. One kicked whatever was lying there, and that provoked another yelp.

"Is that a person?" Carter asked.

"No," said Turnbull, moving down the alley, making his plan, his hand inside his coat on the grip of his .45. "It's a dog."

The pair circled the panting animal, which was lying on its side, and they were laughing. They looked young, early twenties, and they were thin – maybe 150 pounds compared to Turnbull's 200 plus. The one had a goatee. The other had something in his right hand that curved into a hook at the end – a crowbar.

Carter saw Turnbull's hand inside his jacket and knew where it rested.

"You can't," she said.

"Yeah, there'd be paperwork," Turnbull said, still walking. "We do have a plane to catch early tomorrow." He pulled his hand out of his jacket.

"Let's go," Carter said.

"No," said Turnbull without slowing down.

The pair had still not noticed the agents. Crowbar lifted his weapon up over the animal for a final blow.

"Hey," Turnbull said, evenly.

They both looked over at him, puzzled, then they looked at each other, and then back at Turnbull. Crowbar lowered his weapon and began slapping it into his palm. In that time, Turnbull took several more steps toward them, and halted about five meters away. Carter was behind him.

"Oliver," she said.

Turnbull ignored her; he was assessing the two men. The dog moved and drew back Crowbar's attention for a moment before his gaze returned to the big man standing there watching.

"Hey," Turnbull said again. "What's going on?"

"What the hell do you care?" asked Goatee. Crowbar continued slapping the weapon and faced Turnbull. They stood there, Goatee left and Crowbar right, in the center of the alley.

"I'm concerned," Turnbull replied. "It seems like you two were hurting that dog."

"We are PBI agents," Carter said, stepping forward and flashing her People's Bureau of Investigation ID. "You should go. If you do, we won't arrest you."

The men laughed, and they did not go. They figured if they did not see a gun already, the pibbies were not packing. And they might have some nice stuff.

Turnbull stopped, just out of crowbar range. The dog, a stout mix with white splotches on black, was panting. No blood, but it was definitely hurt.

"I don't think you two are going to go," Turnbull said. "Right?"

"This is our dog," Goatee said. "We caught him, we're gonna eat him."

"It's a girl dog, dummy," Turnbull said. "I should run you in for felony canine misgendering. And did you just say you think you're going to eat her?"

"Yeah. We're going to eat *her*," said Goatee.

"So Barack, you think it's okay to kill and eat dogs?"

Goatee furrowed his brows, unfamiliar with the locally-beloved ex-president's notorious epicurean experimentation.

"It's our culture, asshole," said Crowbar, grinning. "You got no right to interfere with our culture."

"Your culture? You're *white*. You're mayonnaise white. What are you, Belgian? Is this some sort of Flemish thing?"

They were equally baffled by the words "Belgian," "Flemish" and "mayonnaise."

"Yeah, it's our culture, and you're racist. So, get out of here before we do the same thing to you," said Crowbar, slapping the bar in his open left palm.

Turnbull assessed. It would be three steps for Goatee to reach him, maybe two for Crowbar to get into swinging range. But neither was tensed or moving – they were also still assessing. Turnbull completed his plan.

"Well," Turnbull said. "I have a culture too, and that creates kind of a dilemma for us. Maybe you can suggest how we solve it."

They stared, so Turnbull went on.

"See, in my culture, people who hurt dogs get the living shit kicked out of them. I mean, we really hurt them bad. That's a pretty important part of my culture, too. So, your culture is telling you to hurt the dog and my culture is telling me to hurt *you*. Do you see the problem? But I think you can solve it by leaving now."

They made no move to go.

Turnbull sighed. "You two walking away was never in the cards, was it?"

"How about I smash your head in?" Crowbar suggested. He once again slammed the crowbar into his filthy left hand, then lifted it up.

"If you raise that crowbar at me again," Turnbull said politely. "I will take it and make you into an idiotsicle." More bewilderment. Then it occurred to him that they did not know what a Popsicle was. Carter probably didn't either.

"Okay," Turnbull said. "That's another way of saying that if you don't put that bar down right now, I'm going to take it away from you and shove it up your ass."

Crowbar charged, not coordinating with Goatee, and that was Turnbull's opening. He charged too, but at Goatee, and he was inside the arc of Crowbar's swing before Crowbar was ready to strike. Crowbar was past him a couple of steps before he stopped to turn. By that time Turnbull was on the shocked Goatee.

Turnbull hit him under the left armpit, slamming him back into the building wall and thrusting upwards on the underarm with all the force his legs could generate. It was more than enough to do the job. The joint gave way with an audible *pop*, as the ball came out of the shoulder socket. The Goatee slumped against the brick, his lower left leg exposed. Turnbull kicked down into it with the heel of his shoe, snapping the fibula below the kneecap.

Letting the screaming Goatee fall to the ground, Turnbull pivoted to face the other target in time to see the crowbar swinging his way. He dodged, and the steel hook smashed into the wall, kicking up a spray of brick shards.

The crowbar was at the end of its swing arc, leaving Crowbar's body fully exposed. Turnbull launched forward, his meaty right fist firing like a piston into the man's unguarded gut.

Three times.

Crowbar dropped the bar and folded forward. Turnbull grabbed him by his baggy People's Jeans and his greasy hair and thrust him face-first into the brick.

Twice.

Teeth frags scattered on the alley floor and the wall was painted with blood.

Turnbull threw the moaning man onto his back on the ground, and picked up the crowbar. Carter stood frozen. The fight had taken perhaps twenty seconds.

Turnbull glanced at Goatee, who was writhing in agony. Then he walked over to Crowbar.

"I told you," he said evenly.

"Fuck you!" Crowbar sputtered from behind shattered teeth.

"I hear dog is tough. It's probably going to be pretty hard to eat one with no front teeth. But hey, look at the bright side. Now you've got a challenge overcome."

Crowbar started to say something obscene about his assailant's parentage, but Turnbull spoke first.

"You should stop talking."

But Crowbar repeated himself, and Turnbull smashed the crowbar into the man's lower leg. The man's tibia gave way. Now Crowbar stopped talking; he was too busy weeping.

"We need to get medical aid," Carter said, surveying the carnage.

"Like a veterinarian?" Turnbull tossed the crowbar down the alley, where it landed with a *clang.* Carter looked at him, annoyed. "Oh, wait, you mean for these two? Nah."

Turnbull ignored the groaning men and knelt by the dog. A large abrasion ran across her rib cage. She was breathing hard. Turnbull gently picked her up. The dog cried a little.

"We need to go," he said. "Because now I'm starting to get angry with them and I might *really* hurt them."

Carter nodded and led the way. Turnbull, dog in hand, took a step, paused, and turned to kick Crowbar in the face one last time. Crowbar was quiet as Turnbull followed his partner out of the alley and to the car.

Rios-Parkinson leaned back in his chair. Inspector Cooley stood nervously as the Director read the transcript of the recorded call.

"So, the general will be visiting our Pennsylvania Avenue establishment," he said absently. The report indicated what the general was seeking. No wonder he needed to pay for it. Rios-Parkinson wondered how a man of such responsibility could be so irresponsible. He looked up at his subordinate.

"Inspector, when he comes in, put the usual procedure into effect. And alert me. I will handle the aftermath personally."

Cooley nodded, a bit of sweat flowing down his temple and leaving a trail of mascara behind it. Personally? It was usually his job to cocoon the flies they caught in their spider web, so Rios-Parkinson obviously considered this an exceptional opportunity.

"Now go," Rios-Parkinson said. Cooley left, and the Director turned his attention back to the thick binder of telephone intercept transcripts his various monitoring directorates had prepared for him.

Carter knocked on the front door again, and then a light came on inside. There was some shuffling, and the front door opened a crack. An eyeball scrutinized them and after a moment Ernie Smith pulled the door open.

Turnbull stood there, the dog in his arms.

"I didn't know where else to come," Turnbull said. "I kind of forgot we don't have veterinarians anymore because I forgot dogs are illegal."

"Owning dogs is racist," Smith said, stepping forward to pet the pooch. "Though I never understood why. Come on in."

The dog lay on Ernie's couch, covered with a threadbare blanket. It was a spartan place near the sector wall, sparsely furnished, entirely functional and spotlessly clean. There were pictures of Ernie with a woman, but there was no evidence she was there. Dead or divorced, but definitely gone.

Ernie had made them all some responsible tea, and each held a matching china cup. It was fairly strong, probably only the second or third steep. No lemon, of course.

"Like I said," Turnbull began. "I didn't know where else to go. We're flying out tomorrow for a week or so, and the dog..."

"It's okay," Smith said. "I like dogs. Grew up with them before the Split. Wish I could have one now."

"Look, here are a bunch of rat cards," Turnbull said, handing over a fistful of coupons. Carter's eyes went wide; people would kill for that much food. "I don't want her to be a burden."

"Nah, she's a good dog," Smith said, petting her. "I can watch her 'til you get back. After that though, what are you going to do?"

"I don't know," Turnbull said. "I'll figure it out."

"So, what about the folks who did this? You need a restock on ammo before you fly?"

"He didn't shoot them, thankfully," Carter said. "Broke one's arm."

"No, I *dislocated* his arm," corrected Turnbull. "I *broke* his leg. And the other one's leg too. And some other stuff."

"Sounds like they got off easy. A man who hurts a dog isn't a man," said Smith. "Or a woman," he added, correcting his omission.

"Can I use the bathroom?" Carter asked. Smith smiled and pointed, and Carter disappeared into the back of the little house.

"So," Smith said. "Who the hell are you, Agent Warren?"

Turnbull rubbed the dog's ears. She was lying quietly, still unsure about these strange humans who did not seem to want to hurt her.

"I've got a special mission," Turnbull finally said. "I can't say any more than that. That's for your safety too."

"I'm not so concerned about my safety," Smith said. "I have nothing to lose. My wife died a few years ago of whooping cough. They stopped doing vaccines years ago. Said they didn't need to because the People's Republic was a model of public health. But the whole hospital was jammed with people with the same cough. It was an epidemic. They never said anything on the TV about it."

"I'm sorry," Turnbull said.

Ernie shrugged. "I guess what I'm saying is, like with the dog, I'm willing to help you if you need it. We old vets gotta stick together."

"I may need some of your special skills."

"I'm here to help. And the girl?"

"Carter? She's along for the ride, but she's not dialed in. You get my meaning?"

"I get it."

There was a flush down the hall, and Carter came back into the living room.

"We should go. The flight is at nine," she said.

Turnbull stood. "You good?"

"I'm good," Ernie replied, standing to show them to the door. "Say, what's her name?"

"I don't know," Turnbull said. He paused in thought for a moment. "Clay. Wait, she's a girl dog. Cleopatra. Yeah. Clayopatra."

"This is awful," Turnbull said, putting down the cup on Kristina Carter's counter. She looked stricken.

"That's my good wine," she said.

"Sorry," Turnbull said, seeing her feelings were hurt. He looked around her quarters. There was a small kitchenette, a living room and presumably a bathroom and bedroom in the back. Unlike Ernie Smith's mostly bare house, these walls were decorated with pictures, mostly of flowers and landscapes, but also with a poster of a racially ambiguous anime-style woman with a sword.

Carter followed his eyes. "That's Kimba," she said, as if he ought to know what that meant. "Kimba," she repeated, but slowly this time. That did not help.

Turnbull shrugged.

"You're probably too old. Kimba was the main character in *People's Justice Warriors*. You know, the cartoon? It was huge when I was a kid. She was this warrior who fought hand-to-hand with racists and sexists and homophobes from the red states who would come and try to subvert the People's Republic."

"I missed that one. Before my time. You ever see Bugs Bunny?"

"Who?"

"Forget it."

"She made me want to be a PBI agent and protect the People's Republic from racists. Kimba was so inspirational for my whole generation of women and womyn. Before the Split, back when it was all racist and red, there were never any non-cis het male heroes. Ever."

"I'm not sure that's so."

"Oh, it is. I majored in the literature of colonial dismantlement at Princeton, and we studied it. There were no female heroes at all in any major, mainstream popular entertainment in the old United States. It was actually illegal. Yeah, there were revolutionary and subversive texts, but you could get sent to a camp if you tried to make art outside of approved sex roles. Look it up."

"Isn't our job to send people to camps for things like making stuff with unapproved sex roles?"

"No, what we do is different. We enforce tolerance." Carter shook her head. "You are so weird, Oliver. Is everyone from a field office like you?"

"Doubtful."

She sipped her wine, and thought it was good. "What you did at the foyer today…"

"You don't have to thank me."

"I wasn't going to. I've been thinking about it, and I didn't need you to white knight for me. I had the situation under control."

"They were about thirty seconds from torching you at the stake."

"If you weren't non-binary, I'd swear you were totally..."

"Totally what?"

"Sexist. Racist."

"Now I'm racist? Against girls?"

"Those guys and the dog. I mean, it was their culture."

"You bought that bullshit?" Turnbull replied.

Carter looked confused. "We can't judge their experiences and values."

"Our whole job at the PBI is judging people's experiences and values."

"That's different," insisted Carter. "At the PBI we only prosecute bad people."

"I think people who hurt dogs are pretty bad."

"How can you judge that?'"

"You just said we prosecute bad people. How can you judge *them*?"

"Because...," she said, then thought for a moment. "It's obvious."

Turnbull rubbed his head. "Tell you what," he said. "How about I beat the crap out of people who hurt dogs and you stand back and watch."

"I could have taken them if I needed to," Carter sniffed.

"You're a hundred and ten pounds dripping wet," Turnbull said, then he realized his mistake. "Fifty kilos."

"So?"

"So? They both outweighed you substantially."

"That's sexist."

"Physics is not sexist. It's *physics*. I don't care what your Kimba show says. They would have pummeled you. That's why you carry a gun. Use your gun. Leave the hand-to-hand to me."

"Oh, because you identify as male?"

"Not because I'm a man. Because I weigh a hundred kilos and I know how to fight."

"I can –"

"No, you *can't*. Forget Kimba. If you get cross-wise with a big dude, shoot him with the Glock, center mass, until he dies."

They stood there in awkward silence for a few moments. At last, Turnbull spoke.

"You've been taught a lot of things, and some of them are wrong and some of them might get you killed. I'd prefer you not get killed."

"You think I always do what I'm told," she said. "Well, you're wrong."

She went back in here room and returned with an old iPhone.

"I don't accept just everything," she said. She put the phone down on the counter and tapped the screen. "One of our jobs in Social Media and Internet Ops was blocking access to illegal music. Well, I was cleared to listen to it to determine if it was illegal and I..."

"You what?"

"I kept some."

"You kept some?"

"Yeah, I kept some." She tapped the screen. The tiny, tinny speaker came to life with a roaring guitar riff.

"Is that," asked Turnbull, "Joan Jett?"

"*Crimson and Clover*, yes. How do you know? It's illegal."

"If I told you I'd have to...what's so bad about Joan Jett?"

"See, I don't know. I don't understand why it's forbidden. It's a girl singing about another girl, so it breaks the cis het hegemony over LGBTQN3#@FZ voices."

"How did you remember all those initials?"

"Stop it," Carter said. "Don't you see? I don't know why that song is illegal, but it is, and I still have it on my iPhone 13."

"So, you're a rebel," said Turnbull.

"I just like the song," she said. "And I don't understand why that's wrong. I'm starting to question a lot of things, and I don't understand it, and I don't like it. But you question everything. Why?"

She seemed on the verge of becoming emotional.

"I have to go," Turnbull said, and he went out the front door toward his own shabby quarters.

9.

Lufthansa flight 4055, an Airbus 350-900, would take them into Frankfurt, and then they would clear customs and wait to catch another plane to Munich. Kelly Turnbull was tired and annoyed as they boarded, but Kristina Carter was wide-eyed with excitement. Even the inevitable pre-boarding debate over who was the most oppressed, and therefore entitled to load first, could not bring her down. She had not flown on a plane since she was a little kid, before the Split.

Coach, of course. There was no way Rios-Parkinson would spring for first class. Unlike on Justice Air, the People's Republic's government carrier (and its only remaining airline), the Germans made no attempt to hide the air travel hierarchy. Carter gaped at the front-end passengers clinking champagne glasses in their own special sanctuary until her partner had to gently shove her back toward their seats in steerage.

Turnbull stored the diplomatic pouch overhead. It held their guns, and since it could not be inspected the security folks had waved it through without taking a peek. That was not much less than the rest of the carry-ons got. The machines that used to scan carry-on luggage had long since broken down, or had been removed due to the protests of "radiation sensitive individuals" who insisted that exposing their luggage to x-rays "irradiated" their bags and somehow caused them to have bizarre reactions when they picked then up at the other end of the conveyor belt. The x-ray activists had descended on the airports, screaming "You're murdering us!" and eventually the People's

Republic stopped trying. After that, carry-ons received, at best, a half-hearted once-over by the bored security timeservers poking through bags at the end of interminable lines of frustrated passengers.

The Germans did not approve of the inefficiency; it grated on them, and the Capital City flight out of what had been Dulles International was universally dreaded by the air crews. So, to the flight attendants, all blonde, Turnbull and his eager partner Kristina Carter were just two more uncouth PRNA citizens in bad suits acting like yokels. The Europeans gave them the stink eye, but Turnbull ignored them. That was his default reaction to those from the dying Old World. He just did not care what the damn krauts thought.

Turnbull collapsed into his aisle seat and shut his lids, but some woman passenger was screeching about how some other passenger's male gaze was "literally murdering her" – to which the offender responded by demanding to know why the woman was assuming xe was male. This colloquy kept Turnbull from drifting off to sleep immediately. Eventually, the statuesque stewardesses refereed the dispute, and he dropped off into slumber.

He got a couple hours before waking up. Somewhere over the north Atlantic, one of the attendants started the meal cart down the aisle, which fascinated Carter. Turnbull passed on the ham and *spaetzle*, but his partner was delighted by hers.

"Airline food is amazing," she said, digging in. Turnbull had a Bitburger *pils* and then went back to sleep.

Along with the rest of the passengers from Flight 4055, they wandered through the endless corridors in the bowels of the Frankfurt International Airport to reach baggage claim and get their checked bags before they moved to customs. A fair number of flyers were complaining that the ground crews in Capital City had pillaged their stuff.

The airport itself was on the cutting-edge of 1970s design and it had not been updated in decades. Germany was still the economic powerhouse of Europe, but its coffers were running dry paying for the social programs the government used to buy peace with its millions of unassimilated, largely unemployed immigrants. As a result, they had delayed infrastructure investment, especially after the Greeks and Italians defaulted on their tens of billions in loans from Berlin. Eventually, the Germans abandoned the idea of improvements. Germany was now focused on maintaining the façade, buttressing the status quo. Once sparkling and modern, the airport, and the country as a whole, had taken on a certain un-German shabbiness as it slowly wasted away.

At the customs desk sat a bored German wearing the green uniform of the *Bundesgrenzschutz.* He had longish brown hair and a drooping moustache, and he was scanning the passports of the arriving passengers. An older woman with a cinched face began to complain about something – Turnbull caught the words "sexist" and "white privilege" – but the border guard shrugged and said, "*Ich spreche kein Englisch.*"

The guard pointed to a screen on the counter; the passenger put her finger tips on it for a biometric reading. Then he handed back her bright pink People's Republic of North America passport and she stomped past through the exit doors.

Turnbull and Carter stepped forward, pulling their bags. Carter kept the diplomatic pouch in her hand.

"Passports, please," said the guard. Turnbull handed him both – they were orange, meaning diplomatic. The guard paused to look them over, then tapped on the screen.

"*Nein,*" Turnbull said. "Diplomatic. We're exempt from biometrics."

"Okay," said the guard. He scanned the passports and handed them back. "You are free to go. Welcome to Germany."

Turnbull nodded and pulled his luggage to the exit door. He did not see the border guard trip the face-level hidden cameras built into the walls.

The short hop to Bavaria took less than an hour, though they spent nearly five waiting for its departure in the Frankfurt departure lounge. There were a lot of German *Bundespolizei* on patrol, many packing MP7s or G36s, and none of them were of foreign extraction. Germans tolerated multiculturalism when it came to working stiffs, but if you carried a gun, you were almost certain to be a Teutonic homeboy.

Frankfurt was still the key hub between North America, Africa, and the Middle East, and foreigners passed between gates under the watchful eye of the security forces. Disembodied voices repeated announcements in German, English, and several other tongues. The linoleum floors were well-swept, but worn down and dull.

Turnbull wanted to sleep, but Carter could not – she wandered through the shops and restaurants, wide-eyed and amazed at the bounty. He trudged along, but only to keep her out of trouble.

"It makes me sad," Carter said after visiting every single concession. "The People's Republic would be like this if it weren't for the racist red states undermining and sabotaging our economy. But our principles require sacrifice."

Turnbull excused himself to go get a stein of lager. Except before he got that beer, he darted into an electronics shop and bought a simple cell phone with an international calling chip. He pulled the battery out and stuffed it in his pocket, then got his lager.

On the ground in Munich, they went to the Eurorent counter and hired a 2033 BMW 435i Hybrid. Carter had never ridden in anything like it before. Turnbull drove, but first he retrieved his .45 and stuck it in his belt.

The *Flughafen München* was northeast of Munich proper and relatively close to where they needed to be. Turnbull wheeled the BMW onto the A92 autobahn and, contrary to the promise of the speed limit free open road, promptly came to a stop in the midst of a particularly ugly *stau*. That made it easy for the Mercedes sedan carrying two agents of the *Bundesamt für Verfassungsschutz* to follow them in their white Audi.

It took Turnbull and Carter 30 minutes to go the few kilometers to the northern suburb of Lohhof, where they had reservations at a discount hotel chain called Ingel Hof. Carter was fascinated by the BMW's radio and kept fiddling with the stations, stopping only when a heavily autotuned voice over a bass-heavy beat came pumping out of the speakers.

I will give you a happy ending

To our love story

Oooo oooo oooo oooo

You must touch my horny!

"Tatiana Sexxxy is an important voice of female empowerment in a phallocentric culture," Carter announced. Turnbull turned off Mrs. Putin's warbling. The rest of the way, Carter's face was pressed against the glass of the passenger side window, looking out.

"So many cars," she said. "Does everyone have a car here?"

"Yeah," Turnbull said. "Same as in the US."

She snorted. "Oh, okay. Sure."

"You know that before the Split, almost everyone in what's now the PR had a car. Sometimes two. And there were traffic jams in Washington before it became Capital City."

She laughed softly. "You're funny, but you shouldn't be. And I shouldn't be laughing."

"You're a laugh criminal," he said but she looked stricken. "Oh, that's a thing, isn't it?"

"That's really offensive," she said, and turned back to watching the traffic.

The Hotel Ingel Hof was a large three-story white rectangle lying on its side just off the main road through town. There were no balconies, only rows of windows. It was perfectly functional, almost militant in its rejection of anything beyond its pure utilitarianism. It was a place for sleeping, and nothing more. But one did not come to the quiet suburban town of Lohhof as a tourist. There was nothing there but homes and light industry, and its only stab at historical significance was its proximity to the town of Dachau. You checked into the Hotel Ingel Hof for a roof and a bed and perhaps an undistinguished meal before making an early departure.

The bored blonde at the front desk effortlessly switched into English upon seeing their clothes – the appearance of citizens of the People's Republic was usually considerably shabbier than that of the fastidious German businessmen who made up the vast majority of the clientele. "Heike" read the name tag above her left breast. She made no effort at small talk. She took their passports to scan, then handed them key cards, and pointed them to the bank of three elevators at the far end of the lobby. All three worked.

The room was small and functional, with the typical low furniture and tight spaces alien to American travelers' eyes – at least to Turnbull's, who never got used to the smallness of European living spaces. It was so unTexas. But Carter was thrilled.

"Look at this!" she said, rushing in, tossing her jacket on the bed's *decke*, a white comforter. She peered around the corner into the cramped bathroom. There was no tub, of course, only a very narrow shower stall with a shower head that sat about 1.5 meters high off the floor, ready to spray any man of average height in the sternum.

Turnbull went to the bank of windows that overlooked the parking lot in the back of the property. The windows did not open except for a few inches at each side of the frame. Turnbull had asked for a second-floor room, too high to break into easily, but possible to jump from if it came to that.

While Carter played with the weird German water faucet on the tiny sink, Turnbull did a quick check for listening devices. He doubted he would find any in the unlikely event the BfV had planted them – the Germans were good at this stuff. He figured there was a decent chance he had been made at the airport – he had passed through Germany dozens of times in the past, so they had his biometric info. Not having to give over his fingerprints might delay them, but they were likely to make him with facial recognition eventually. Still, as long as he behaved – as long as they did not know he was misbehaving – the krauts were likely to let him go about his business and depart.

"I'm taking a shower," Carter announced from the bathroom, and then it occurred to him. There was just one bed.

Carter walked out of the shower with her top off and immediately undid and removed her threadbare tan bra.

"What the hell?" asked Turnbull. She looked at him, baffled, and unbuttoned her pants.

"What? You want to go first?"

"You want to put on a towel?"

"What do you care?" Carter replied, genuinely puzzled. "You're non-binary."

"Just..." Turnbull sat on the edge of the bed, looking away. "That's a microaggression. Can you put a towel on?"

"I should not have to hide my body..."

"Towel!"

"Fine," she said, tossing her bra onto the bed and returning to the bathroom.

He put the .45 next to the phone and the TV remote on the small wooden nightstand that was built into the wall, then lay down. In the bathroom, the water went on. Turnbull retrieved his European cell phone and reassembled it. It powered right up. From memory, he dialed a number in the United States. Aware that the BfV was going to be listening – at least electronically, using algorithms to flag keywords – Turnbull waited until it went to voicemail.

"Please leave a message," said a generic voice. Then a beep.

"Broadsword calling Danny Boy," Turnbull said. "Broadsword calling Danny Boy. Call back at midnight your time. I'll be listening for ten."

Turnbull hung up and removed the battery again. No sense in carting around a tracker. If Clay Deeds was alive and able, he would call back at seven the next morning and Turnbull would have the phone turned on and be waiting.

If.

Turnbull squirreled away the phone and the loose battery and lay back over the comforter. The water was still going. Carter was going to enjoy her first long, hot shower maybe in ever. He shut his eyes and tried to sleep.

"This is amazing," Carter enthused, stuffing the *doner kebab* into her mouth. Bits of pita fell away onto the hotel room floor.

"I can go get more," Turnbull said. "The *imbiss* is just down the block." He took another sip from his bottle of local *pils*.

"It's so good," she said. "So, this is traditional German food? I love it!"

"It's Turkish. The Turkish guest workers in the nineteen sixties and seventies brought it with them and the Germans adopted it."

"Multiculturalism is fantastic!"

"Yeah, yeah. Look, we need to get to the factory, scout it out, and see if we can get inside, and we need to do that before dawn, so can you hurry up?"

She nodded, taking another bite of the foil-wrapped sandwich.

Turnbull pulled her Glock out of the diplomatic pouch and slid in a mag, then racked a round into the chamber. Carter finished her meal and held out her hand; Turnbull passed her the gun.

"Let's try not to spark an international incident," he said.

"I don't think I'm the problem, Oliver," she said, putting the weapon in its holster under her jacket.

Hebertshausen was almost indistinguishable from Lohhof. It was neat, orderly, and functional – German through and through. The Feldschall Fabrik Gmbh factory was on the north side of town, off on its own at the end of a narrow road and surrounded by high fences. There were lights inside the main building; it was operating an overnight shift, but there was not much visible activity other than a guard at the front gate. He was holding an old HK MP5 submachine gun.

"If the Germans let him carry, there's something interesting in there," Turnbull said. The info on Feldschall that Rios-Parkinson had been able to discreetly obtain – he certainly could not go asking for it from the PIA – was pretty sketchy. The company designed and built custom scientific equipment, and rumor had it that it was not too particular about who it did so for.

Somehow, whoever was growing Marburg X had gotten his laboratory from Feldschall. And who knows – maybe they were looking to replace what they had abandoned in Siberia.

The pair watched for a while. There was enough light around the gate to observe what was happening. The guard checked the papers of everyone going in, but he waved anyone going out through.

"We could climb the fence," Carter suggested. They were observing from a parking lot two hundred meters from the gate. The BMW was parked out of sight – any vehicle coming down the road was going to the factory so they had gotten out well away so as not to draw attention.

"No, it's got concertina running along the top. Plus, there will be sensors."

"What do you suggest?"

"I could shoot the guard and we could walk in."

"What happened to 'no incidents'?"

"I'm not seeing a lot of other options...wait, yes I am."

There was a rumble to their rear. A work truck was coming slowly up the road from behind them. It looked like it belonged to some sort of cleaning company, and it had an open rear bed with some boxes in it.

"Follow me," Turnbull said as it passed, and he darted off with Carter following.

He got his hands on the rear drop-door and pulled himself over and into the flat bed. The cab was out of sight, blocked by several large boxes. Carter was running along behind. He got her hand and pulled her inside. They crawled around to the far side, away from the guard shack. As the truck slowed to a stop, Turnbull drew his weapon.

Just in case.

There was an exchange in German and in bad German – the driver was clearly speaking *Deutsche* as a second language. The gate swung open slowly and they ducked down as the truck entered the compound.

It came to a halt by a large, open bay at the edge of the main building. Turnbull peeked over the edge of the bed and determined that it was clear – or at least as clear as it was going to get. They tumbled over the side and onto the asphalt.

A dark man with a moustache dressed in work clothes who Turnbull thought looked more than a little like Donkey Kong's nemesis Mario stepped around the back of the truck and came face to face with the pair. Then he turned to the truck bed and began retrieving his gear. It was unclear to Turnbull whether the man thought they belonged there, or whether he knew they did not belong there and had no desire to inject himself into some kind of trouble. Regardless, Turnbull and Carter headed inside the building.

"Then we have an agreement, Herr al-Afridi," Spetters said into his cell phone.

"We do," replied the Arab into his. It was a high price, but worth it if the German kept his promise. The al-Baghdadi Brigade's plan to blow up the Ric Grenell Annex of the United States embassy in Berlin was not his operation, but anything that might lead to dead Americans he would cheer on, even if Allah's work was being done by rivals. Spetters would now roll up that whole network based on the information al-Afridi had just disclosed. It was a delicious irony that the price of saving the Americans had been the life of an American agent.

"My men are already there," Spetter said. "Yours need to hurry to collect your prize." The Arab grunted and hung up.

Al-Afridi handed a paper with the address to his man Hassan. Hassan was unimaginative, but pious, brutal and reliable. At this time of night, Hebertshausen was perhaps a half-hour from central Munich. Spetters would ensure the *polizei* were nowhere around, and that the van full of armed Arab men would move unmolested through the suburbs past the routine checkpoints and patrols.

"I want Turnbull alive," al-Afridi said. Hassan nodded and left him.

"What are we looking for?" Carter asked. They moved slowly, lurking in the shadows when they could.

"Offices," Turnbull said. There were doors at the end of the open bay. Turnbull pushed one open. It was a long, dingy corridor. They could hear clanging and grinding from what was apparently the main factory floor on the other side of the wall.

Turnbull went first, weapon in his jacket. At the far end of the corridor was another door, and beyond it, the stairs. A sign pointed upward. It read "*Verwaltung.*"

"Is that it?" Carter asked.

"Search me, I don't speak their weird-ass language. But most big shots like to be on the top floor, so I'm guessing that if what we want is here, then it will be upstairs."

The second floor did contain offices, and some of them were

still lit. But there were no people visible. The only noise as they entered was the distant clanging from the factory floor.

And then another noise – mumbled words in German. Plus...mooing.

Turnbull's gun was up and pointing to an office with an open door and a light on inside. Someone was speaking quietly in there, but there was only one voice, and its German was slurred. And there was something that sounded like a ruckus in a barnyard. Turnbull peeked around the corner and saw something that did not surprise him.

There was a chubby middle-aged man at his desk, drinking glasses of schnapps poured from an open bottle, his black rimmed glasses reflecting the farm-themed pornography he was watching on his computer monitor.

Turnbull stepped in, his gun raised. The man stood up, his belt flapping and crumpled paper napkins scattering.

"Geez, sit the hell down," Turnbull shouted, not too loudly but loudly enough. "What is it with naked people today?"

The man sat and began fixing his pants, mumbling. Turnbull and Carter entered the office and shut the door behind them. The .45 stayed on the German.

The man finished arranging himself and looked up, confused and afraid. The video clip on the screen continued.

"Is that a pony...?" asked Carter, horrified.

"Freaking Germans. Fritz, turn it off!" Turnbull said. The man grabbed the mouse and closed the window. Turnbull leaned over the desk.

"I need to ask you some things. Then we leave and you can return to your sexy zoo party and this never happened. Okay?"

"*Kein Englisch*," replied the German.

Turnbull put the barrel of the Wilson X-TAC to the German's forehead. "This is my universal translator. You still *speaken* no English?"

"Is that even German?" asked Carter.

"I can speak English," said the man, quivering.

"Great. I have a few questions for you then we go away and you can get back to your animal husbandry."

"I don't know..."

"Shhh." Turnbull pushed the barrel of the Wilson X-TAC against his skin. "You don't want to die with your browser history uncleared."

"What do you want to know?" The man smelled like fear inside a distillery.

"There was a special order recently, the last few months. Same as one from maybe a year or so ago. A full lab set up. Very specialized. You sent the first one to Siberia."

The man swallowed.

"Ah, rings a bell," said Turnbull. "Who made the order?"

"I can't..."

"You can. And you will."

The German swallowed again – Turnbull could see the wheels turning inside his schnapps-clouded head. The man was thinking over his options, and none of them were good. It was time to offer the man an out.

"No one will know. You tell us, and we go. It'll be just like we were never here."

Hope was sometimes as powerful as a pistol. The man nodded.

"The Arabs," he said.

"What do you mean 'the Arabs'?"

"The buyers. They were Arabs. They met with Herr Teuffelmann this morning to complete the latest agreement. They have bought from us several times."

"Who is Herr Teuffelmann?"

"Our CEO. I saw them meeting. I reviewed the proposal. Please…"

"A few more questions. What did they order?"

"A specialized laboratory package, complete and air transportable."

"Where was it supposed to go?"

The German gestured toward the computer and Turnbull nodded.

"Careful." He wagged the gun in his hand. The German nodded and used the mouse and keyboard to find what appeared to be a bill of lading.

"These are the shipping documents. The shipment left the factory this afternoon."

"Print it." The German moved the cursor and right clicked. The printer next to Carter hummed to life. She grabbed the paper and began reading.

"It's to a company, no doubt a front. They are flying it into Washington – well, Capital City but this says 'Washington.' How many hours are we off from PR time?"

Turnbull thought for a moment. "Six."

"It lands in an hour."

"Turn Rios-Parkinson's cell phone on. Take a picture of the bill of lading and text it to our friend back home. Don't write anything – the BfV might catch it."

Carter nodded and set to work.

"This is a very sensitive transaction," the German said.

"I'll bet," said Turnbull.

"It was *approved*."

"Approved? You mean by the government?"

The German nodded. "As a German, I am very conscious of such matters. Especially living here." He gestured at the schnapps; apparently that helped him cope with the moral quandary.

"I wish the rest of you Germans were as caring," Turnbull said. He looked over to his partner. "You finished?"

"Yes."

"Turn the phone off and check the hallway." She moved out the door. Turnbull turned back to the German, pointed to the shot of schnapps on the desk, and gestured with the weapon. The terrified German threw it back in one quick motion. Then he poured another.

"It's *slightly* to my advantage not to shoot you, so I'm not going to. You would be well-advised to forget we were ever here. Perhaps you will wake up tomorrow after having blacked out."

The German drank the shot, then poured another.

"Good," Turnbull said. "Now, if we walk out of here and hear an alarm, I'm coming right back here to this office." The German drank the third shot, and poured himself a fourth.

"*Ja*, I understand."

Turnbull gestured toward the shot glass. The German picked it up, stared at it uncertainly for a moment, and then downed it.

"*Auf wiedersehen,*" said Turnbull, and he left.

The German poured another shot, but before he swallowed it he took the mouse and cleared his browser history.

There was a small motor pool of light trucks, and the keys were on pegs behind a vacant counter. Turnbull went behind it, took one and picked up a work coat that had been left behind on a chair.

"Number 67," he said, putting on the blue coat as they went to the designated box truck.

Carter got down in the well of the passenger seat of No. 67; Turnbull lay his .45 on the console for easy access. The Volvo cargo truck fired right up, and Turnbull backed out of the parking space and headed toward the gate after a three-point turn.

The gate was ahead, and the guard shack was on the other side. Turnbull pulled the Volvo up to the white line a few meters inside and idled. A head popped out of the guardhouse door, then disappeared back inside. A moment passed. Then another. Turnbull's hand was inching toward his pistol when the gate began to swing open. When Turnbull and Carter passed by him, the guard was inside the shack, seated and illuminated by a flickering television screen.

Turnbull drove the truck up the narrow road and then took a right, and the gate disappeared from view behind a white building that evidently held a farm supply warehouse store. The BMW was parked at the far end of the lot among several other vehicles. Turnbull stopped the truck nearby, turned off the engines and the lights, and they exited. He tossed the work coat inside the cab then slammed the door.

"Let's get..." began Turnbull, but he was interrupted.

"Halt!" said one of two large German men, stepping out of the shadows.

"Good evening," said Turnbull, assessing. No weapons in hand. Someone with a rifle up on the roof pulling over watch?

"Your identity papers," said the taller of the two.

"How about *your* identities?" replied Turnbull. "Who are you?" The pair was now about two meters away. Why no weapons?

"We are *polizei*," said the other one.

"I'll just call you Brint and Meekus. That okay?" asked Turnbull. They seemed to not understand. "Never saw *Zoolander*, huh? It's a classic."

"Your identification," Brint, the taller one, said impatiently. He was looking at Carter, who was looking right back at him.

"Okay," said Carter.

Shit, thought Turnbull.

Carter launched a vicious strike with her right hand directed at Brint's solar plexus, throwing her full 110 pounds behind it. But Brint was a solid 220 pounds. When the blow landed, he looked down, surprised, and then launched an open-hand right across Carter's face. It took her off her feet and sent her sprawling on the ground.

Meekus, distracted, did not have time to defend from the right Turnbull drove into his gut, followed by the left to his face as he crumbled.

"Halt!" shouted Brint, his Heckler & Koch P10A compact 9mm pistol out and aimed center mass directly at Turnbull.

Brint's head jolted sideways as Carter's Glock went off. He fell over. Turnbull drew his Wilson X-TAC and put two rounds into Meekus's head as the German tried to grab his own weapon.

The encounter had distracted them, and they did not see what was coming up the road. There was a tire squeal and a tan Opel panel van with Arabic script on the side screeched to a stop perhaps 10 meters away. The side door flew open, revealing four men in black knit masks bearing a variety of handguns.

Turnbull opened fire with the Wilson X-TAC, fast and with minimal aim – luckily, they were packed tightly together in the back. One wavered and dropped; the other three rushed out directly at them. But they seemed hesitant to fire.

Turnbull was not.

He blasted off the rest of the mag, and when his slide locked back he shouted "Reloading!" Another attacker staggered and fell.

Carter continued firing from their flank, drawing the attention of the last two away from Turnbull. He did not go for another mag. Instead, he dropped to the pavement and pulled the P10A pistol the rest of the way out of the German's holster then slapped his left hand around his right for a two-hand grip.

"Reloading!" shouted Carter as her slide locked back, just as Turnbull had trained her at the PBI gun range. She reached for her next mag.

Turnbull assessed his targets. One was on his feet maybe five meters away and probably not hit; he had some sort of SIG Sauer, probably a 226. A second was standing there, dazed, probably hit. He had a Beretta M9. The driver was probably intact; he might have a long weapon in there.

Turnbull took aim center mass at the SIG guy, firing off two fast shots. He hit – the guy's shirt erupted in two holes, but he did not go down. Vest, or just the 9mm ammo?

Turnbull took no chances. He pivoted up at the target, who was now facing him, and fired twice toward the nose. The first smashed into the bridge, the second into the man's right eye. As he fell, Turnbull aimed at the driver, firing again and again at the shadowy head. The glass cracked and shattered and the van lurched forward. Turnbull kept firing off rounds until he went dry.

Two more gunshots went off to his right. The wounded attacker collapsed; a wisp of smoke curled out of the end of Carter's Glock.

Turnbull tossed the HK aside and retrieved his Wilson X-TAC, sliding another magazine into the well and sending the slide forward. He got up and charged the van, which had rolled to a stop after bumping into the side of the Volvo truck they had stolen.

Turnbull cleared the rear cargo area – he noted the zip ties and duct tape – and carefully opened the driver's door, weapon up. A black-clad figure slumped out of the driver's seat. The 9mm round might not be the most powerful slug out there, but if you shoot a guy a half dozen times it tends to resolve the situation.

"Shit, Oliver," Carter said, standing.

"Security!" Turnbull yelled, and Carter took up a position to engage any new threats. "You hit?"

"I'm okay," she said.

Turnbull hopped up on the van's running board and reached inside and across to the glove compartment, grabbing what appeared to be the van's registration papers. Then he stepped over to the dead men from the van. Kneeling, he pulled off SIG's ski mask.

"This guy is an Arab," he said. He reached over to another one and removed his mask. The same. What the hell?

"I don't understand," Carter replied.

"See anything?" Turnbull said.

"No, nothing yet," Carter replied, scanning the empty streets.

"That won't last." He stepped over to Brint's body and dug in for his papers. There was a small leather case in his jacket. Turnbull opened it. There was Brint's photo on a card identifying him as a member of the *Bundesamt für Verfassungsschutz*.

"Who were the Germans?" Carter asked, not taking her eyes off the approaches.

"Kraut secret police," Turnbull said, tossing aside the ID and digging into the guy's pockets. His hand came back with a set of Audi keys. Turnbull hit the button with the picture of a horn. A few feet away, a white Audi honked and its headlights flashed. Turnbull pushed the trunk button as he jogged over. In the back were two black plate carrier rigs, a G36A2 assault rifle and a totebag full of loaded magazines. Turnbull took it all.

"Let's roll," he said, heading toward his BMW. Carter joined him.

"Check under the wheel wells," Turnbull said, throwing the gear and the gun into the back seat.

"For trackers?"

"Good girl," Turnbull said. He checked the two wells on the driver's side.

"Got it," Carter said. She was holding up a small magnetic transponder.

"Get rid of it." Turnbull sat in the driver's seat and took out the knife. Eurorent had installed a recovery tracker on the inside windshield, apparently not imagining that someone would simply pry it loose and cut the wires. Turnbull tossed the black apparatus out of the car, pulled the door closed, and turned over the engine.

"Where are we headed?" Carter asked as he roared out of the parking lot.

"Not back to our hotel room, that's for sure."

"Where will we go? They're going to be hunting us."

"The Germans and those Arabs both."

"Do you think these are the same Arabs who bought the lab gear?"

"Definitely," Turnbull said. "But I don't get the relationships here."

"The autobahn is that way," Carter said, pointing left as Turnbull made a right onto Alte Römerstrasse, a wide street lined with picturesque homes and businesses until the right side of the road became nothing but a long grey wall with occasional graffiti.

"We're not taking the freeway," he replied. The bad guys would be all over it.

Turnbull made a right after the wall ended and drove back past some houses. At the end of the road was a chain strung between two poles blocking further access, but Turnbull killed the lights and simply drove around the right pole, working his way deeper into what seemed to be an abandoned parking area filled with weeds and broken beer bottles.

"Where are we?" Carter asked.

"I was here before, back when it was open and people came here."

"What is this place?"

"Dachau."

The visitors building was ruined and covered with graffiti. Most of it Turnbull could not decipher exactly, but he got the gist. The influx of unsympathetic Arabs, the break-up of the United States, which had liberated the camp, and exhaustion after nearly a century of national guilt all combined to create a national consensus to forget this place ever existed. So, the memorial was closed and forgotten by everyone but the drunks and the vandals.

They hid the car behind the overgrown bushes and went inside the walls of the camp. There had been two columns of twenty long barracks each between the walls. Nineteen rows had been torn down, leaving empty concrete foundations, while two remained at the south end of the camp, along with the chamber of horrors that was the administration building.

The doors to the two remaining barracks buildings were padlocked with rusty hasps. A solid kick forced open the door and they stepped inside the musty museum. Turnbull swung the beam from the BMW's emergency flashlight across the interior. The displays of photos he remembered were still there, but the layer of dust showed that no one ever came to learn from them anymore.

"We'll stay here tonight," Turnbull said. He put the rifle against the wall and sat down on the filthy floor. Using the flashlight, he examined the registration he had liberated from the van. "It was owned by a company called Salaam GmbH on the *Burgstrasse* in what I bet is downtown Munich. That's where we need to go tomorrow."

"But everyone is looking for us."

"They'll be thinking we're heading away, maybe trying to make a play for France, not going into Sharia central. You're going to have to cover up."

"Do you think we really need to? What if Director Rios-Parkinson got the text and intercepted the shipment."

"We can't be sure. We have to be sure."

Carter walked over to the displays. "What is all this?"

Turnbull got up with the flashlight and illuminated the photos posted on the displays. German soldiers. Barbed wires. Starving men and women in striped uniforms. Bodies.

"I don't understand," Carter said, horrified.

"This was a concentration camp during World War II. The Nazis sent people here to die. Jews. Gays. Priests. Anyone they thought was unworthy of living. The American Army liberated it."

"The American Army?" she said, incredulous.

"Yes, the United States Seventh Army. It was right before the war ended. When the Americans saw what the Nazis had done, they took a bunch of the guards around back and shot them. When the command saw what happened here, no one was ever charged."

"But the red Americans were Nazis themselves, weren't they? I mean before the People's Republic split, America did things like this all the time. Didn't it?"

"Is that what they taught you?"

Carter nodded.

"Did they teach you what the Holocaust was?"

She shook her head.

"Six million Jews murdered. Millions of others. They never taught you about the Nazi genocide?"

"Only about the red American genocides. I've never heard of any of this. Where did you hear about this?"

"Take this," Turnbull said, his lower lip quivering a little. He had to remind himself that it was not her fault. He took a deep breath. "You take this flashlight. You walk through here and you look at every single photo. Then you go to sleep."

He walked away and left her standing there.

10.

Just before seven, Kelly Turnbull ensured he was alone and stepped outside the barracks. It was a clear day, and the sun was already well up in the sky. He walked around a corner and assembled the cell phone he had bought at the *flughafen* then turned it on. He sat on a cement stairway and waited. Ten minutes ran by.

He decided to make another call.

"Broadsword calling Danny Boy," Turnbull said when the voicemail message finished and it beeped. "Today I'm heading into the *Schloss Adler*. Talk to you same time tomorrow."

He hung up and broke down his phone again.

"You look good," Turnbull said, inspecting Kristina Carter's new *niqab*. It was black, which was the style, according to the German who sold it to them who specialized in outfitting fellow infidels who had to dress to conduct business inside central Munich. It covered her whole body except her face; underneath she wore a headscarf that left exposed only her eyes. They declined to go full *burka*, which also covered the eyes with a fabric mesh, and the German warned them that some of the locals would consider her a whore for not doing so.

"I just need to remember that this is really about empowering women and showing respect for your people," she said, and Turnbull detected no sarcasm. She continued: "Now, sometimes dress can be a tool of patriarchal oppression, like in the red states or in *The Handmaid's Tale*. But not this."

"I'm glad you feel empowered. Is your Glock empowered with a fresh mag?"

"Yes. I have it in here."

"Take mine too and stick it somewhere in there. And these mags." He handed them over to her and they disappeared inside the shapeless tent that surrounded her.

Turnbull adjusted his tie and beeped the BMW locked. The area was thoroughly immigrant and primarily Muslim, and he was getting some odd looks from the locals. But he was pretty sure they were safe on the streets. Accompanied by Carter in her outfit, he was either a convert or someone with business there. And the car and the gear in the trunk were safe – thieves from that neighborhood ended up dumped by the side of the autobahn *sans* hand.

They started down the wide, filthy Marienplatz, passing by the coffee houses and *halal* food vendors. The people were mostly African and Middle Eastern immigrants. There were lots of children. The Muslims had hope for the future; the Germans had none, and therefore no reason for the natives to spend their euros on raising a new generation rather than on easing the pain of their nation's decline.

The Rathskellar was a huge gothic building they passed on the left. The lower floor's beer halls had long since gone, replaced by *halal* cafés and coffee shops. The face of the ancient building was scarred, and the niches under its arches empty. It took Turnbull a few moments to realize what was missing – all the statues and sculptures of ancient men and women that had once decorated it had been brutally chiseled off.

The minarets on the new mosques that had been built in place of old German buildings towered over it all. Turnbull had timed the visit to avoid getting caught outside during prayer call.

At Burgerstrasse, they took a left, walking up the side streets toward the address where the van was registered. It was a huge white building, five stories high with a parking garage below, black with soot and bearing a sign in Arabic over the main entrance. In smaller letters beneath the flowing script, it read "Salaam GmbH."

A number of salty looking dudes lurked out front, but people were going in and out, mostly women and children, to whom the guards paid no heed.

"What is it?" wondered Turnbull.

"I bet it's social services," Carter said. "Just like at home. You go there for benefits. It's like for entitlement payments."

"But private, like a charity?"

"No," said Carter, horrified. "Charity is a tool of oppression designed to obscure the patriarchy's solidification of its own power paradigm."

"Did you memorize that in school?"

"Of course. Didn't you?"

"Come on, let's try the garage."

They walked past the wide garage entrance, dodging a van not unlike the one they saw the night before as it exited up the driveway. The driver honked and Turnbull put his right hand on his chest. The van turned left and kept driving. They made their way down into the dark.

There was a security booth, and someone in it. Turnbull carefully peered in to see the back of a head and a television showing a badly dubbed version of the 1980s beach bunny movie *Hardbodies*. The Arab guard was enthralled at the glistening bounciness of it all, and the pair tiptoed past him.

It was cramped, with vehicles parked tight against each other and plenty of chips and scrapes on the walls and the van bumpers. They moved back toward the rear of the underground space, keeping to the shadows as best they could. Toward the far end, there was an elevator and, next to it, what was likely a stairwell door – with a "*Verboten*" sign on it.

A Mercedes sedan came down the driveway and they pulled back out of sight. It stopped in front of the elevator and two men got out of the back.

"Lab coat," said Turnbull. One of them was clearly a thug, the other clearly a geek. The two men ignored the elevator and used a key to enter the stairwell. Turnbull and Carter were moving before the door slammed shut, and Turnbull caught it before it latched. He pulled it open gently. Footsteps and talking – Arabic – were coming from the lower reaches.

"There's something deeper underground here," Turnbull said.

"What is it?" Carter asked.

"I have my suspicions. Look, be very careful. If this goes south, you take that tent off and run, got it?"

"I can..."

"*Listen* to me," Turnbull said. "I know what I'm talking about. If you see anyone who's not ..."

"Not what?"

"Not *normal*, you cap him and run. You got that?"

"Let's go, Oliver," Carter said firmly. Turnbull pushed open the door and headed down the stairwell.

It went down three floors and crossed three landings, none of which had doors, until it came to the bottom and a landing blocked by a steel door with a tiny viewing window at eye level that was closed with a sliding door on the other side.

"I think we've come to the…" Turnbull said as he stepped onto the landing. Even as his foot lowered to the floor, he saw the card reader on the wall to his right.

His foot hit the landing. There was a buzzing – he had tripped something. The sliding door on the viewing window pulled back, revealing a pair of eyes examining them. Turnbull stayed frozen, hoping to look like someone lost and surprised.

The view port slammed shut and the steel door opened. There were two men, wearing plate holder rigs and obviously guards. Each had a Heckler & Koch FP6 tactical pump action shotgun hanging across his chest. They both came out, speaking rapid, angry Arabic. They did not go for their weapons, though they could have. The door slammed shut behind them.

Turnbull shrugged and smiled, trying to look lost. He stepped all the way down onto the landing and Carter joined him, but they ignored her.

It was clear the intruder did not understand Arabic, so they switched over to German and continued their harangue. Turnbull smiled like an idiot and pointed back up the stairs, making to depart. This made them even madder. The taller one put his hand on Turnbull's shoulder to hold him in place. Now the shorter one's hand went to the stock of his shotgun, which hung over his chest via a black combat sling.

The taller one turned Turnbull to face the wall and pushed him against it, not at all gently. He then conducted a quick pat down – nothing – and turned Turnbull back around. Turnbull smiled goofily and put his hands up. The tall one yelled in his prisoner's face in German, then gave a curt order to the short one. The shorter one took his hand off the shotgun stock and put it on the radio handset by his shoulder.

Carter moved quickly and was on him before he could react, pressing up against the stunned guard and forcing him against the wall.

He yelped once, drawing the tall one's attention, and then there were two *cracks* from between his and Carter's bodies. He spit up a gob of blood all over Carter's *niqab*.

Turnbull could smell the cordite as he brought his fist hard against the tall one's temple. The man staggered under the blow and fell with his head on the lower stair. Turnbull brought his boot down hard on his neck and there was an audible *snap*.

The short one had collapsed on the floor – if not for the bloody hole under his plate carrier, he would have looked like he was just sitting there napping. There was a smoking, blackened hole in the middle of Carter's costume. She pulled the *niqab* off and the Glock was in her hand.

"Nice job," Turnbull said. "I bet you no one heard that through that door."

"I've killed two or three people in twenty-four hours," she said, a bit shell-shocked.

"It has been a little slow," Turnbull said. "Get his 12 gauge and some shells. I think we're done with subtlety."

He knelt down to the twitching body with the broken neck and took his corpse's key card as well as his weapon. Turnbull swiped the key card against the reader and the door buzzed open.

"I hate long, dark halls," Turnbull said, stepping through with the short-barreled shotgun pointed downrange.

Carter followed, her weapon up too. There were a couple of chairs in the hallway against the wall where the guards sat, and there were cell phones out on both.

"Guess they got wi-fi," Carter observed.

There was no window on the locked door at the far end, and Turnbull tried the key card. Nothing.

"What do we do?" asked Carter.

"We knock," said Turnbull, and he rapped hard on the door.

They waited.

Nothing.

"Well, it was a ..." began Carter.

The lock clicked and the door opened inwards.

Turnbull kicked it, hard, smashing it into the face of the thug behind it. The thug staggered back and went for the SIG in his belt. That was a mistake. Turnbull put two loads of double-aught buckshot into his chest and he sprawled back across a table, knocking Bunsen burners over and sending beakers crashing to the floor. The science geek stood there with an iPad, stunned. Carter covered him. His mouth moved, but no words came out. It was an Arab, not Dr. Maksimov.

It was a cellar converted into a lab. Obviously, some of the equipment had been removed already – it looked like Turnbull had just missed moving day once again. On the wall was a red panel with Arabic script and a German word: *STERILISIEREN*. There were tanks in one corner with the "inflammable" symbol. Against the north wall was a large refrigeration unit that was running loudly. It had a biohazard sign on it.

Turnbull fed two replacement rounds into his weapon and cleared the big room quickly and efficiently, ending up at the door at the back. It had a large biohazard symbol on it too.

"No, no!" said the geek in the lab coat.

"Shut up," Carter hissed.

"Do not go in there," the tech said in accented English. He was clearly terrified, more than of the young woman with the shotgun pointed at his guts.

"What's back there?" Turnbull said, though he had a feeling he knew.

The lab geek swallowed. "The cells," he said quietly. "They are all gone or dead. But it's still dangerous."

Turnbull put his ear on the door. Nothing.

"Get me a mask and a suit."

Turnbull put on the gas mask and the white plastic suit the geek had directed him to and slowly pulled open the door, weapon up. Carter and the geek were huddled at the far opposite end of the main room. She had strict orders if it went south.

Shoot the tech and run like hell.

The lights came on automatically. There was a row of perhaps a half dozen cells. Shapes lay silent at the bottom of each of them.

He pulled the door closed and removed the gear. Then he walked to the lab tech and slammed him hard in the gut with the butt of the shotgun. The geek fell to the floor, groaning.

"First thing. How do you speak English?"

The geek struggled to catch his breath. When it looked like Turnbull was about to slam him again, he suddenly caught it.

"I studied in the United States, at UT – University of Texas."

"In the red?" Carter said, as if she was evaluating a bug.

"Okay, longhorn," Turnbull said. "I know your pals left for the People's Republic yesterday. One of them was Dr. Maksimov, right?"

The geek nodded.

"And he's off to Washington?"

"To Capital City."

"Yeah, yeah. Now, who are they?"

"Who?"

"Yeah, who? Who are they?"

"They are freedom fighters, martyrs, carrying out the will of All-"

Turnbull smashed him across the face with the butt of his 12 gauge.

"Listen, you start that shit with me and I will hurt you. I mean bad. Who *are* you people?"

"We don't have a name. Not like the others who fight *jihad*. We represent all true Muslims."

"Really? I've killed a lot of *jihadis*, and most Muslims thought they were assholes too. So, why are you going to the PR?"

"Why?"

"Yeah, why?"

"To bring judgment to the infidels," the geek said, proudly. "There is nothing you can do. What is in progress cannot be stopped."

"We'll see."

"And I will be a martyr too."

"You are not in any position to do anything *but* be a martyr, dude," Turnbull said. "And your pals don't think so either. They left you behind to clean up."

"No, you are wrong. I volunteered to be one of the pilgrims."

"What the hell does that mean?"

"It lives only in hosts. That is why we had to take the *kaffir* German addicts and scum and use them. To keep it alive inside them until they died." He looked over at the reefer unit.

"Holy shit," Carter said.

"It incubates quickly. I would have to get on a plane and I'd should show no symptoms before Capital City."

"You were going to carry it over?"

"As a back-up, a fail-safe. It's already there! The other pilgrims have already gone." The geek started to laugh, spitting blood from where Turnbull hit him.

Then he stopped. "You are the one al-Afridi talked about. The American. You were to come here last night."

"American?" asked Carter.

Turnbull ignored her. "Yeah, your pals' plan kind of went awry. Terminally awry. This al-Afridi guy – who is he?"

"You speak of him with respect!"

"Not likely. Al-Afridi...is he Iraqi?"

The geek nodded. "A prominent family of freedom fighters from Baghdad."

"Yeah, I think I waxed his brother. Twelve gauge in the nutsack. So, it's personal, huh? Hey, I bet you could call him over there in Capital City."

The geek suddenly smiled and giggled.

"Oh, I can call him with the iPad. A video call! I think he'll answer." The geek giggled again.

"Let's do it," Turnbull said, handing over the iPad.

"Do you think this is a good idea?" Carter said.

"I think it's the best idea I've had in a long time." Turnbull handed over the iPad. "Go ahead. Remember, I got this shotgun and I have a track record of blasting *jihadi* jerks in the junk, so you be cool."

The geek took the iPad and punched up Skype, then giggled again as he hit an account on his favorites that had no avatar. It rang. And rang.

And it picked up. The video focused. An Arab man in a sunny room. He said something in Arabic, and sounded impatient.

Turnbull took the iPad and stared into it.

"Hey, asshole. I'm who your boys were looking for. I smoked their sorry asses. Oh, and by the way, your pudgy brother died crying like a little bitch, but he got off easy compared to what I'm going to do to you."

"You?" al-Afridi said, stunned.

"Yeah. And when we meet, it's going to be my choice of time and place."

Al-Afridi composed himself. Then he smiled, and began to laugh, a bitter, nasty little chuckle.

"No, Turnbull, I think I know the time and the place." Al-Afridi maneuvered his iPhone so that the camera picked up what was behind him out the window.

The minaret-filled skyline of Munich.

"Run!" Turnbull shouted, dropping the iPad.

The geek roared in laughter for about a half-second, then Turnbull shot him in the face.

They ran toward the door but Turnbull stopped at the red panel. "I bet I know what *STERILISIEREN* means," he said, breaking the seal and pulling the red handle. In the far corner of the lab, the tanks of inflammable gas began to hiss.

"It needs time to fill the whole space," Turnbull shouted as they sped across the guard corridor.

"How long?" Carter said, following him out the door and onto the landing where the two dead guards lay.

"Maybe a minute," Turnbull said, rushing up the steps.

One flight.

Two flights.

Noise – people descending.

Third flight, the garage level.

Three Arab men rounded the corner above them coming down, all with handguns. Turnbull fired first and kept firing as Carter joined in – though at a slower rate because of the recoil and need to pump.

The first Arab took it in the chest and the second took it first in the upper thigh then in his gut. The third stopped, turned around to take cover and got a blast in the back of his neck. They collapsed in a pile and began to tumble down the steps. Turnbull's ears roared – Carter was saying something but he could not hear. He shouted "Reload!" at the top of his lungs – they would probably have to shoot their way out of the garage.

Two more appeared at the landing above them and the carnage below, and Turnbull was sliding a shell into his weapon as they spotted him. He ducked back and several rounds hit the wall behind where he had been standing. Carter got off one blast – she missed, taking out a chunk of plaster, but it gave them pause.

And then the lab exploded. The building shook, and the sprinklers went off.

Carter was thrown off her feet and hit the ground first, then Turnbull landed on top of her. The two attackers were falling down the stairs – one had kept his balance until his foot hit a splotch of goo that had been the contents of one of his predecessor's abdomen and had been made even slipperier by the cascading water. They tumbled out onto the landing just as Turnbull let the slide go forward. One shot each solved the problem they posed.

He and Carter got to their feet and paused by the door to the parking garage.

"All right, let's do it," Turnbull said, slipping two replacement shells into his weapon as the water rained down on them.

She nodded and pulled open the door to the parking level. Turnbull rushed out into the garage, gun up, looking for targets to engage. For some reason, the sprinklers had not engaged there. The perplexed guard was standing out in the open, unsure of what was happening.

Turnbull clarified the situation for him, terminally, then racked another shell.

"Keys in!" Carter yelled, jumping into the driver's seat of one of the tan vans. Turnbull leapt into the passenger seat and Carter pulled backwards to execute a three-point turn to exit the garage. Turnbull covered the stairwell and elevator doors as she did. The elevator doors opened up and Turnbull opened fire until the shotgun went dry – suppression, since he could not see inside. Now pointed toward the driveway, Carter gunned it and the vehicle took off up the ramp. As they went upward, the rear right window shattered and the windshield cracked from the inside as a round flew through the van directly between them.

The van leapt out onto Burgerstrasse and Carter cranked a hard left, barely slowing.

"Give me yours," Turnbull said, taking her FP6. He checked the feed. Empty.

"Any loose shells?" he asked.

"I'm out," Carter said. She dodged a Fiat that was pausing in the street for no apparent reason. Turnbull looked back. There was smoke billowing from the Salaam GmbH building, and people were streaming out the exits.

It was rapidly disappearing behind them as they tore up the street.

"Which way?" Carter asked. This is not the route they had come – they had walked from the BMW down the pedestrian-only Marienplatz.

"Next right," Turnbull said.

"Great idea with al-Afridi," Carter said. "What were you doing?"

"Trying to get a clue about where he was."

"Oh, well that worked."

She hit the brakes. The BMW was right there. They rolled out of the van, leaving it idling, then jumped into the sedan. Passersby stared, unsure of what they were seeing, but that shotgun the big man carried made it clear that interference was not a wise course of action. The locals minded their own business as the two kaffirs roared away up the street.

Al-Afridi watched the flames engulfing his building; the German firemen had taken their sweet time waiting for the *polizei* to gather and escort them into the immigrant zone. Finally on scene, their attempts to put out the fire seemed half-hearted. Bastards, but maybe it was for the best. The more thorough the destruction, the fewer questions to answer.

A dozen of his men stood around him, waiting – they knew better than to interrupt him while he was deep in thought.

He turned to the most senior of his followers who was still alive and still in Munich.

"Gather the brothers, Ahmad. All of them. Find those two. They arrived with People's Republic passports, so I expect they will be heading to France."

"But the checkpoints –"

"I will make a call. You will not need to worry about passing through the checkpoints."

Ahmad nodded. "If they are clever, they will keep to the countryside, but there will be trouble with the *kaffirs* if we follow. We may have to break our truce with the Germans."

"Then break it, Ahmad. But I want the infidels dead."

Ahmad nodded again, and shouted instructions. Dozens of cars would be leaving soon. Al-Afridi put his hand on his man's shoulder.

"And I need to be driven to the airport. It is time for me to go to Washington."

11.

Martin Rios-Parkinson stood by the SUV, a pair of armed People's Bureau of Investigation special tactics officers with AK-47s flanking him on the tarmac. The rest of the team was scouring the Airbus A220 with yellow and brown AvecAir livery that sat in front of the hangers at the northeastern cargo area of what had been Dulles International.

Inspector Cooley trotted over to his superior. His mascara was running from the exertion.

"Gone," he said.

"What do the pilots say?" asked the Director.

"Nothing. They are French. They deny any knowledge of the cargo. They were hired, they loaded, flew over, and unloaded, and the passengers and equipment were picked up by cargo trucks and left right away. We missed them by ten minutes."

"Paperwork?" Cooley handed it over. They had already determined what they expected; the receiving company was a front. Rios-Parkinson noted the customs stamp.

"Medical equipment," Cooley said. "The crew denies seeing it. Well, they saw sealed containers, but not what was in them. And they were told to stay in the cockpit and not interact with the passengers."

"Bring me the customs officer," Rios-Parkinson said. Cooley nodded and left.

Kristina Carter's cryptic text had been right – they had flown into Capital City, but they were gone now. He drummed his fingers on the black hood of his ride. As a practical matter, they could be anywhere by now.

"Director," said Cooley, frog marching a dead-eyed woman in a disheveled People's Customs Service uniform into his presence. She was thin, with hollow cheeks and a half-open mouth.

"Who were these people?" Rios-Parkinson asked, anticipating the answer.

"I don't know," the woman said and Rios-Parkinson slapped her across the left cheek hard. She staggered back, but Cooley lifted her up again.

"This aircraft flew in here not an hour ago. It unloaded cargo and passengers and you were in charge of clearing them. And you did. This is your stamp and your signature, correct?"

The agent nodded slowly. It was occurring to her that she was in a situation.

"You listed zero passengers entering the People's Republic and you cleared at least ten cargo units in five minutes. I am guessing your inspection was cursory at best."

The agent stared, the wheel in her head turning.

Rios-Parkinson sighed. "You simply put down what they told you to put down and stamped and signed it. Am I correct?'

The agent looked down at the tarmac.

"Reach into her pockets," said Rios-Parkinson. Cooley did, and withdrew a thick wad of ration cards.

"You are a traitor," Rios-Parkinson said without emotion. "You understand what happens to traitors?"

The agent did understand that. "I just –," she began.

Rios-Parkinson nodded.

"They were *official*," she said.

"The people on the plane?"

"No, the ones who came here before and told me what to do when the plane landed. They had suits."

"You betrayed your country because someone in a suit told you to?"

"They had identification. Government identification."

"What *kind* of government identification?"

"PBI," she whispered.

Of course.

"What did they *say*?" Rios-Parkinson asked.

"They said a plane would come. I was not to inspect it or ask questions, just put down what they told me and not ask questions," she answered.

"And they would pay you in ration cards for your trouble?" Rios-Parkinson asked.

"They were *official*," she replied, miserable.

"I am *official*," snapped Rios-Parkinson. He turned to Cooley.

"Take her. And the crew. Get anything else you can out of them. Everything. And they talk to no one." Cooley hustled the customs officer away.

Rios-Parkinson felt the cold tingle of fear he so hated. Wildfire had arrived.

"It is not to either of our advantages to be seen meeting," said the Vice-President.

"This hotel is secure," replied Louise Stenz. Both her and Richard Harrington's security officers were in the hallway outside the suite. Adam Marshall sat a few meters away, close enough to be summoned, far enough to be excluded.

"It's a PIA hotel, Louise," he said. "You've doubtless memorialized our little meeting electronically. But I accept that. That's part of why I am so intrigued by you. You are thorough."

"We both have assets that we bring to the table," replied the Chameleon.

"That we do. But tell me, are the assets you bring to the table greater than anyone else's who I might choose to work with?"

"What are we talking about, Mr. Vice-President?"

He laughed. "I have no doubt that the Chameleon has anticipated exactly what is likely to happen in the coming months and that she has a plan. I am just curious if she believes that I fit into it."

"Go on," she said.

"You know President De Blasio is suffering from dementia. Oh, it's difficult to tell considering the nonsense that fool spews, but the fact is that he is weak and the sharks are circling. Alliances are being made. The presidency will come open, sooner rather than later, but perhaps not soon enough, considering the chaos enveloping the Republic. How long do your analysts give it before it all falls apart, Louise?"

She paused, considering. "Six months. The food situation is untenable."

"Too many mouths, too much socialism."

That seemed to take the Chameleon back a bit. It had been a long time since she had heard such blunt speech from a fellow member of the ruling class.

"Come now, Louise, we all understand that the socialism we all praise on television is utter nonsense. The People's Republic's flirtation with it will go on the list of the times socialism was tried but was never *actually* tried. Everyone sentient understands that this country needs reform. I don't propose we return to the pre-Split days. I prefer my capitalism controlled, harnessed, and obedient. I propose retaining a firm hand."

"And you wish to be that firm hand?"

"Can you think of a better candidate?" Harrington asked. In fact, she could, but she did not name her.

"You mentioned assets. Mine are different than that of others you are likely talking to," she said. This was, she realized, an audition.

"You know who I'm talking to, I suspect."

"Information is my asset. I don't have an army like the generals. I don't have the secret police like Rios-Parkinson. I have information," Stenz said. But so did Harrington. One of those sources was in the PIA and had revealed a certain lab in Siberia to the Vice-President, who revealed it to the Director of the PBI. That source had since disappeared, probably dead in a PIA dungeon. Neither the Chameleon nor the Vice-President would be so vulgar as to speak of that unpleasantness.

"You also have some small direct action elements," the Vice-President said, taking a sip. "Let's not be modest, Louise."

"If I were to be able to influence the situation, might that be useful to you?"

"It might. I'm intrigued. What do you mean by 'influence the situation'?"

"You said it yourself, Mr. Vice-President. The situation is unstable. We've both read the unfiltered reports. Riots. Looting. Five People's Security Force officers murdered by a mob in Detroit last night. The security forces are losing control. And while you seem to have Rios-Parkinson's PBI in your pocket, you don't have the military. At least, not yet."

He silently acknowledged her shrewd assessment. Though the law had him as next in the line of succession, what did that really matter. It would be a knife fight, and he needed allies. His approaches to the leaders of the military had met with failure. The military stubbornly retained its independence from his control.

"The military still has President De Blasio's confidence, or rather, the confidence of those who change his diapers and feed him mush with a spoon."

What if something happened to make them lose that confidence? And if that something solved some of the resource issues…"

The Vice-President looked the Chameleon over. "Fewer mouths? Yes, that could change the calculation. And lost confidence means they would have to support a leader who was actually capable of leading."

"The vice-president would seem to be a natural choice to lead in a crisis," Stenz said. "The president would doubtless direct the military, to the extent it was itself unaffected, to pledge its loyalty to his successor, whoever that was. Obviously, if that loyalty was weakened…"

"So, what kind of event might allow us to achieve those laudable goals?"

"A significant event."

"You have a plan, don't you?" asked Harrington. Of course, he suspected how the pieces might fit together. But he was not prepared to abandon his deniability quite just yet.

"I have an expectation that if a crisis develops that demands a unified, forceful response that allows you to seize power that you will share it with those who helped create that opportunity."

Harrington smiled. "I think you would make a fine senior official in my administration."

"I would make a historic vice-president."

"You might indeed."

"Even if you previously promised that position to someone else."

Harrington admired the ice in her veins. "Your information is very good. I am told that such a person almost befell an unfortunate fate in Mexico City recently. I assume this significant event might solve that problem too."

"I would expect it to. And I would expect the security domestic portfolio in addition to my present international security area of reasonability."

"If you deliver what you promise, it is yours."

"Then we have an understanding, Mr. Vice-President."

"We do," Harrington responded. "I expect it is useless to ask for more details."

"It is best that you do not know."

Harrington grinned; he was now sure he had guessed correctly.

"And when will whatever this is you have planned begin?"

The Chameleon smiled. "When it happens, you will know."

"I look forward to it." Harrington was well-satisfied. One of the two rivals would prevail; either way, he would.

The staff was cleaning up after the meal. Harrington and his personal security detachment had slipped out of the hotel unseen. Stenz and Marshall adjourned to an adjoining room.

"The video is perfect. You have him conspiring," Marshall said.

"He would just claim we manufactured the footage," Stenz responded. "And, of course, it would paint me as a traitor too. No, we will proceed with the plan. How are our fanatical cat's paws doing?"

"They are out of sight now. We don't have access or contact. It's too hard to get close to them inside there." Marshall did not tell his boss that he had sent two agents to observe the Arabs, and neither had returned. That would just upset her.

"We don't need to watch them. We know what they plan to do. Is the construction completed?"

"It is," said Marshall. "The entire PIA complex area is now a control zone, complete with a wall."

"Make sure you have the personnel to person the wall when it happens," Stenz directed.

"And the Capital City Control Zone wall has been analyzed. We'll take it down to allow them in at key locations when the time comes. They think their wall will keep it out; instead, they will be trapped inside. Their wall is a death trap."

"Rios-Parkinson might escape. They have a few operational helicopters."

"True," said the Chameleon. "But where would he go?"

12.

They pulled off the main road before sundown and took the dirt track back into the woods several kilometers until they were confident that they were far away from any people. Turnbull took the first watch, and Kristina Carter fell asleep almost immediately in the passenger seat.

Turnbull exited the car quickly, shutting the door as soon as he was out to kill the dome light. He went to the trunk and opened it, removed the G36A2 rifle and shut the boot again, quietly. Then he unfolded the stock as he walked about 25 meters away to a tree where he could sit and have a good view of both directions of the dirt road.

He sat still and silent, listening. He learned that in the service, the power of listening. At first, the wood seemed silent. But soon he was picking out noises – crickets, wind, bird calls, perhaps a dog, and off in the distance, cars passing in the night.

He watched and listened, the weapon on his lap. For hours.

They were back on the road. It was about 11 a.m. when a green and white *polizei* Mercedes passed by them heading northeast without drawing even a bored glance from the cops inside.

"Still no BOLO to the fuzz," Turnbull said. He had been concerned passing through the checkpoints around the Munich city center, and he was wondering if the authorities would be looking for them out here in the countryside.

"What?" asked Carter.

"BOLO. Be on the lookout." He paused as she stared. "Fuzz? Cops, from the nineteen sixties? Like 'groovy?' Whatever. The cops don't seem to be looking for us."

"After all the people we've killed in the last of couple days? It seems like they would all be looking for us."

"Maybe not. Those weren't German cops we iced. They were secret police, intel guys. My guess is that they aren't telling their regular pals what's up. But I bet they'll be looking for us, and not in uniform."

"Plus the Arabs."

"Plus the Arabs, if they want us bad enough to risk coming out into the countryside looking for us. The local Bavarian boys won't take too kindly to a bunch of immigrants showing up on their turf."

Turnbull accelerated down the country road. They were heading southwest, down toward the Alps. The countryside was green and clean, except for the random burned-out barn and destroyed house. It seemed most of the outlying buildings were deserted. And when they passed through a village, the locals watched them carefully.

"American," Kristina asked, apropos of nothing.

"What?" asked Turnbull.

"They called you an 'American.' Why did they do that?"

"Habit from before the Split. They call anybody from the PR or the US an 'American'."

"And what was that about shooting his brother in the genitals?"

"You know I can't talk about that stuff."

"Who are you, Oliver?"

"I'm just a non-binary trying to survive in this business. Can you stop talking?"

"You are not PBI. That's for sure."

"I am if you believe I am. Now look at the map. We need gas. How far to the next town?"

She stretched out the paper map – Turnbull did not want her using electronics – and pored over it for a moment.

"Bad Kohlgrub. A few kilometers ahead."

"Sounds charming."

Bad Kohlgrub had been charming. Now it was a sullen little town with whitewashed buildings and red roofs dulled with soot. A church steeple loomed overhead. Turnbull took a moment to confirm it was not a minaret. It was not – a minaret would not be flying a German flag.

There was an Aral gas station, white and trimmed with blue, toward the center of the town. The pumps were under a large, flat roof structure. Then there was a rectangular building that housed the cashier and the snack shop. No one was at the pumps, but a German with a large brown bottle of something, undoubtedly beer, was staggering about out front.

Turnbull pulled into the lot and next to a fuel pump.

"There's no line," marveled Carter. "Do we need rat cards?"

"Nope."

"You can just buy gasoline?" she said, still baffled. "Anybody? Who decides if they need it?"

Turnbull was not ready for a discussion of her flawed underlying premises, not before noon, not without a big brewski like Gunter over there was guzzling.

"I'll pump. Take these Euros," he said, handing her some candy-colored bills. "Buy some gas and get us some food inside."

"But I don't speak German."

"I bet they speak money." He popped his door. "I'm hitting the head."

He got out and walked over to the pump and inserted the hose in the tank and Carter disappeared inside. He waited until she had time to pay, added some time for the communication delay – she had probably never bought gas in her life, much less in a foreign country. The numbers went to zero and he started pumping, locking the handle. As the liters flowed, he went to the restroom.

When he pushed open the door, there was a blue Opel sedan parked on the other side of the pumps from the red BMW. Three swarthy men were walking into the store. A forth waited by the car.

Arabs?

They seemed to be walking with a purpose. And the guy by the Opel did not seem interested in pumping gas. He was watching the several surly German men gathering across the street.

He had a jacket on and it wasn't that cold.

The three disappeared into the store. Carter was in there. There were no windows, so what was going on in there was a mystery.

If the Arabs were looking for them, they were looking for a man and a woman. But did they know they were looking for a red 4-series?

Almost certainly. The license number? Maybe.

One of the Germans across the street, a scruffy guy in his early twenties who had probably already quaffed a couple, shouted something. Turnbull didn't peak German, but he spoke fluent Angry. Whatever Fritz had said was not "Welcome, my new Arab friend."

The Arab guy shouted something back, in German, and whatever it was likewise was not nice. The Germans returned the insult in kind.

Great. A Bavarian rumble.

Turnbull exited the restroom quietly and unnoticed, the Arab focused on offering obscene gestures to the half dozen Germans across the road.

He wasn't afraid of getting his ass kicked. Meaning he was strapped.

Turnbull walked up behind the guy and pulled out his M1911. The Germans saw him and stopped shouting, and the Arab turned just in time for Turnbull to bring the heavy metal pistol hard across his temple. The man went down on the ground.

Turnbull walked around the Opel, glancing inside through the open driver's window. The black stock of a long weapon was peeking out from under a coat in the backseat. They were baddies all right.

He continued around to his vehicle and pulled the fuel hose out of his car and shut the door, then dragged the hose over to the Opel and stuck the nozzle inside and squeezed. Gasoline splashed across the dash and the seats. He kept his eyes on the door of the store the whole time. Satisfied, he splashed more gas on the outside of the driver's door and the pavement leading over to the BMW. Then he hung up the pump and walked toward the store.

He pulled the doors open and was greeted by a large cardboard cut-out display for Happy Jus, a citrus drink that was enthusiastically recommended by a pair of half-naked blondes. He stepped around it and saw Carter marveling at the selection of weird chip flavors – lots of them seemed to involve cumin and/or paprika. And the three Arabs were converging from the merchandise rows behind her.

"Hey assholes!" Turnbull shouted, but if the Arabs didn't understand his spoken language, they understood the international language of his .45 pistol.

"Oliver?" Carter said, suddenly aware she was not alone.

"Come on," Turnbull growled. The Arabs stood still, Turnbull's weapon tracking from one of their faces to the other then the other, reminding each of his own personal mortality. Carter ran for the door and the Arabs went to ground.

Turnbull fired three rounds into the beer cooler door behind them, collapsing the sheet of glass on top of them.

Carter passed him heading out the door. One Arab leaned outside an aisle endcap with a beer bottle display, a Glock in hand. Turnbull fired three times fast. He missed the target but shattered a dozen bottles they exploded in a cascade of suds and foam that soaked his target.

Turnbull reached over with his left hand and snagged a red plastic lighter out of a bowl on the counter – the German clerk was crouched down behind it, hiding – and then he ran out the door.

As he hit the pavement, several rounds passed through the door from inside. He ran to the BMW and got in, as did Carter. Across the road, the Germans were shouting and hooting. They loved whatever the hell was happening, and they were too buzzed to think to take cover.

Turnbull took a second to take care of one last thing, then hit the ignition and gunned the engine of the BMW as the Arabs burst out the door, firing a few shots at the escaping infidels.

As the BMW whipped around the corner and out of sight, they ignored their prostrate pal and piled into their Opel. Pulling their doors shut, they noticed it – the wetness, the smell. The driver looked out his window and the wet pavement leading over to where the BMW had been parked.

To where a red lighter lay on the ground, burning.

He shouted something to his pals as the pavement erupted in blue and orange flames that ripped across the moist fuse Turnbull had laid right to the driver's door and up the side into the interior. The gas fumes ignited, the Opel blew apart in an orange ball of flame and smoke.

Across the road, the drunken Germans cheered, and when the baffled *polizei* rolled up a minute later with a fire truck, the witnesses denied seeing anything at all.

"How did they find us?" Carter asked. "Did they just get lucky?"

"Not luck. Numbers," Turnbull said. He gunned the engine and the BMW responded, gripping the hill country road tightly and accelerating as they left Bad Kohlgrub behind. A black finger of smoke was rising above the church spire. "They must have a bunch of them out looking for us, and the *BfV* told them who to look for."

"But why are the German secret police helping Arabs?"

"Duplicitous krauts? I'm shocked. Shocked!" Turnbull said. "Probably buying peace here in *der* Fatherland by letting them do whatever they want to the *untermeschen*. You know, us."

"They let the terrorists buy the equipment and send it to the People's Republic," Carter said, the perfidy of their hosts dawning on her.

"No doubt. And we're a couple of loose strings."

"What do you mean?"

Turnbull sighed at the metaphor gap with his partner.

"It means they need us dead. Dead men tell no tales."

"Nor dead women," she corrected him. He shook his head and accelerated.

"We need to get to France and get home," she said.

"That's exactly what they think we'll do. They'll be watching the border. Our only edge is they won't get the regular *polizei* involved. Too many questions. They'll let Hamid's boys do the dirty work."

They continued to drive fast to the west, keeping to the back roads where possible. After a while, near the tourist town of Schwangau, Carter froze, staring at something looming above them through the windshield.

"What is that?" she said.

"That's Neuschwanstein Castle," Turnbull said. The immense white structure stood on a hilltop, framed by mountains, with white towers and dark roofs. "They say Walt Disney used it as a model for the Disneyland castle."

"Disney was the Nazi ringleader, right?"

"Not quite. He made children's movies."

"Yes, him. That's who I mean. The Nazi."

"I'm guessing you've never been to Disneyland."

"I don't know what that is. Sounds horrible. But I know his propaganda was banned after the Split."

"If you're ever in the US, visit Disney World in Orlando. Not EPCOT though. It sucks, except it sells booze. So actually, maybe it's better after all."

"You've been to the US, haven't you?" Carter said. "That was your mission. You were inside the red with all the racists. That's why you're so damaged. I'm starting to understand your challenge overcome."

"I'm not authorized to talk about any of this."

"You don't have too. I just want you to know I validate your pain."

"Oh good. I yearn to be validated."

"Where will we cross into France?"

"I'm not sure. I think we need to lay low somewhere."

"The faster we get out of this country the better."

"Haste makes wasted," Turnbull said.

"So where do we lay low?"

"I'm thinking inside the Black Forest."

He spent the next ten minutes explaining to her why the term was not inherently racist. At the end, she still did not believe him.

13.

Adam Marshall closed the door of his office on the top floor of the People's Intelligence Agency building and walked to his desk. The windows opened up on the Virginia countryside. In the distance, the new wall around the complex cut through the green like a scar. The workers were putting the finishing touches on it – time was running out.

His assistant had told him about the call; he was concerned enough not to have told her to blow the caller off. He sat down in his leather chair – they had snuck it into his office to avoid protests by the militant vegans in the Agency – and picked up the secure phone on his desk. Then he punched the blinking red button.

"Herr Spetters," he said in English. He knew the man at the other end of the line understood. "To what do I owe the pleasure of this unexpected call?"

"Deputy Director Marshall, unfortunately, this is not a pleasant call to make."

Marshall sat up. Did the German intelligence chief know? The Arabs had flown into Washington already with their equipment. They were situating themselves at that moment in the People's Republic, so if this call was about the project, the BfV director's ability to influence events going forward was minimal at best.

"I am sorry to hear that, Herr Spetters," Marshall said. "How may I help?"

"Your agents have caused us...an inconvenience."

"My agents? I am afraid I don't understand."

Spetters sighed at the PR man's denial. This was the dance, and he had to move with the music.

"Your agents. They have...misbehaved. It is unacceptable."

"Now I am very confused, Herr Spetters. Perhaps you can start from the beginning."

Spetters sighed again, louder.

"Your agents flew in three days ago and have killed...actually, I've lost count of the exact number of people."

Marshall was truly confused. Was the German referring to the Arabs as "agents?" That would be odd. But even if so, what had they done?

"Herr Spetters, I assure you I have no idea what you are talking about. What agents?"

Spetters kept his irritation in check. "They came in under the names Oliver Warren and Kristina Carter."

Marshall sat up in his chair. "Say that again. Say those names again."

Spetters assessed the surprise in Marshall's voice as genuine. Now he was intrigued rather than merely angry.

"The names were Oliver Warren and Kristina Carter. Traveling on People's Republic of North America diplomatic passports through Frankfurt to Munich."

Oliver Warren. Rios-Parkinson's man.

"Those are not *my* agents, Herr Spetters."

"Come now, Deputy Director, I am no fool...."

"They are not PIA. I can assure you of that."

"Then who do they belong to, may I inquire?"

"I know who. And I will act accordingly. Whatever outrages they have committed will be punished, I assure you. Where are they now?"

"At last report, a few hours ago, they killed a number of individuals at a gas station in Bavaria. I expect they are making their way to France, and then back to the People's Republic."

"Unless you get them first."

"*Ja.*"

"You have no objection from the Director to your taking whatever action is required to deal with these rogue agents, Herr Spetters."

"Rogue agents. So, some sort of power struggle within your government? An opposing faction. Yet you know their aliases."

"I know them, and who they work for. Carter is no alias. 'Warren' I have always believed to be a cover identity."

"Then perhaps I can help you address this unacceptable situation. I know who Oliver Warren really is."

"You do? What's xis name?" Marshall said, going to the inquiry window on his desktop and poising his fingers over his keyboard.

"Not xis, Herr Marshall. Our file on him, while sketchy, indicates he is actively – how do you say in English? – cisgender. His name is Kelly Turnbull. He was, at least one time, a member of...."

Marshall sat upright. He finally remembered.

"The United States Army," said Marshall, before typing in the inquiry into the PIA database.

"Yes," said Spetters, a bit taken aback. "He was associated with the United States on prior entries into Germany. Before your...how do you say?"

"Split."

"Before your Split. So you know this agent?"

"I met him," Marshall said, remembering back a decade. "In the red states, years ago."

"I assume the encounter was unpleasant."

"It was. But nowhere near as unpleasant as our next encounter will be. For him."

"It seems you have business to attend to on your end, Herr Marshall. And I on mine."

"Yes," said Marshall. "And Herr Spetters, should you take him alive, I would be indebted if you allowed some of my people to conduct their own interrogation after you are finished."

"We can certainly discuss that, if we take him alive. *Auf wiedersehen*, Herr Marshall." Spetters hung up and the line went dead.

"So, Captain Turnbull," Marshall said aloud. "Whatever are you doing working for Director Rios-Parkinson?"

He got up and headed down the hall to see the Chameleon.

"I'm hungry," Carter said.

"Me too," Turnbull said. They had been on the road for hours heading west. The gas gauge was getting low too. "But we can't stop. Not yet."

Turnbull gunned the engine as they passed a sign announcing that they were entering the Schwarzwald.

"We're in the racist forest," Carter said, not ironically. Turnbull refused to take the bait.

Then there was another sign, this one yellow and talking in German about curved roads, but what was spray painted on it in was the interesting part. It was a crescent with a slash through it.

"I don't think they like Muslims here," Carter observed. "You must feel extremely otherized as a Muslim yourself."

"Oh, I sure do," replied Turnbull. "I think we're in the West Virginia of Germany, where they don't dig strangers."

Ahead, it was wooded and hilly, even mountainous. Other signs pointed south to Zurich and southeast to Basel, both in Switzerland and both off-limits to most travelers these days. The Swiss, as was their habit – a habit that had kept them free for centuries – was hunkering down again and largely shutting the world out. Of course, they did not exclude the world's money – in the last decade, it had reembraced its essential self and re-imposed its strict bank secrecy laws. Stubbornly unaligned Switzerland was the refuge for the monies looted by the European elite – the same elite that publicly excoriated the Swiss for their stubborn refusal to conform.

Straight west was France – it was chaos there, but friendly enough that a couple of People's Republic agents could likely find help.

They tore through a valley and a little town called Grafenhausen – it was probably pretty in better times – and paid little attention to it. The locals paid attention to them, though. They got plenty of stares. And not friendly ones.

There was a blue Audi A6 parked on a turnout off the road as Turnbull and Carter passed the village limits sign. The Audi's occupants noticed the BMW and made a phone call even as the driver pulled onto the country road.

"Which way?" Turnbull asked. Carter consulted the map on her lap.

"You need to keep going north, then left," she said

"Here?" They were approaching a T-intersection.

"Yes," she replied. He sped up, glancing at the rearview.

In the mirror, the blue vehicle made the same left.

"Hand me the rifle," Turnbull said.

"What's wrong?"

"My gun's in the backseat and not in easy reach and that makes me sad. Grab it for me. Now."

The blue car looked like an Audi. It was matching his speed.

Carter reached back and brought it up to the front seat. The G36 was awkward inside a vehicle even with the stock folded up; the designator and fore grip below and the optic – a sweet Zeiss RSA reflex red dot – made it hard to handle in the cramped quarters.

"You take it," Turnbull said. He pulled out his Wilson X-TAC and held it between his legs. "And arrange those vests against the back seats."

She slid the rifle into the well at her feet and arranged the vests. Then she looked behind them.

"That blue car?"

"Yeah, seems a bit too interested in us," Turnbull said. "Just sitting outside of town, where they would not draw attention? Probably nothing. Pulled out as we passed it? That happens. Making all the same turns as us? Okay. Matching our speed? Now I'm getting interested."

She looked out the back window. "They're a couple hundred meters back. I can't see the passengers clearly."

"Passengers plural, huh?"

"Yeah, at least three – no, four."

"Four adults in a sedan. That's kind of weird."

"Maybe they're sharing a car," she said, still looking back. "You know, because of climate change."

"That's called 'carpooling,' and I don't think the Black Forest has a rush hour. They're presumptively dirty."

They were on a long stretch, maybe a half kilometer with woods on each side.

"What do we do?"

"We stop."

Turnbull hit the brakes and came to a stop in the middle of the lane.

"Could I have the gun, please?" Turnbull said, shifting to "P" and putting his .45 on the center console. Carter handed over the G36. He did a chamber check – there was a 5.56mm round ready – and glanced at the rear-view. The Audi had slowed to a crawl about 100 meters behind them.

"If they weren't interested in us, they'd have gone around us. Now, you may want to cover your ears." He flicked on the optic.

"Oliver –"

Turnbull was out the door with the German assault rifle going to his right shoulder.

Maybe 80 meters away, the four Arabs tumbled out of the doors of the sedan, all with long weapons.

Turnbull's mind assessed the threat as it unfolded – multiple targets, moving in different directions, with weapons that could reach out and touch him. He was outgunned, but he did have one advantage.

The initiative.

Turnbull was aiming while they were scrambling.

The first burst was pure suppression – send a swarm of hot lead in their direction to keep them moving. They only needed a few seconds to set, acquire, aim and fire, and Turnbull wanted to deny them that.

The rounds zipped around them, with a few blowing out the flung-open front door's windows and some stitching across the windshield.

It was enough to keep them moving for cover – they kept low and moved fast toward the rear of the vehicle. But the driver was a little slow. He showed his back.

Turnbull lay the red dot between the man's shoulders and squeezed. The weapon roared and an arc of empty shells flew out of the open bolt. The unlucky man dropped on his face onto the asphalt.

Turnbull ripped another burst through the Audi's windshield to keep their heads down below the trunk. The bad guys were huddling back there now, and they were only a few seconds from returning fire.

Turnbull shifted his aim to the sedan's body, particularly the driver's side, and steadied himself against his own doorframe.

Turnbull fired, peppering the front tire, and blowing it out. He shifted to the rear tire and fired until the G36 went dry. The tire didn't blow out dramatically like the front one did, but he saw the rounds tear into the rubber and it started deflating. A couple feet away, the driver lay motionless.

Turnbull tossed the empty weapon into Carter's lap and shouted "Reload!" as he swung into the driver's seat and shifted back to "D."

"And duck," he added, just before the rear window shattered.

Even as they roared off down the road, Turnbull could hear the rounds slamming into the rear deck of his ride. The protective vests lying against the rear seats jolted and jittered as they stopped the rounds that made it through the trunk into the passenger compartment.

There was a lot of firing – probably G36s – but fewer hits as the BMW got farther away. Within a few seconds they were around a bend and the impacts ceased.

"That sucked," Turnbull observed.

"They're going to call us in," Carter said.

"Yep," Turnbull said. "Real soon this place is going to be crawling with 'em."

"What do we do?"

"My first choice would be to get over the border ASAP, but I don't think we're getting into France in a car that looks like sieve. The borders aren't open anymore. You can't just drive across. The *gendarmes* will have questions."

"We have to try," she replied.

"Not sure that's in the cards either," Turnbull said. "Look."

He pointed to the dash display. Among the digital gauges and readouts was one that gave kilometers left on the present tank of gas.

It read "82."

"Before we had our close encounter of the 5.56 kind, that gauge read 143 klicks. Those shitheads put one in our gas tank."

"Can we make it?"

"I don't know, but every mile we cover is a mile we don't have to walk."

"Why are you always talking about miles? What did they do to your head in the red?"

"Just navigate," Turnbull said.

The roads were empty as the sun set, but the signs were pretty clear. More slashed crescents, and no *polizei*. With about 40 klicks to the French border, they were in the wild west of *Deutschland*.

"That's it," Turnbull said as the BMW sputtered and died. The "Fuel Reserve" light had gone on a few minutes before. He glided another 100 meters to wring every meter of distance out of their ride and pulled the car over to the shoulder of the country road. "We walk."

He cut the headlights and they got out. Turnbull and Carter each put on their vest – the rounds had not shattered the ceramic plates – and Turnbull took the rifle and the ammo bag.

"Maybe we can get a ride in the next town," Carter said. "Here, shine that light."

Turnbull turned on the flashlight attachment on the rifle and shined it on the map. Breaking light discipline by using the white light made him queasy – his Army training again. Anyone could see them out there. As Carter studied the map, Turnbull looked around. The woods were impenetrable – utterly black.

He was not happy with their tactical situation, to put it mildly.

"Todtmoos," she said.

"Excuse me?"

"The next town. Todtmoos. A couple kilometers west."

"Let's go," he said, turning off the light and taking point. The G36 had no sling, so he carried the weapon in the ready position. They moved off down the road.

Carter started to say something, but he shushed her.

"Listen to the silence," he said. So she did.

They had walked for about ten minutes when Turnbull held up his fist. Carter kept walking and Turnbull realized she did not know to stop.

"Don't move," he whispered. "No matter what. And don't go for your –"

"*Halt*!" A German accent; the word meant the same in *Duetsch* as it did in English. The shout came out of the darkness; Turnbull could not determine where. However, unarmed single individuals rarely gave orders to a pair of people, one of whom was carrying a loaded assault rifle.

Turnbull halted. Discretion was the better part of getting shot to pieces.

He lowered the rifle, safed it, and dropped it on the gravel of the soft shoulder. Carter stayed perfectly still.

There was movement on both sides of the road, a lot of it, and a pack of German country boys emerged from the darkness. All strapped.

Turnbull marveled. He couldn't help himself.

"Are those MP-40s?"

The Germans were kind enough not to tie them up for the walk into town. Naturally, they were relieved of their weapons, body armor and phones.

"Don't lose that," Turnbull said as one of the Germans took his black Wilson X-TAC Elite and examined it. "I'm going to want it back."

Their escort consisted of about a dozen locals, a few carrying old school Karabiner 98k bolt action rifles but most packing "Schmeissers," metal machine pistols familiar to anyone who had ever seen a World War II movie.

Which Carter had not.

"It's a 9mm submachine gun," Turnbull said. "The Nazis used it in the war. Very potent. It's not .45, but used properly it'll wreak your day. These things look brand new."

One of the Germans shushed him. Since he was holding one of the classic weapons, Turnbull complied.

The town of Todtmoos was closed, literally. A couple buses blocked the road into town and more armed locals warmed themselves at fires while they stood guard. There was beer, of course.

The town itself was in a shallow valley, with the town itself spread over the surrounding hills. Like others they had passed through, it was probably quite pleasant at one point.

The escort took them through the barrier and into the town. Lots of locals were coming out to have a look. It occurred to Turnbull that strangers did not often go traipsing through the Black Forest at night in these dark days.

Their captors led them to what appeared to be the main watering hole, a packed guesthouse called *Gasthaus Ludwig*. A caricature of a jolly king – probably Ludwig – graced the exterior. The festivities stopped when the strangers entered. Even the band stared.

"*Ein pils, bitte*," Turnbull said. His escort pushed him forward toward the head table and the moon-faced *burgermeister* who sat there with his mug. He sipped as he regarded his captives.

"*Amerikaner,*" said the head of the hunters. He held up the G36.

"We're –" began Carter, but Turnbull intervened.

"Stop talking," he hissed.

"Why are you here, wandering around our forest at night with guns?" asked the mayor.

"Because some bad people are trying to kill us," Turnbull said. "And we are merely passing through."

"On foot? At least, not very quickly."

"We had an...incident."

"Outside Grafenhausen. We know. Word travels fast in the forest."

"Then you know who is after us."

"Oh yes. And any enemy of theirs might just be a friend of ours. Would you sit?"

Turnbull and Carter sat down on the wooden benches at his table. A crowd was gathered around them, and the band was back on. It was playing a version of Louis Armstrong's "It's a Wonderful World." The mayor motioned to a waitress in a traditional blue and white dress who looked like the St. Pauli Girl's divorced older sister. She took his order and disappeared into the back.

"I learned English in America, at college. Notre Dame, long before you split your country apart. Germans know something of having their country split in two by leftists. I remember when it happened to you, the bloodshed and then the ripping apart of the most powerful country in the world, all over leftist ideology. The world was stunned. But I saw it coming. I was not blinded by the comfortable lies of the fashionable fools in the cities. And I think that this may happen here in Germany once again."

"You do seem to have your own set of problems."

"The foreigners," the mayor said. "That fool, *mutti* Merkel, she invited in half the world to our country and imagined they would become Germans in Germany, when in reality they became Syrians or Afghans or Turks or Nigerians in Germany. And now, chaos, which the cowards in Berlin refuse to face. So, we must act for ourselves. Our *jaegers*, our hunters, will do what the *polizei* and the *Bundeswehr* refuse to do – defend our people."

"Diversity is strength," Carter said, fuming. Turnbull, as he clenched his fist in irritation, observed that despite the Split, some Americans still retained their natural inclination to tell other people how they should live.

"Does Germany look strong to you, *fräulein*?" the mayor replied. Carter did not realize that the term had decades ago gone from merely unfashionable to *verboten* in the cosmopolitan circles of German society. He was being condescending, and she did not realize it.

But Turnbull did.

"I assume we are not going to be thrown in your jail," he said.

The mayor smiled. "I do not think so. I see you less as prisoners than guests."

"Perhaps, as your guests, we could trouble you for a couple of rooms."

"Two, not one? Yes, of course. At least in this part of Germany, we have not lost our *gastfreundschaft* – our hospitality."

"Why don't you check our rooms?" Turnbull said to Carter. She did get what that meant.

"I can –" she began.

"No, you can't. Go check out the rooms."

She stood up, visibly annoyed, and was led away upstairs. The waitress came and dropped off a large glass mug of amber pilsner.

Turnbull turned back to his host.

"I think you would appreciate plain talk," Turnbull said.

"I would."

"We are being hunted, both by Arab terrorists and by your government, or at least a part of it."

"A strange circumstance for two citizens of the People's Republic of North America."

"It's a long story, and I'm guessing you served in your country's military."

"I did," said the mayor. "Active and then for years in the reserves."

"Then you know that some matters are classified."

"So, a secret mission?"

"One that is not against Germany or its interests. One that Germany does not want to see fail, even if some of its officials do not see that right now."

"You fought Arabs. This makes you an ally. What do you need?"

"We need to get out of the country. We need to do it tomorrow."

"The French are already expecting you. It is unofficial, but they are waiting for you. You will not be allowed in."

"We are not going to France. Not after tonight."

The mayor laughed. "Switzerland? The border is sealed. And they do not care for your kind there."

"Don't worry about my kind. We just need to get over the border. Someplace quiet. And remote. And dry. I bet you know one."

The mayor smiled slyly. "Here, to some extent, borders are just lines on a map. In this region, we are all – what is the word? – 'interconnected.'"

Turnbull nodded. Whoever this guy was, he was probably interconnected as hell – and he was probably interconnected with every shady, shadowy deal getting done in this remote corner of the Fatherland.

Could he be trusted?

Turnbull did not bother to think about that. There was no reason to. If they wanted him disappeared, he and Carter would be dinner for the wild boars at a snap of the *burgermeister's* ruddy fingers.

"I will help you," said the mayor.

Turnbull lifted his mug. "*Prost.*"

The mayor walked beside Turnbull down the streets of Todtmoos, glad-handing the residents as he passed. Several *jaegers* with MP-40s accompanied them. Every few minutes one would wander up and whisper in the boss's ear in German. The mayor mostly did not mention what he was told, but occasionally he did.

"They are here in the Forest," he said after one such message. "There are dozens of cars in the Forest this morning. Too many for us to eliminate. One or two, perhaps. But there are too many."

Turnbull could well imagine the fate of carloads of terrorists entering the Forest and never coming out – and never being heard from again.

"They used to raid us. They would come out from the cities in packs, and we were defenseless. The *polizei* were outnumbered and ordered to be gentle. And, of course, the leftists in Berlin forbade us from having guns of our own. They even banned hunting rifles. So we were helpless, or so they thought."

They stopped at a large, plain stone building with no markings and no windows. One of the *jaegers* opened the ancient padlock on the front door.

Inside was a large space with a blonde hardwood floor. It was totally empty. It looked like some community center for dances or concerts or whatever.

The *jaeger* walked to the far corner, knelt down and pulled up a metal ring that was flush with the floor. A trap door opened, and he descended down the wooded stairs, pausing only to flick on the lights.

"You first," said the mayor. Turnbull went down.

At the bottom, he looked around and gasped. "Holy shit."

Guns. Lots of guns.

Racks of Karabiner 98k rifles, some MG-42 machine guns, and MP-40s. At least 200. Plus ammo boxes piled to the roof. That was all he could see from where he stood – there was certainly more.

"What is this place?" he marveled.

"It is what has allowed us to protect ourselves. You see, Hitler wanted us to fight to the death," the mayor said. "Even if we were overrun, we were to rise up at an opportune time and throw out the allied invaders. So, he built these armories, secret armories, in many villages so that when the time came the Reich could be restored. Of course, that day never came. We had had our fill of that fool's war. Most of the armories elsewhere were discovered decades ago. But here, in the Forest, we know how to keep secrets. There was no hurry to revolt, but no hurry to give up the means to do so either. So we kept it. And when the communist threat appeared, we were ready. Even after we reunified and that threat faded, we still kept our secret."

Turnbull walked to the rack of machine pistols and took one off. Its stock was folded and there was no mag in the well. He ran his finger in the empty space where the magazine went and looked at it. No dirt, light oil coating.

"You maintained these all these decades? It's been almost a century."

"Yes, of course. They would decay otherwise." The mayor seemed to think Turnbull was slightly cracked for imagining the villagers might have done anything different. "And we train with them, out in the Forest, every young man. There is plenty of ammunition, enough for another century."

"You know, my G36 is a nice weapon."

"Oh, it is, very nice. I used one in the *Bundeswehr.*"

"It's not good in a vehicle though. Too bulky."

The mayor grinned. "Perhaps we can arrange a trade for something more suited to your needs."

Turnbull pulled back the bolt on the submachine gun. "Yeah, I think we can do that. But I'm going to need two of these. And a lot of mags."

Rios-Parkinson left Cooley and his security team in the lobby behind him, where his agents had about a dozen girls decked out in bikinis and low-cut gowns up against the wall. The women were quiet and cooperative – this was not the first time this had happened, and they were all grateful it had not happened to them.

There were doors evenly spaced along the hall and the dirty bulbs in the sconces on the walls cast a dull light. The last door on the end was open. A couple agents hung around outside it; there was a low animal moaning issuing from inside.

"Is he ready to see me?" the Director asked.

"Yes, sir," the taller People's Bureau of Investigation agent replied. Rios-Parkinson frowned at the faux pas, and the agent caught himself. "I mean 'Director.'"

Rios-Parkinson ignored the microaggression and stepped inside. This establishment had been a hotel before the Split, before the previous PBI director had converted it and before Rios-Parkinson inherited it. There was a desk/cabinet assembly of black fiberboard against one wall. A bottle of whiskey – real stuff, Jameson's – and a trio of glasses were on a tray on top of it. A large, dirty mirror was above the structure, affixed to the wall. Some of the cameras were behind it. Others were hidden, with mics, around the room. There was a utilitarian bed with a frayed cover and graying sheets. They were streaked with red now.

Two women, conventionally pretty and blonde, both wearing cheerleader outfits with big "A" varsity letters on their chest were laying on the cover, quite obviously dead. On the floor was a naked man, head in his hands, weeping. Next to him was what Rios-Parkinson recognized from his own youth as an Orange County high school student as a letterman's jacket.

"General Zisk," Rios-Parkinson said, his voice devoid of pity.

The Air Force officer looked up. It took him a moment to focus, because he was still groggy.

"Director Rios-Parkinson?" he said.

"That is correct, General. Can you say what happened?"

"I don't know..."

"Of course, General," the Director replied. "Everyxone sometimes loses control." Rios-Parkinson was familiar with the General's pronouns and careful to use them.

"I didn't…"

"I understand, General. Fortunately, they contacted me instead before anyone else. So, I can help xoe."

"Help xi?" replied the General. There was hope in his voice and his eyes.

"Help xoe," said Rios-Parkinson. "Help xoe ensure this unfortunate situation never becomes public."

"I'm not…," the General said.

"I understand," Rios-Parkinson said.

"I don't understand. I'm not like *this*," the General insisted. Rios-Parkinson nodded, and suppressed a smile. They always said that.

General Zisk's file, which Rios-Parkinson had read closely since being alerted that the officer had scheduled a very specific session at this PBI-controlled brothel, had him as registered "Omnisexual/Trans Questioning." You could not do better if you were ambitious and seeking promotion in the People's Republic military. But the reality was something truly appalling, a trip through the forgotten bourgeois perversions of pre-Split America.

"The cis paradigm of blonde cheerleaders and the football team captain," Rios-Parkinson said, shaking his head ever so slightly. "I don't think the command would react well to this revelation of your preferences. Obviously, the trauma of having developed in the era of institutionalized sexism and cis tyranny scarred you."

"I can't help it," the man sobbed.

"I understand your shame, but I am not going to judge xoe, General. Xoe cannot control the urges xoe feels. Even ones that are technically criminal."

"I'm not like that normally," the General said, imploring. "I just, I just wanted to play the role. It was like a game. I didn't mean to, to, reinforce hateful gender roles." His chest heaved with a swarm of sobs.

"Luckily xoe have friends," Rios-Parkinson replied.

"Xoe're my friend?"

"We will be friends going forward," replied Rios-Parkinson, extending his hand. The General took it in both his own hands, grateful. The Director called out to the agents posted outside. They came in, barely suppressing their distaste for the creature before them on the filthy carpet.

"Help the General clean xisself up and see that xe gets back to Fonda Air Force Base," Rios-Parkinson said. Andrews had been renamed for a movie star whose Vietnam-era resistance to the fascist American Air Force was an inspiration to millions of oppressed peoples before the Split. Then he gestured to the corpses. "And get rid of those."

The mayor stood next to the white 2017 BMW 530i. It had seen much better days, with dents and rust at the fringes, but the engine was good. A map of the Black Forest was spread out on the hood, with Turnbull and some other men poring over it. A pair of immaculate MP-40s and a khaki bag holding about a dozen loaded 32-round magazines lay inside over the tan front console.

Turnbull looked up to make sure Carter was still inside grabbing some food. Confirming she was absent, he looked back down. One of the *jaegers* was pointing out the correct road. His finger was over a patch of dark green.

"There's nothing there," Turnbull said.

"There's nothing on the map," the mayor corrected him. "The road is there. There's a small wooden barrier at the end, but no permanent guardhouse at the border."

"Got it," Turnbull said. He committed the image to memory. That's how he would navigate.

"Remember, once over you must surrender yourself to the Swiss immediately. Do not defy them. They are...not friendly to intruders. And I expect that this is how they would classify visitors from the People's Republic." The mayor looked at Turnbull's face for a reaction.

"Thank you for your *gastfreundschaft*, Mr. Mayor," Turnbull said, handing the map back to the *jaeger*.

"Someday, during better times, you must return to Todtmoos and tell me who you really are," replied the German.

"Let's hope someday there are better times," Turnbull said. Carter was coming out of the *Gasthaus Ludwig* with a couple of bags.

"We ready to go?" she asked.

Turnbull nodded and turned to the mayor. "Thank you for the car."

"Thank you for yours. Our boys brought it in on a flatbed last night and we will strip it for the parts that do not have bullet holes in them, if there are any."

"And thanks for those." Turnbull nodded at the MP-40s.

"Now, are you certain you do not wish to trade that big American pistol for a vintage Luger or Walther?"

"I'm certain. I'm all about the .45 caliber."

"So be it. Good luck to you."

They entered the BMW, Turnbull driving, and pulled their doors shut. The mayor leaned into the open driver's window.

"Our reports say that there are many of them on the roads. The *polizei* are completely gone, ordered into their stations, and unofficial word has been passed for civilians to stay off the roads this morning in this region."

"It's only 35 kilometers to the French border," Carter said. "We'll make it."

The mayor looked at Turnbull and thought better of commenting. Instead, he simply said, "Good luck to you."

Turnbull pushed the ignition button. He fiddled with the dial on the console to make sure the display showed the vehicle status, not the car's nav map.

"*Danke*," he said, and he pulled away and down the road.

"Are you going the right way," Carter asked. "Where's the map?"

"I have to go a little east to go west," Turnbull said. She shrugged.

The most direct route to the Swiss border was directly south, but the problem was that the border there, and for most of this stretch of frontier, was the Rhine River. The bridges would be guarded by the Swiss and under observation by the Arabs. But further to the east, the border was across dry land. He hit the gas.

"He was right. There's almost no traffic," Carter said a few minutes later. She looked at the road signs. "We're getting close to the Swiss border. How far is France?"

"Not far." Turnbull was grateful the People's Bureau of Investigation did not bother training its agents on land navigation. He'd learned it at Fort Benning, and he always knew which way was north.

"I'm ready to go home," Carter said.

Ahead, a green Ford crested the hill coming their way.

"Duck down," Turnbull said.

Too late. The sedan passed them and it was full of men.

Turnbull hit the gas and behind them the Ford flipped a huey.

"It's on," Turnbull said, punching it. "Gimme a machine gun."

She did, and opened the bag of mags on the console between them.

He pushed the "SPORT" setting button and the suspension tightened and the accelerator instantly got significantly torqueier. The speedometer in the BMW read in kilometers per hour. He was already at 140, and this was not much of a road. Behind them, the green Ford was giving chase.

"We can outrun this assbite," Turnbull said. "I'm more worried about the friends he might have called out to meet us up ahead."

"I don't see anything," Carter replied. She looked down at her submachine gun. Turnbull had given her a block of instruction on it, but she had never fired it or anything like it.

Turnbull took two small packets out of his breast pocket. They each contained two orange rubber earplugs. "A gift from our host," he said, passing one over. "You'll want them if it gets going."

He bit open his own packet and stuffed the orange rubber plugs into his ears while Carter did the same with hers.

"Do you know where we're going?" Carter asked.

"Yep," Turnbull said, then he spotted movement up ahead. "Uh oh."

A beige Opel, closing on them from the front. Three hundred meters.

"Get ready to rock and roll," Turnbull said. He took his MP-40 in his left hand and hung it out the window on the side mirror.

Someone hung out of the rear driver's side window of the Opel with what looked like an MP5.

Turnbull fired.

The MP-40 hopped and skipped a bit, but it was designed to be fired off the side of vehicle and even had a fin on the bottom of its barrel to facilitate it. Unfortunately, the open bolt ejector was on the right, meaning the spent shells cascaded into the passenger compartment through the window, clattering as they landed across the dash and the seats.

"Shit!" Carter yelled – one of the pieces of hot brass went into her open collar and down her shirt. Cordite smoke filled the passenger compartment.

Turnbull ignored her and the haze and adjusted fire to walk the spray into the oncoming Opel. The Opel's occupants were returning the favor; the BMW's windshield cracked across the center top as a round from the Arabs connected. But Turnbull was more accurate. A burst hit the Opel directly in front of its front seat passenger and blew out its windshield. The Opel swerved and spun out on the open shoulder.

Turnbull jammed on the brakes, but the anti-lock system kept the sedan from skidding. As the car came to a stop, Turnbull dropped the empty mag on the floor and reloaded, then grabbed a second mag from the bag as he rolled out of the car.

The Opel was on the grass, driver's side toward Turnbull, maybe 20 meters away. The back door came open and the guy with the MP5 stepped out as Turnbull brought up the machine pistol.

The burst caught the Arab square in the chest – he was flung back against the rear quarter panel, but he didn't go down, validating Turnbull's faith in the venerable .45 round.

Turnbull cursed the light hitting power of the 9mm Parabellum bullets and squeezed off another burst. That did the trick.

Turnbull emptied the rest of the magazine into the idling Opel, shattering glass and stitching lines of holes across the unibody. There was no return fire. He dropped the empty mag, slammed in another and sent the bolt forward. The firing from behind startled him. He pivoted. Carter was opening up at a target on the road back the way they came. Her left hand was holding the mag, exactly as he taught her not to do it – the proper grip was on the solid mag well – but he wasn't about to correct her technique right then.

She was shooting at the Ford that had been following them. It had caught up and was barreling toward them fast. She was getting hits, but they were not stopping the oncoming hunk of metal. She needed help.

Turnbull brought up his own machine pistol and squeezed the trigger. For a few seconds both gunners were emptying their weapons at the oncoming sedan. A line of holes erupted across its windshield and some of the rounds must have connected. The car spun and flipped over twice before coming to a rest in the middle of the road.

Behind it, in the distance, were at least two more cars.

"Let's go!" Turnbull shouted. To his right, a shot – someone was alive in the Opel. He tossed the empty MP-40 into the BMW and drew his .45, emptying it into the Opel as he slid behind the wheel of his own.

The BMW roared off down the road, with Turnbull clicking his seatbelt. After all, safety first. Carter was reloading both machine pistols without being told to – at least she was learning something. He handed over his .45 for a fresh mag and she took it.

Turnbull scanned the way ahead. There would be a left ahead, the unimproved road, whatever that meant. But it would take them into Switzerland.

Carter handed him the loaded pistol and looked behind them. "They're closing."

Turnbull looked at his speedometer – over 150 klicks per hour on this country lane? The bad guys were gaining. They really were seeking martyrdom.

"Shoot at them!" Turnbull said.

Carter was holding her weapon, unsure.

"Through the rear window. Shoot it out!" Turnbull yelled.

She raised the weapon and fired. It was deafening, even with the plugs in. Glass shattered. The smoke inside grew thicker. She fired again. And again. A hot shell fell in Turnbull's lap and he thrust it off him.

"They're still back there!" she shouted. His ears were ringing.

The turn.

Turnbull braked hard, and the anti-locks slowed the sedan 90 kilometers per hour in just a couple seconds. He cranked the wheel hard onto the road.

The BMW took the turn, clipping a tree at the corner and tearing up some brush, but it made it. The first of the pursuit vehicles was not so lucky – it smashed head-on into the tree. One of the passengers was evidently not wearing a seat belt – he was ejected out into the underbrush.

The second vehicle, a white Mercedes, slowed and took the turn, then accelerated.

The BMW buckled and jostled at the uneven track. Maybe a klick, Turnbull thought, remembering the maps. Beside him, Carter fired again until the bolt locked empty. Turnbull glanced in the rearview. The rear window was just a jagged memory now, and the Mercedes was back there. He saw flashes. They were firing.

The BMW hit a pothole and they were jolted hard, but their belts kept them tightly in their bucket seats. Low branches flailed against the cracked windshield.

"How far to France?" Carter shouted.

Turnbull did not reply – this was going to be awkward.

Ahead there was a padlocked wooden barrier gate across the road, and a halfhearted fence stretching east and west from both sides. There was a sign with the words "KEIN GRENZÜBERSCHREITENDER." The pictogram of the skull and crossbones indicated that whatever it might mean, it was probably not "Welcome to Switzerland."

Turnbull accelerated and smashed through the barrier, sending splinters and timbers in every direction. The windshield shattered, but from the inside – the Mercedes was following closely and its occupants were firing furiously. Bullets ripped through from behind.

The BMW jolted, the tires losing their grip – had one been blown out? The BMW slid to the right, over the shoulder and across a small embankment, smashing hard into a pair of trees.

The side airbags deployed, their acrid chemical smoke making the passenger compartment even more unbreathable. His ears were ringing like a cathedral bell tower on New Year's Eve. Turnbull beat down his airbag enough to see the Mercedes pull up to a stop a few meters away and its doors fly open.

Show time.

Arab guys, with a couple MP5s and a couple G36s were spilling out, rushing toward them. Turnbull reached for his machine pistol but it was gone, thrown into the back seat by the force of the crash. He went for his .45 – gone.

The Arabs stopped, looking around. Someone was shouting – no, *lots of people* were shouting, but Turnbull couldn't understand any of it. Now the Arabs were shouting too, and there was more shouting, and one of the Arabs raised his G36 and then there was roaring from every direction as the Arabs were caught in a hail of gunfire and shredded before they could get a round off.

All four collapsed to the ground, torn and bloody rag dolls. There were still rounds slamming into their bodies for a few moments until there were more shouts and the shooting stopped.

From the woods, men in camouflage appeared, lots of them, weapons at high ready, aimed at the Arabs.

And, Turnbull realized, aimed at him and Carter too.

"Don't even move," Turnbull told Carter.

A trio of troops appeared in his driver's side window, SIG 553 carbines pointed at his face. The Swiss soldiers seemed extremely unhappy.

There was a shot. Behind the guys to his front, he saw the Swiss dispatching a wounded Arab.

This was getting real.

"Anyone speak English?" Turnbull shouted. The Swiss stared, aiming. Time to lay down his cards.

"I'm an American citizen, a citizen of the United States of America, and I demand political asylum!"

14.

The white paint on the huge man's face made it look like a skull. He had a cavalry saber at his side slid though the belt of his tattered cargo shorts. His bare, chiseled chest and arms were covered with crude prison tattoos, a collection of tribal symbols, patterns and random words mostly in gothic script.

But Hamid al-Afridi focused on the man's wild, bloodshot eyes.

"I am King Leon IV!" the man said, and he did, in fact, wear a crudely fashioned crown on his unkempt hair. Behind him, the six men of his personal bodyguard – all large and well-fed, but smaller than their sovereign – were all similarly outfitted, carrying clubs, machetes and spears. They also held torches to cut through the darkness; the burning rags threw a weird and disorienting orange light on the walls.

Al-Afridi said nothing to the godless savage. Behind him, his own half-dozen guards waited with their AK-47s, ready.

The King surveyed the eerily calm man before him. His shouting and obvious madness usually caused his opponents to fear him. This Arab seemed unafraid. Perhaps it was those guns his men had – where would one get guns like that except from the blues?

The guns would be nice, yes. His warriors had a few guns, but more would be very nice indeed. His army, with guns! Then they could grow and expand outside, into the air, into the sunlight. The blues did not fear him out there, only in here, where they never dared come anymore. Someday they would fear his people outside, though; his people would march out, defeat the People's Security Force patrols that kept them trapped inside, that kept them from doing any serious pillaging. They would conquer.

He was truly a great king.

But should he take the guns before him now? Tempting. These Arabs could not kill all of his multitudes, and his followers would charge into the bullets if he told them to. He knew that. But for six guns when they offered so much more?

No, King Leon the IV would play along, for now. He would keep with the deal, if they kept with the deal.

"I will keep with the deal," King Leon IV said to al-Afridi, as if the conversation in his head were happening in real life.

"Do you have what you promised?" asked the Arab.

"You have the turf," the monarch replied. The Arabs had moved in undisturbed, as promised. In fact, the King had provided bearers to carry the heavy cargo down down down into the dark, where even his own warriors feared to go. Keeping them safe had taken a great deal of firmness. Some of the residents resisted displacement. They died. And some of his subjects from upstairs had failed to obey his directive to leave the Arabs' trucks be as they moved their goods inside. A pair of his subjects decided to try and steal from the trucks; normally that would be good initiative and laudable, but the King had given his command and they disobeyed. Intolerable. Their heads decorated the south entrance as a warning of the price of misbehavior. The remainder of their skinny carcasses were recycled, as it was called in the Kingdom.

King Leon IV demanded obedience. Sometimes, obedience was tasty.

"The rest of it," replied the Arab. "The rest of what you promised to us."

"Oh, I have them. Strong. Prime! Right down the corridor, awaiting my summons. And do you have what you promised me?

Al-Afridi nodded. He had brought the payment from Germany. It would have brought millions of Euros on the street, but it was a small price to pay for the treasure he sought in this life and the next. The Arab nodded to Azzam, who shouldered his rifle and brought forward a silvery metal case.

He laid it on the ground and opened it. Clear plastic-wrapped bricks of white powder. At least two dozen.

Even the King gasped.

Al-Afridi could only imagine what the negotiations had been like that brought this deal to fruition, and he was glad not to have partaken in them. The infidels had arranged it all before he arrived, and there were rumors that the first two sets of envoys to King Leon IV had disappeared into the giant bubbling stewpots that sat cooking night and day in the central courtyard. The third set of ambassadors had managed to make contact and make the deal, instead of being made into a meal.

"Another like this one," said the King. "Every single week,"

"Another one, every single week," replied the Arab. "*If* you keep your bargain. A dozen more. Healthy, strong. Every single day. Then you get another one, every single week."

But Al-Afridi was lying. Within just days, the ungodly king would receive a very different kind of tribute.

"Yes, yes," the King nodded. He turned and snapped his fingers at one of his minions, who took off at a run back up the corridor. Every single week, he thought, marveling.

He was truly a great king.

The minion returned with others, maybe four dozen. The Arab security team stood up straighter, but it was no threat. The minion held a rope, and the rope led back to dozens of captive savages bound in a line, their eyes wide with fear, driven forward with kicks and strikes from the sticks of their captors.

One of the Arabs took the end of the rope from the minion and pulled the captives forward. A European emerged from the shadows. Dr. Maksimov had a flashlight, and he looked over each one, one at a time. They were all under thirty, all dressed in rags, and all were healthy, relatively speaking. Dr. Maksimov nodded and Azzam said something in Arabic and his companion pulled the terrified line of prisoners back into the darkness.

"What are you doing with them, anyway?" asked the King. "Are you eating them? I told my men to choose tasty ones."

"Here, this time, next week," said al-Afridi, ignoring the degenerate's query and delighting in his own lie. This animal and the rest of these creatures deserved their fate. Allah would have no mercy upon them, nor would Hamid al-Afridi.

"You are eating them!" the King said, smiling at what might or might not have been a joke.

Al-Afridi was not amused. In fact, feeding his men was quite a challenge. With their sacrifice at hand, maintaining their purity by eating only *halal* food was essential, and the logistics of it were a burden.

"Just ensure we are not molested."

"If you are molested, you tell me," said King Leon IV majestically.

"We won't be, if you keep your word and ensure no one comes near."

"I shall," the monarch pledged. "For I am truly a great king."

222 | KURT SCHLICHTER

"But Director, there are no leads," said Inspector Cooley. They were in the operations center at PBI headquarters and the monitor was displaying a map of the greater Capitol City metropolitan area. Several sections – including the one they were located in – were sealed off controlled areas depicted in pink.

"Several large trucks load up at an airport and we have no idea where they went?" Rios-Parkinson asked.

Cooley looked down. He had already explained to his superior that the traffic monitoring directorate had been in a racism confrontation stand-down the evening the charter flight had arrived and were busy purging themselves of hatred when the vehicles were on the road.

"I assume every entity that provides trucks has been contacted and audited," he said. He knew the answer. His team had all the truck movement carbon waiver requests directly from the newly-renamed Bureau of Climate Salvation.

The trucks had to be provided by another agency, one that was not accountable to the normal monitoring channels. Rios-Parkinson had an idea of who that might be.

"Our contacts in the Muslim Community?" he asked. "I know they will be eager to assist us in protecting the Republic from racist false-flag attacks."

"No one in Shariatown has seen anything," Cooley said, and then he realized his mistake. "I mean the Muslim Community."

Rios-Parkinson glared, as did several of the other directorate heads. But Rios-Parkinson was mostly irritated by the constraints he operated under without Turnbull. They were looking for Arab Muslim terrorists, and he could not say so. The informal working story among his senior subordinates was that this was agents of the United States pretending to be part of the Muslim Community in order to cause dissension by falsely slandering the religion of peace. But they all understood the reality – they just could not speak it.

Because of this, Rios-Parkinson missed Turnbull, which added to his annoyance.

"So how do we find them? Internet?" he asked.

The internet monitoring director, a biologic male whose card stated a gender identity of "Ethereal Spirit," listed the searches that they were monitoring especially closely, in addition to the usual ones that gave evidence of treason like "freedom" and "Constitution."

"Telecom?"

The director of telecommunications monitoring, a thin woman who simplified things by identifying as a woman, spoke up. "We are monitoring every communications channel. We have added the key words you suggested to the algorithms." The computers recorded every conversation and text for review. She had been puzzled at the words the Director had personally instructed her computers to sweep the conversations for – words like "Marburg" and "incubate."

"Stay behind," he instructed her. "The rest of you, go."

Rios-Parkinson knew it was all necessary, but he knew it would not be enough. Their quarry would not be so foolish as to communicate with anyone here. They would be preparing for their attack.

The telecom director stood nervously before him after the others departed, shifting her weight from one foot to the other.

"Do you have what I asked for?" he said. She nodded and handed over the papers. She knew tracking People's Intelligence Agency telecommunications was serious business, and only her greater fear of her own agency director motivated her to perform the task.

He scanned the report on significant calls over the last 48 hours. "Did you record this conversation with Germany?"

"Yes, of course, but it was scrambled, Director."

"Can you unscramble it?"

She swallowed. "The deciphering algorithms got some words with over 80% reliability, which is the threshold for our decryption model. But not many. The words are in the report."

Rios-Parkinson looked at the paper. One word caught his eye.

"Turnbull."

"Turnbull," said the Swiss intelligence major, sitting down across the institutional metal table from the American in the interrogation room. The Swiss had separated Turnbull from Kristina Carter at the border and driven them separately to the building housing the *Nachrichtendienst des Bundes* (NDB) in Zurich. At least, Turnbull assumed Carter was somewhere in the same building – he had not seen her in several hours.

"You know who I am," Turnbull said.

"Oh yes," said the Major. His uniform said "Strasser," but there was no chance that was his real name. "Your file with us is...significant."

"You people owe me," Turnbull said.

"Whatever we owe you for is above my clearance."

"Then maybe you should pull whoever has the clearance away from his cuckoo clock building or chocolate making or whatever you do for fun in Germany Lite and get him in here so we can talk."

"You are a very unpleasant man, Mr. Kelly Turnbull."

"Which is what led to Switzerland owing me."

The major got up and left. He was gone a half-hour. In that time, Turnbull got up and kicked the door until they opened it and took him down the hall, with five guards, to drain the lizard.

He was sitting back in his institutional metal chair at the institutional metal table when Major Strasser returned and sat across from him.

"My principals have instructed me to provide you with all the assistance you require, Herr Turnbull," he said. "Whatever you did for our country, consider the favor returned."

'That's more like it."

"I have been instructed to clarify exactly how you came to enter our nation, illegally, pursued by four men we have identified as Islamic radicals."

"I think they wanted to convert me," Turnbull said. "Not into a Muslim. Into a corpse."

"Imagine that," the major replied drily. "And what is your mission?"

"Can't say much. Except that you'll lose a lot of customers if I fail."

"So, what will you say?"

"You guys understand discretion. That's why I like you Swiss. Always have, since I saw *The Sound of Music* as a kid."

"You are confusing us with Austrians."

"Yeah, I feel like that when Americans get confused with Canadians. I meant that the Von Trapps *went* to Switzerland," said Turnbull. "You know what I mean."

"Go on."

"I'm a United States operative."

"Paired with a People's Republic operative."

"Only she does not know it."

"My colleagues are trying to talk to her. They tell me she is extremely confused."

"Is she cooperating?"

"No, she is most uncooperative" said the major.

"Good girl."

"She tried to hit one of our men and we had to restrain her."

"Well, I warned her about that. In any case, she needs to believe I am a PR agent, that the USA agent thing was a hoax."

"I want to be clear. You are an American agent pretending to be a People's Republic agent who pretended to be an American agent when we arrested you and who now wants to pretend to be a People's Republic agent for the benefit of your partner who actually is a People's Republic agent?"

Turnbull took a moment to diagram it in his head.

"Yeah," he said. "That."

"How can we help you, Herr Turnbull?"

"I need travel docs back to Washington," he said. "I mean Capital City. Preferably Swiss passports."

"Now you want to be Swiss?"

"No, I want to get back to the PR alive. Everyone's going to be looking for my real ID, my fake ID, and her ID."

"Which is real."

"Hers is real."

"But now she needs a false one."

"And so do I."

"Well, you have cleared that up," said Major Strasser. "I will discuss your request with my principals."

"Discuss it quick," Turnbull said. "Because a lot of people are going to die if I don't get back there quick and stop the friends of those guys who your troopers turned into Swiss cheese. Or do you guys just call it 'cheese'?"

The Swiss intel officers had cleared all the very irritated business travelers out of the Skyview Lounge at Zurich *Flughafen* so that Turnbull and Carter could await their Swissair flight to what had been Dulles in privacy.

One of them dumped a pair of new passports and their old ones, plus their pistols and accessories, and other personal gear, on the bar and stepped away. Turnbull racked in a round and slid the Wilson Combat .45 into his belt at the small of his back. Carter took her Glock sullenly. They then perused their new identity papers.

Turnbull went behind the bar and poured himself a glass of 2027 Robert Gilliard les Murettes Fendant. The Chasselas grape white wine was tart and dry. He poured one for Carter, who stood fuming.

"This," he said, "is good wine. And it's better because it's free." She took her glass sullenly and waited until the Swiss officers left them alone.

"What the hell is going on?" she blurted out. "Who the hell are you?"

"I'm me. I said what I had to," Turnbull replied. "We're going back with new IDs. So it worked."

"I'm going to text the Director that we're returning."

Turnbull shook his head. "Text him from Dulles when we land. I mean 'Diversity.' I don't want a welcome home party."

She put her phone away. Turnbull took his European cell phone from the bar.

"I do have to make a call," he said. She shook her head.

Turnbull walked off to one of the privacy booths and put the battery in his phone. It powered up and he dialed. He awaited the voicemail. He got a voice. It was weaker than he remembered, but it was unmistakable.

"Hello Broadsword, this is Danny Boy."

"Good to hear your voice, Danny Boy. How are you feeling?"

"I've been better. The question is how are you doing?"

It was an open line, so they had to be careful. Turnbull went on:

"I'm in Zurich. I'm returning to where you sent me."

"Vacation?"

"Business trip. Trying to nail down an account. Looking to have a sit-down once I get back where I'm going."

"Who's the client?"

"Old friend. From Siberia by way of Baghdad."

"You had old friends in Iraq?"

"The brother of one. Accounting industry."

"I see. You think you can close the deal?"

"If I get face to face with him, I'm going to settle the account permanently."

"Sounds good. You know how to arrange a ticket home?"

"Yep."

"Good luck. Broadsword. Call for a ride. See you back home."

"See you there, Danny Boy. And make sure my dog is okay."

The line went dead. Turnbull stepped out of the booth. Carter was waiting.

"So, who were you calling?" she demanded.

"Ordering a pizza. No pepperoni out of sensitivity to those of Italian heritage."

Carter was puzzled – she had learned about Chris Cuomo's courageous struggle against the "Pizza man" stereotype in college, but the PR was far past that kind of hateful imagery.

"Wait," Carter said. "You're just messing with me."

"What? That's so insensitive," he said. "Next you're going to make an organ grinder and monkey joke. I think I need to go back into that closet and cry."

"Who the hell were you calling, Oliver?"

"Theodore," Turnbull said, holding up their fake Swiss passports. "Until we get back, I'm Theodore. But you can call me Ted."

"You need to answer my question."

"Nope. Not so," he aside phatically. "I don't need to answer your question. Not even a little. I told you, this is bigger than you understand. Stay in your lane and you might come out of it alive."

"I need to know what's happening. You need to trust me."

"I do. I'm protecting you." Turnbull took the battery out of his phone and put it in his pocket.

The Swiss intel agent watching them from a few meters away answered his cell, muttered something and put it away.

"It is time to board," the Swiss officer said. "Follow me."

Nothing.

Not a whisper, not a hint.

Nothing.

Martin Rios-Parkinson leaned back in his chair, one of the most powerful men in the People's Republic, utterly powerless.

Inspector Cooley stood in front of him uncomfortably. He had stood there for 20 minutes as the Director devoured the day's intelligence reports. Cooley was in a difficult position. He had been told to turn the entire internal security apparatus of the People's Republic toward a single objective, finding a group of mysterious Arab men from Europe, and even he had no clear idea who they were or why they were so important. That was necessary – the internal spying agency was itself full of spies. But Rios-Parkinson was not interested in excuses.

"I find it difficult to believe that a gaggle of foreigners can somehow be setting up a complex laboratory inside our country and we cannot find them," the Director said. His voice was cold, but then it was always cold.

"They clearly are not using comms. They aren't moving. They aren't interacting. They are hunkered down."

"And someone out there knows where. Are you incentivizing our patriots?"

The patriots were the PBI's network of informers, and Cooley had made clear to the PBI's army of handlers who worked with the network of civilian spies located on every block and in every large building and work complex what was being sought, and what the reward for finding it would be.

"We are. But so far, all the leads have turned out to be false. Our field agents are being stretched thin checking them out."

"Bring in more agents from New York, Baltimore, and Philadelphia. You have no higher priority."

Cooley nodded.

Rios-Parkinson went on. "Are you closely monitoring the PIA communications?"

"Yes, as closely as we can without revealing our surveillance," Colley said.

Rios-Parkinson was not worried about that. The Chameleon would assume that his PBI watchers would be scrutinizing the communications of everyone in her organization, even more than usual. They would not be in contact with the Arabs.

"They are somewhere. Find them."

Cooley nodded, nervous. "And there is the Buffalo issue. The riots are completely out of control."

"No doubt our comrades in the Army will pretend that insurrections are in the wheelhouse of the police and not the military. They should act decisively against these traitors," Rios-Parkinson said. He wistfully recalled the solution that a then-obscure Congressman from the San Francisco Bay Area named Eric Swalwell suggested for American citizens who insisted upon their rights. At the time, a nuclear strike on an unruly American city seemed extreme. It turned out he was a visionary of petty tyranny. Swalwell would go on to run the People's Bureau of Investigation after the Split, and he pioneered the building of the network of reeducation and reintegration camps that dotted the rural reaches of the People's Republic. They housed the social criminals, such as gun owners and dedicated Christians and Jews, who were not lucky enough to be executed. The camps were heavy on reeducation, mostly through labor, fear and hunger, but not so much on reintegration.

"The local area is also experiencing...instability," said Cooley. "Across the river, a group of People's Volunteers on a pacification operation near Manassas was ambushed. They lost at least a dozen AK-47s."

Rios-Parkinson grunted. The loss of a dozen guns was more significant than the loss of a dozen paid thugs. There was an endless supply of those. If you paid them off in food, the same punks who would riot would happily accept a firearm and a commission to go suppress rioters.

"Enlist another 200 locally. Take the food to pay them from the local community feeding centers. These ungrateful animals can support their captors."

Cooley nodded.

"Go," Rios-Parkinson said. "And find those criminals and their lair. I expect results, not excuses. Do you understand, Inspector Cooley?"

Cooley nodded again, then departed.

Rios-Parkinson drummed his thin fingers on his desk. The Chameleon was playing it exactly as he would. Hide them. Leave them alone so you could not give away their location. Let them prepare. Then one day, suddenly, there would be a plague spreading across the land and the PIA would be safe behind its brand-new walls. The PBI would get the blame, and his arrangement with Vice-President Harrington would vanish beneath a tsunami of blood-crazed lunatics.

That would be the end of Martin Rios-Parkinson.

No. He would not lose. He would not be outplayed, not after all the years of climbing the ladder. He would not end up against a wall after losing a power struggle like his predecessor Director Swalwell did.

He had one more card to play. But where was that card? Where was Kelly Turnbull?

The People's Republic Welcome Service officer barely acknowledged their presence as they handed over their Swiss passports at Diversity International airport. The scanner was working and it pinged as she swept the bar codes over the red lights then handed them back.

"Welcome to the People's Republic," she said, bored. "Hate and intolerance are not tolerated."

"*Zergut*," Turnbull said. The officer did not respond and he and Kristina Carter walked through into the dingy terminal.

What had been Dulles Airport until the Split used to consist of several terminals serviced by a set of tall white shuttles that carried passengers between them. The shuttles were rusting off in a corner of the airfield now, and only the main terminal, with its swooping roof, was still in operation. There were only a few passengers arriving today. The flight had been nearly empty, and the Swiss intelligence agents had ensured that they were the only passengers in the first-class section. Carter spent the whole flight in a nearly catatonic state, almost unable to comprehend the luxury of it all.

Turnbull, for his part, drank beers and thought about his options when he was not sleeping.

After the customs check, they moved toward the ground transportation area. The few dozen foreigners on the flight were all being picked up by prearranged transportation. There were no taxis, but even if there were any, neither had the carbon credits for a lift into the city.

Carter used her cell to call Rios-Parkinson. She talked for a moment, then hung up.

"Transport is coming," she said.

Transportation did come, after a half-hour, in the form of four People's Security Force squad cars. Three were Fords, one was a Chevy, and none was newer than 2020. The pair slipped in the back seat of the third car in line – it smelled like vomit and fear – and the mini-convoy headed into the Capital City Control Zone with lights flashing.

There were three cars when they got to the main gate and were waved through. One of the vehicles blew a tire and there was no spare, so they abandoned it on the side of the old 267 Freeway near what had been the Wolf Trap exit. Animal rights activists had complained this name was traumatizing; it was now called 'Wolf Justice.'

They crossed the Potomac on what had been I-66. Turnbull looked south at the smoky haze hanging over Arlington and the Pentagon. There was no traffic. The People's Republic was at least good at keeping the roads empty.

Turnbull and Carter went straight past Blue Hair and into Rios-Parkinson's office without pausing to acknowledge her. She ground her teeth at the slight, but she would have her revenge. She opened a drawer and pulled out the burner phone Marshall had given her and typed out a text, then hit "Send." She had earned the 10 pounds of beef she would be receiving that evening. Marshall always paid what he promised.

Carter shut the door behind them as Turnbull walked to the desk. Rios-Parkinson assessed him coldly.

"My feelings about your resurrection are mixed," he said.

"Our mutual friend says 'Hello,'" Turnbull said.

"I am so glad he survived," Rios-Parkinson replied. From the tone of his answer, it seems that he felt the precise opposite.

"Back to the business at hand. Where are they?" asked Turnbull.

"They landed just as you two said they would."

"So, where are they now?"

"We were too late to the airport. They were gone," Rios-Parkinson said. "The people who arranged it used PBI identification."

"That's a nice touch," Turnbull said. "You have spies everywhere. You monitor all the comms. And you still can't find them?"

"They are not moving, they are not communicating."

Turnbull nodded. It made sense. "They've gone to ground. They won't come up until they are ready. Until the bug is ready."

"That is what I would do."

"Me too, if I was a terrorist asshole."

"Do you have any ideas, since you apparently interacted with some of them?"

"Our interactions were pretty terminal. Not a lot of chatting."

"Except for their leader, this Hamid al-Afridi," Carter piped up as she joined him in front of the desk. Turnbull realized he was standing, and slumped into one of the leather chairs. Rios-Parkinson ignored the disrespect.

"You spoke to him?" the Director asked.

"By video call. We just reminisced about old times with his brother."

"You knew his brother?" the Director said, leaning forward.

"Well, yes. Technically," Turnbull replied. "A decade or so ago, I shot that rapist piece of shit in the balls with a twelve-gauge shotgun."

"And, not surprisingly, his sibling holds a grudge," observed Rios-Parkinson.

"I know, right?" asked Turnbull. "I figure we have 72 to 96 hours until these guys breed up enough carriers to unleash the Marburg X effectively. So, we need to find these assholes, and quick."

"And do you have any ideas that might help?' asked the Director.

Generators," Carter said. "Running non-stop, since they cannot rely on constant power."

"We are always looking for generators as a matter of course," Rios-Parkinson said. The PBI had a whole unit devoted to stopping "climate/energy criminals."

"People," said Carter. "He needs people to use as incubators for the virus. So they have to be somewhere where there is a supply of people who no one will notice are missing."

"I will ask Cooley to monitor all missing persons reports, though few people bother to make them to the People's Security Force anymore. Any other ideas?"

"Yeah," Turnbull said. "I was thinking about it on the plane."

"Care to enlighten us, Inspector Warren?" the Director said.

"Sure," Turnbull said. "The sons of bitches gotta eat, don't they?"

"What does '*halal* mean anyway?" Carter asked. She was in the back seat of the sedan, with a scarf around her face. They were parked on a street in what used to be Fairfax, Virginia. He was watching the storefront establishment at the end of the block. The hand-painted sign above it was in Arabic script.

"Your xenophobia and Islamophobia are sadly apparent, Agent Carter," Turnbull said. "I feel unsafe."

Carter waited for a moment, then realized that he was messing with her again.

"I'm serious. It's a serious question."

"I'm not sure of the specifics. It's like kosher, except for Muslims."

"What is 'kosher'?"

Turnbull sighed. "There are religious rules regarding the preparation of food. This is the only place the Directorate of Religious Affairs licenses as *halal* for miles."

A trio of men in Middle Eastern garb walked by them, staring, and then went back to conversing. There were no women in sight.

"It's so calm here," Carter said. Was that approval in her voice?

"Yeah, they take care of their own business in these Shariatowns."

"You can't call them that!"

"Arrest me when this is over," Turnbull said absently. He was scanning the street. Empty. "Let's go."

"We're just supposed to observe."

"We could be observing forever. Time for a chat."

"You may spook him if he really is feeding them."

"Oh, I intend on spooking him." Turnbull started the sedan and pulled out into the vacant street.

He parked across the street from the storefront, and they got out. She was careful to walk behind him.

"You feeling empowered back there?" Turnbull said as they approached the door.

"Kind of," she replied.

The store had an OPEN sign and another with both English and Arabic script. The English part read "Muslims Only."

"Guess I'm cool," Turnbull said, heading in through the door.

There was a meat counter, with surprisingly abundant wares, and a variety of packaged goods. It appeared they also sold produce. There was a door to a back area, and a puzzled man came through it wearing a dirty apron.

"*As-Salaam-Alaikum*," he said, but it was almost phrased as a question. Carter turned the OPEN sign around in the window and stood by the door. Turnbull went up to the counter.

"Hi," Turnbull said, flashing his Inspector Oliver Warren identification.

"No, this is not right," the man said. "You should not be here bothering me."

"Really? Do you have a special arrangement not to be bothered?"

"This is an Islamophobic attack on..." the proprietor began. Turnbull held up his hand.

"You need to stop," he said.

"You are a racist!"

"Muslim is not a race," Turnbull replied. "Now, let's take a walk in back."

Turnbull crossed behind the counter and the man moved into his path. Turnbull grabbed him by the top of his apron and pushed him through. Carter followed.

The back room held a storage area and a walk-in refrigerator, which probably got little use since the power was so unreliable. It was dingy and dirty. There was a large sink and some metal tables – a food prep area. The sink was piled with unwashed pots and pans.

"Who are you cooking for?" Turnbull asked.

"I feed observant –," the man began.

"No, you're cooking for some very special folks. And, frankly, this is not looking super *halal* to me."

"Get out!" the man ordered.

"Nope." Turnbull pushed the man back so his ass was pressed against the steel prep table, and then Turnbull loomed over him.

"Someone hired you to cook *halal* meals for a bunch of the brothers," Turnbull said.

"It was one of you! Your own people!"

Whoever made the arrangements used PBI credentials. Clever. And the fact he actually had meat in stock – supposedly *halal* butchered meat at that – indicated that whoever hired him had some pull.

"Tell me all about it," Turnbull said.

"No," the man sputtered.

Turnbull drew his .45 and put it to the man's forehead.

"Tell me all about it," he repeated.

"No," said the man.

"These are 230 grain hollow point rounds, which is bad enough. Except, these are special. I dipped them in pork drippings back at the cafeteria. So, when I start shooting at your feet and working my way north, that's going to mess you up in this life and the next."

The man laughed. "You pigs don't serve pig."

"He's right," Carter said. "It'd be racist."

"Muslims aren't a race," Turnbull snapped. He stepped back from the proprietor and holstered his weapon. He was annoyed that his go-to interrogation tactic had failed.

Carter removed her scarf; the man was appalled.

"I guess he doesn't scare you," she said. The man smiled, defiant.

Carter returned his grin. "But I should. Inspector, hand me that big knife."

Turnbull took the dirty blade out of the sink and handed it over to her, handle first.

"I'm going to cut off your balls," she said pleasantly. "A woman is going to take away your manhood. Do you think I am bluffing?"

He laughed. She stabbed him in the thigh; not just a poke either. It went in a half inch. The man screamed and covered the spurting wound with his hand.

"Do you still think I'm bluffing?" she asked.

"Whore –," he began, but her next jab, into his other thigh, turned his epithet into another scream. Turnbull assessed that it went in nearly an inch this time.

"You have children," Carter said. "Think what I will do to them after I finish with you?"

The man looked to Turnbull, silently pleading. Blood was oozing out of the wounds under his hands. Turnbull shrugged.

"I would just tell her what she wants to know," Turnbull said. "I haven't seen this side of her before, and frankly it scares me a little."

"Look at me," Carter said, drawing back his attention by snapping the fingers on her left hand as her right readied the knife for another jab.

The man complied and stared into her eyes.

"Tell me everything, and you and your family are safe. That's all you have to do to go free and be safe. Just tell us a few little things. Start now."

They left the store in the hands of Cooley's agents and returned to the PBI building back in the Control Zone. The agents were keeping it quiet – no sense riling the locals and somehow passing a warning to the bad guys that they were compromised. The proprietor himself was down in the dungeons below getting acquainted with Rios-Parkinson's interrogators even as Turnbull and Carter passed by Blue Hair heading into the Director's office.

Carter spoke first as Turnbull shut the door behind them.

"He was cooking for them all right. He gave up the location where they meet every evening at five to pick-up the food," Carter said.

"Inspector Warren is most persuasive," Rios-Parkinson said, and Carter looked crestfallen.

"No, it was your young protégé here," Turnbull said. "She seems to have learned a lot from you."

"It was just basic interrogation skills, right out of the Academy," she said. "Pain. Threats to family. Promises of false hope. It wasn't hard. He broke quickly."

"Excellent work, Agent Carter," Rios-Parkinson said. He hit a button on his desk and one of his video monitors flashed up a map of the Capital City region. "So, where do they meet?"

"Here," Carter said, pointing to a location in Virginia near the river. "National Landing, in the ruins of the old Amazon Complex." The merchandise giant had opened an enormous new headquarters campus there just before the Split. Not long afterwards, the blue government could no longer contain its greed. President Elizabeth Warren declared the company a "profit crime enterprise," and what assets that had not been relocated into the red at the corporation's new headquarters in Atlanta were seized. The company founder, Jeff Bezos, became a fugitive from the People's Republic, and he still resided in the Caribbean Island nation of Grenada, which he bought in 2026.

"We have that area well-covered," Rios-Parkinson. And then he saw it. As did Turnbull.

"The Pentagon," Turnbull said.

"Yes," Rios-Parkinson said. "Estimated population, twenty to thirty thousand, both inside and in the surrounding shantytown. We send in enough food every day that they are not so hungry that they march out and invade the surrounding area, but we have no assets inside. Not anymore."

"You could run generators 24/7. Obvious, plenty of warm bodies."

"But it's complete chaos in there," Carter said. "There's no law and order."

"That's a feature, not a bug. Make a deal with the locals," Turnbull said. "Trade them something. Hamid al-Afridi is a drug dealer. That seems like he might have something to bargain with for some space to do his thing."

"We cannot raid the Pentagon," Rios-Parkinson said. "I simply do not have the forces to search the entire structure within the time we have available."

"I can see where this is going," Turnbull said glumly.

"When you find them, you alert me to the specific location. I will have a PBI tactical response unit ready to launch and take out the entire group.

"Recon job," Turnbull said, shaking his head. "Inside the freaking Pentagon."

"Do you have a better idea?"

Turnbull didn't. "I'm going downstairs to the armory. I bet your people have ingress and egress routes for when they do try to see what's happening in there. I'll need those marked on paper maps." Rios-Parkinson nodded, and picked up his desk phone to pass the request to Blue Hair.

"I'm going with you," Carter said firmly.

"Of course you are. Do you think I'm some kind of idiot, wanting to go in there alone?"

"Oh," she said. "I just thought you'd tell me I couldn't come along. That I would get myself killed."

"We both probably will, but there's a marginally better chance of survival with someone along watching my back," Turnbull said. "You stay here and get the maps. I'll get you some mags and gear downstairs. We need to move quickly. When they come to meet their Grub Hub guy and he's a no show, they may get spooked and jump."

"Grub hub?" Carter asked.

"Forget it. We just need to move fast. The rendezvous is less than six hours from now."

"You're back," Ernie Smith said over the armory counter. He seemed little surprised to see Turnbull standing there in one piece.

"How is she?"

"Your dog is doing fine. Where is your partner?"

"Getting some other gear. We got a mission. I need a suppressor for her Glock. And mags."

"How many?"

"How many you got?"

"That kind of mission, huh?"

"Yeah," Turnbull said. "We'll need some other stuff. Med kits, flashlights, lightweight vests."

"Uniform or civilian clothes."

"Civilian. Low profile. Got any?"

"I don't see anything about you as being low profile. But yeah, we have some duds."

"This time I want to avoid attention."

"But I bet you want to be able to deal with it if you get some?"

Turnbull nodded.

"What's the scenario?"

"Close quarter battle. Inside, cramped areas."

"Ranges?"

"Five to twenty meters."

"That's close."

"Lots of targets. And I gotta stop 'em."

"Sounds like .45."

"Hard to go wrong with .45."

"You'll want it quiet."

Turnbull nodded. "I don't want to blow out my eardrums."

"The .45 rounds are subsonic," Smith said. "You need a good suppressor."

"It's got to be small. Concealable."

"I get it. No attention, until you have their attention."

"Yeah, and when I do I want to smoke every son of a bitch in my way and not worry if I just wing them."

Smith smiled. "I think I got something for you." He disappeared into the back and returned a couple of minutes later with a 2' x 2' black case.

"I don't get much business in here," Smith said, laying it on the counter. "So I do projects to kill the time. Ideas that catch my fancy. This one is one of my favorites." He undid the latches and opened it up.

Turnbull whistled.

Nestled in the foam cut-outs was a gray metal weapon, about a foot long, with straight angles of chromed stamped steel, very boxy, but also familiar. Turnbull recognized it immediately, but also noted the special additions Smith had made to it. A long tube sat beside it in the case, the suppressor.

Smith lifted the weapon out and held it up.

"Original Military Armament Corporation from the early nineteen-seventies," he said. "Some of our close protection guys still use them. But they aren't like this one."

Turnbull took the weapon and examined it in the light.

"MAC-10," Turnbull said.

"Well, not quite a MAC-10. Not anymore."

"What did you do to it?" Turnbull asked, working the bolt on the top of the upper. Solid.

"I reworked the action to smooth it out. Made a lot of little tweaks here and there. I spent a lot of time on the feed ramp. It won't jam, not even with hollow points, even though Gordon Ingraham designed it to run with ball ammo. The cyclic rate is still just a hair under 1100 per minute."

"Sweet," Turnbull said. He extended the reinforced stock. It was still a metal wire frame, but this new one was a bit more rugged than he remembered from firing the original weapon during familiarization back in the Q Course.

"Pachmayr?" Turnbull asked, examining the black rubber wrapped around the pistol grip.

"Yep. Modified for this weapon. The finger grooves will help you keep control on full auto."

"Is it select fire?"

"I guess," Smith said, pointing out the selector switch on the lower left side of the receiver. "But you don't pack a MAC-10 to shoot it semi."

"No, this is for lots of lead headed downrange at close targets. Exactly what I need."

"The bolt on the top of the upper receiver means no picatinny rail, so I had to do some custom work to attach the accessories, like the Aimpoint red dot over the sight," Smith said. "I put the laser designator up front on the side to help compensate for lift when you fire. Flashlight too. Makes it a little bulkier, but you can take them off if you want."

"No problem. I'm carrying it hanging down under my coat," Turnbull said, attaching the long black loop sling to a swivel under the stock. "Easy access."

"Now the best part," Smith said, beaming. Look here."

He reached into the case and took out the suppressor. It was thicker than the weapon itself, and just as long. "With the subsonic .45 rounds, this will keep things on the down low."

Turnbull took the silencer and screwed it on to the MAC-10's protruding barrel. It felt nicely balanced, even with the accessories. He tried out the laser designator and a red dot appeared on the ceiling. He flicked the flashlight on and off.

Turnbull smiled. "Let's go across the hall to the range and try it out."

Carter looked over the maps Blue Hair brought into the Director's office. They were the structural plans of the Pentagon, which had been the largest office building in the world at one time. And there were tactical maps showing ways in and out. But it had been years since the squatters took over the building – who knew what had happened inside? And whether the routes in and out were still good was an open question.

"We sent in a reconnaissance team six months ago," Rios-Parkinson said. "Our persons never came back. The inhabitants appear to have some sort of feudal society inside there. Very primitive. The rulers distribute the rations we drop off every day. That appears to be one of the ways they hold power."

"We will find the laboratory," Carter promised.

Rios-Parkinson nodded. "I need you to take this." He handed her a dull green, metallic device that looked somewhat like an old-fashioned cell phone.

"What is it?"

"Transponder. It is very powerful. It can work even deep underground. Activate it when you find the laboratory. It will send out a signal that the tactical team can follow to raid the target."

Carter nodded and pocketed the device.

"When you locate them, stay nearby and observe until the tactical team arrives. We need to be absolutely sure no one leaves, that we take them all out."

"I will not fail," Carter said. "I'll tell Inspector Warren."

Rios-Parkinson frowned. "You may have noticed that Inspector Warren is unusual."

"I have," she replied. "Xe is definitely challenge overcome."

"Yes, challenge overcome. The mission comes first, Agent Carter. Tens of thousands, maybe millions of lives are at stake. You understand that too?"

"Yes, Director."

"Warren may seek to try to resolve the situation xisself. Xe may not allow you to activate the transponder so that xe can kill al-Afridi personally. This is short sighted, but not unusual in one with xis challenge overcome."

"I won't tell him about it until I activate it."

"Good. Very good. Accomplish this mission and there is a bright future ahead of you here at the PBI. Very bright."

"I won't fail the People's Republic," she said.

"I know," replied the Director. He watched her leave, then went to his desk and pulled out a drawer that revealed three dozen secure cell phones. Each was plugged in and charging. Rios-Parkinson rummaged through and found the one he was seeking. There was but one number on its speed dial, which linked to another cell phone that itself had only one number in its memory – the very number he was calling from.

A male voice answered. "Yes."

"General Zisk," said Director Rios-Parkinson. "It is time to return my favor."

Carter walked out past Blue Hair without a word. The assistant scowled. Carter did not even notice, nor did she notice when the assistant began a short text that read "Pentagon."

15.

"You look like a hobo puked up by another hobo," Kelly Turnbull said, assessing Kristina Carter as the unmarked PBI vehicle pulled away. They were standing outside a massive trash dump at the west end of what had been the Arlington Memorial Bridge into Washington, DC

"What's a hobo?" she asked.

"Someone who is home and hygiene challenged. Come on."

They both looked the part. Turnbull wore some dirty tactical pants and a wool shirt under a dark suit jacket, which came complete with tears and stains. The MAC-10 hung inside by the loop around his neck and right shoulder, and his Wilson .45 was in his belt at the small of his back. The pockets were packed with mags, as was the knapsack he carried. There was a light Kevlar vest under the shirt, but no plates so it would not stop a rifle round. He wore tactical gloves and a pair of black Corcoran combat boots that Smith had been saving in his endless back room, size 11.

Carter looked equally disheveled. Under her rags was her Glock and the dozen mags Turnbull had brought her.

The beacon that Rios-Parkinson gave her was in her jacket pocket, and she had not mentioned it to Turnbull.

They went through the wall surrounding the dump by stepping over the rubble where a section had collapsed. Actually, it had probably been knocked over by one of the hundreds of garbage trucks that made their way through the area every day. Looming above them, on the hill to the west, were ruins. Turnbull got quiet, more than usual.

This had been Arlington National Cemetery until the People's Republic had decided to make it a landfill.

They were not alone, but no one paid much attention to two more derelicts as they headed generally south through the wasteland. The place was packed with people, all wending their way between the towering piles of trash in the access lanes or on the garbage hills themselves, digging and rifling through the fresh debris and stuffing their treasures into the filthy pillow cases most used as bags.

Turnbull and Carter kept close as they moved. The green grass that used to cover the ground was gone. The pathway beneath their boots was not even mud but trash, pounded and compacted by passing trucks. In fact, every few minutes the horn of a garbage truck would warn them to move out of the way and it would rumble by them and over the mounds, followed by a dozen or more filthy men and women eager to get a first chance at the spoils when it finally dumped its cargo.

The smell was as one would imagine.

"I don't understand this," Carter said. "These people, living like this."

"Yah socialism," Turnbull said.

"It's not socialism that did this," Carter insisted. "It's – the racism inherent in society."

"And whose society is it?"

"We're still trying to undo the fascist legacy leftover from before the Split," she replied. Was there a hint in her voice that she was a bit unsure of what she was saying?

Turnbull did not care. He was too angry, because he knew exactly what the People's Republic had dumped its refuse on.

"Mine!" shouted one of the scavengers and he pulled at what may have once been the maroon chassis of a child's bike that another one held tightly in her hands.

"No, it's mine!" she yelled, but the man was stronger and he pulled it away. Satisfied at his prize, he failed to pay attention, and the women sprung at him with a rusty kitchen knife she had hidden under her rags. He howled as it entered his back, and he spun about trying but failing to grab it and pull it out as the woman seized the bike chassis and fled. The wounded man staggered and fell, twitching, and he was immediately set upon by several others, who proceeded to fight each other over the contents of his pillow case.

Turnbull and Carter plowed on, keeping their heads down, avoiding eye contact.

It was slow going. Turnbull was grateful for his boots, and could not even imagine the trek without them. A light rain had made the surface soggy and rivulets of liquid filth wound through the bottom of the canyons between the hills. Above them, a weak sun peeked through the smoky haze. It was just past one in the afternoon, but it looked like it was near dusk.

Carter lifted her arm and pulled back her sleeve to check her watch, and a tall man rooting around in the flotsam and jetsam took notice and stood in their path.

'What you got there?" he demanded.

Turnbull and Carter stopped.

"Nothing," she replied.

"That's mine," the derelict said. He was under the influence of something. "I lost it and that's mine."

"No, it's mine," Carter said, moving around him. He shifted to block her path.

"Give it to me!" He pulled a long three-pronged cooking fork out of his tattered jacket and waved it with his left hand.

Turnbull saw Carter's hand going inside her clothes.

"Hey!" he shouted, drawing the man's attention. "That's my fork."

"Ain't your fork."

"It's my fork. I recognize it."

"It's my fork!" the man insisted.

"She keeps the watch and you keep my fork. Deal?"

"I want both," said the man, and he lunged forward.

Turnbull grabbed the man by the left forearm and pulled him past, firing his knee into the man's gut. There was an "Ooof" and the derelict expelled all the breath in his lungs and folded up. Turnbull slammed his fist into the side of his face, and the man sprawled in a murky puddle, coughing and struggling to breathe. Turnbull picked up the fork and tossed it over the adjacent trash pile.

Wordlessly, he moved on and Carter followed.

The parking lots surrounding the massive concrete structure were packed with shanties and lean-tos. It looked like a refugee camp, without the hygiene, organization or cheer. There were men, women, even some children, filthy, often coughing, sometimes crying. They pushed through, at several points stepping over corpses. The smell of the open latrines on the edges of the lots wafted throughout the settlement. They both struggled not to vomit.

There was a great deal of business going on in the parking lot, from the landfill scavengers trying to trade what they had found in the garbage to the smugglers who got through the People's Security Force patrols on the perimeter and brought in goods from the outside. Food was at a premium, and barter was the name of the game. Food for clothing, trinkets for food, and naturally human beings for whatever use the buyer might desire.

"Capitalism can never die," Turnbull observed.

"This all ought to be stamped out," Carter sniffed.

"Create the problem, then create more problems trying to solve the problems you created in the first place," he muttered.

The dull gray concrete Pentagon loomed over it all. Each face was over 900 feet long, and each facing was five stories high. Fingers of smoke from fires rose upwards from inside. It was obvious that many, if not all, of the windows had been long-ago smashed out. The wall of each facing was marred by graffiti as high as humans could reach up from the ground and hanging down from the roof.

A line of people, each carrying one or two buckets, extended into the Pentagon from the former yacht basin off the Potomac River directly to the east.

The entrance was ahead, and as they drew nearer, the composition of the inhabitants changed. They were less bums and derelicts than primitives, sometimes garbed only in loincloths, often painted with fearsome designs. There was a warrior caste – they were clearly feared and the weak cleared a path for them as they strode through the milling mass of people. Many were shave-headed – badly, as if their styling was done with dull blades – and they carried crudely fashioned spears, axes, and the occasional club.

A mass of people was gathered about the rectangular columns of the entrance façade. There were a few dozen warriors there, allowing some to pass inside and not being so gentle with others. Turnbull and Carter worked their way closer.

"Are those hat I think they are?" Carter said, pointing.

Turnbull followed her finger to the roundish objects hanging down from the roof over the walkway.

"Yep," he said. They were heads.

"Can we get in?" Carter asked. She was no longer sure she wanted to.

"I don't know," Turnbull replied. "They seem to be screening people to enter."

He pressed forward through the stinking crowd to get a better view. A woman with several babies was pleading to be allowed in.

"They're hungry!" she shrieked to a couple of implacable warriors. This made them laugh.

"I need it!" shouted another to a stone-faced warrior with a primitive club fashioned from a baseball bat and nails. The man seemed desperate. He pressed in.

"Back off!" the warrior shouted, slamming the man in the side of the head with the bat. The man stood there for a second, blinked, and a thin trickle of blood ran out his nose as he collapsed. The warriors found this hysterical.

"Now he's got something we want!" shouted the clubber. The warriors found this hilarious.

"Bring him inside and recycle him," he ordered, and two lesser warriors complied by dragging the dead man into the darkness behind them. The crowd quieted for a moment, and then the pleas and begging began again.

"How are we getting in?" Carter whispered after they pulled back to the rear of the crowd. Turnbull had already run through several options, and he was dismayed to realize that the best option he could come up with was to machine gun the savages and walk in.

But, of course, there were undoubtedly more savages inside. More than the number of rounds he was packing, and he was packing a lot of rounds.

"We have to find another way in," he said.

"You want in?" asked a short, thin man, mid-twenties, with wild eyes and spiked hair was grinning before him. He wore what looked like a buckskin vest, tan leather with fringes and no shirt. He had a knife in a scabbard.

"What if we do?" Turnbull replied.

"Well, you got nice stuff. Bet you got something in that bag you wanna trade inside without paying tribute." The man leered, his eyes darting to Turnbull's knapsack and back.

"What if we do?"

"Well, then you gotta let the Sly Boy help you. He knows all the ins and outs."

"Sly Boy? That you?" asked Turnbull, vaguely irritated at the man's use of the third person.

"I'm a Sly Boy ding ding, but you don't have to tell me, over and over again, oh my God! Bleech welch," rapped the man, quickly, his voice going higher as he used the Lord's name, all the while stroking his chin.

Turnbull stood silent for a moment, contemplating this explanation.

"Get away from me," Turnbull growled.

"The Sly Boy knows all the ins and outs, don't you get it?" he said. "You want in, you gotta go through me." For emphasis, Sly Boy tapped his hairless chest.

"You can get us inside?" Carter said. "Quietly?"

"That's what the Sly Boy does, my lady."

"Why are you assuming I'm a lady?"

"Look," hissed Turnbull. "You can get us inside or not?"

"Yeah, sure, I'm the Sly Boy," Sly Boy assured him.

"And can you show us around inside?"

"Like I've been telling you, I'm the Sly Boy,"

"I assume not for free."

"I survive on gratuities," Sly Boy said.

Turnbull looked around – no one else was paying attention to them, so Turnbull pulled a LED flashlight partly out of his pocket. Sly Boy stared – it got his attention.

Turnbull slid it back in. "I bet one of those would be super useful inside there, super valuable."

"Yeah," Sly Boy said, thinking. "Does it work?" Not working would not necessarily queer the deal. There were plenty of tinkerers out in Shantytown who specialized in resuscitating broken devices from before the Split.

"Oh, it works," Turnbull said. "I'll throw in some spare batteries too. If you get us in and help us."

"You sir, have a deal," Sly Boy said. "Give it here."

"No. You get it when we get in and out."

"You know, trust is important in a relationship. We need to establish a level of trust."

Well, Sly Boy, trust this. If you cross us, your head and your balls are going to be hanging over that entrance."

"You are a hard man, sir," Sly Boy said. Then he offered his dirty hand. Turnbull shook it, without removing his glove.

The underground metro station entrance to the Pentagon was supposed to be sealed off. A huge pile of office chairs and desks blocked the path from the old subway station into the building. They had accessed it through ventilation shafts, and now the trio looked over the obstacle from a distance. All quiet, and quite foul smelling. But Sly Boy seemed skittish about the black hole that the tracks led into. He kept glancing over at it.

"King Leon IV ordered this closed off because of the raids," Sly Boy said.

"I have several questions," Turnbull said. "Raids by who, and what the hell is a King Leon?"

"The Fourth," Sly Boy corrected him. "You don't know King Leon IV?"

"We've never been formally introduced."

Sly Boy looked at Carter, who shrugged. "Seems like a paternalistic power paradigm," she said.

"He's the King, man. The boss. He's got the lights, he's got the juice, he's got the eats, he's the Lord of the Streets."

"Sounds like one potent potentate. And what's he so afraid of down here?"

Sly Boy flicked his finger in the direction of the subway tunnel. "The crazies. They live down there. Sometimes they come out."

"Oh good. There are people these lunatics think are nuts. Well, Mr. Boy, how do we get through this pile of stuff and get inside?"

"I got a pathway through. Nobody else knows about it. But you gotta crawl on your belly like a reptile."

"Sounds fantastic. Lead the way," Turnbull said.

They scrambled over to the bottom of the pile. Whoever emplaced it did a good job. It was a tangled mass, all intertwined and very solid.

"Where's your pathway through this?" Carter asked.

"Up a little," Sly Boy said. He climbed a few feet to what looked like the surface of a desk, and then pushed it aside. There was a space behind it leading back into the jumbled pile.

"'Through here," he announced.

There was a shriek from off behind them, from the tunnel. Turnbull saw nothing, only black, but when he turned back around he saw that Sly Boy was pale.

"We should go," he said.

"Her first," Turnbull said, alternately watching Sly Boy and watching the tunnel.

Carter scrambled up and past Sly Boy to the edge of the path. He nodded and she went inside on her hands and knees. The pile groaned and shook a little.

She halted. "Oliver, this is not stable," Carter said.

Another shriek, and noises. Feet.

"They're coming," Turnbull said. "Go now!"

She lunged into the tunnel between the furniture. Turnbull saw her boot disappear and turned toward the tracks. Three thin figures, dressed in gray rags, running awkwardly but fast, shrieking like banshees.

Turnbull whipped open his jacket and brought up the MAC-10, activating the laser designator. The lead one spotted him and screeched, holding aloft a hunk of wood with glass fragments lodged into it. He charged.

Turnbull used his left hand to pull himself up the face of the pile even as he guided the red dot to the wraith's chest with his right.

He fired. The weapon cycled smoothly, like a buzzsaw, and an arcing stream of shells launched out from the bolt on the right side of the weapon. A stream of red splashes followed the dot across the crazy's chest as a half dozen 280 grain Hydra-Shok blew him back onto the track.

The other two clambered over their dead friend as Turnbull pulled himself up to the hole. Sly Boy was paralyzed, but Turnbull gave him a shove and he followed Carter.

The wraiths scrambled to the bottom of the pile and prepared to climb up after him. The red spot found them and Turnbull disappeared into the hole as the empty .45 shells sprinkled over their corpses.

Turnbull manhandled the desk back into position hiding their route. He watched through jumble as another dozen crazies appeared, screeching and howling, looking for their prey. He quietly followed his companions up and through the pile.

When Turnbull emerged, his companions were on a landing at the top of the pile, and it smelled even worse there. Obviously, the big furniture obstacle was a latrine of convenience for some of the residents.

It was dark, but there was a corridor off to the side, and there was an orange light flickering in it. There were hushed conversation and occasional shouts issued from that direction.

"So, we are inside," Sly Boy said. "Now, where do you want to go?"

"We're looking for some friends," Turnbull said.

"With that big gun of yours? How you get a gun, anyway?"

"How about you just dial down the curiosity and focus on helping us find who we are looking for?"

"Sly Boy knows everybody. Who you looking to meet up with?"

"Arab guys. Probably renting out some space from King Leon."

"The Fourth," Sly Boy corrected.

"How do we find them?" Carter asked.

"You ask the folks in the know. They'll be around the courtyard, waiting for their dinner."

"Then let's go," Turnbull said.

The Pentagon contained 6,500,000 square feet of office space when it was used as the headquarters of the United States Department of Defense, making it the largest office complex in the world. But soon after the Split the People's Republic's military had abandoned it for a number of reasons – the movement of the capital, the reduced size of its armed forces, and the chance to crow about how this icon of warmongering was being delivered to the people to house and nourish them.

The corridors – there were five concentric rings of them above ground and more below – reeked of piss and shit. Graffiti and filth marred the walls. The wooden doors were largely gone, burned long ago, and much of the plaster was destroyed in a search for copper and other metal. Most offices were occupied as living spaces. The luckiest were in the outside ring – some of them got windows to the outside breeze. Those windows on the inside opened on fetid open spaces between the rings, which were soon piled high with trash and worse.

There was a torch every seventy meters or so. It was barely enough, but it was something. Apparently, King Leon IV took his role as light bringer seriously.

"He's a beloved monarch," Sly Boy said. "Truly a great king."

Turnbull grunted as they walked, not seeking eye contract with the inhabitants but not signaling weakness by avoiding it either.

They passed by open rooms, the wooden doors long ago taken for fuel. There were often small fires in the dark, sometimes giving light, sometimes warming spoons.

"King Leon IV is the bringer of juice," Sly Boy said, this time not enthusiastically.

"So," Turnbull asked. "What happened to Leon versions 1.0, 2.0 and 3.0?"

"They lost," said Sly Boy.

"Lost what?"

"Challenges. The king is the strongest warrior, so the king is chosen by challenge."

"Seems sexist," said Carter. "That privileges traditionally cis male factors."

Sly Boy seemed puzzled.

"I'm guessing it's to the death," Turnbull said.

"Oh yes," Sly Boy replied. "The loser goes in the pots."

"In the pots?" wondered Carter aloud.

"You can't waste protein," Sly Boy said, genuinely confused.

"King Leon is very concerned with his subjects' nutrition," Turnbull remarked

"The Fourth," Carter said. Turnbull glared.

"I don't want to offend Sly Boy," she explained.

"Sly Boy, ding ding," their guide rapped quietly, stroking his chin. Turnbull shook his head.

They stopped at a doorway. The door itself was absent, torn off its hinges. Through the arch they could see a huge courtyard full of milling people, with shanties and an improvised marketplace. Toward the center there was a hub of activity. Smoke rose over it. There were fires and many dozens of massive cooking pots.

A line of water bearers extended out from the east-facing section into the center of the courtyard. Each individual bearer would come, hand over a full bucket in exchange for an empty one and begin the long walk again. Others, guarded by warriors, pushed heavy carts holding the truckloads of flour and beans dropped off earlier in the day at the agreed location in the former south parking lot.

"Everyone has a job," said Sly Boy. "See, King Leon IV is about full employment."

"Wonderful. This is what a disarmed populace looked like. Living in fear of the biggest and strongest." Now let's go find what we are looking for," Turnbull said.

"Let me make my inquiries," Sly Boy said. "Stay here. Don't talk to anyone." He disappeared into the mass of humanity.

"I can easily not talk to anyone," Turnbull said. He gestured with his head and Carter followed him to an area near the interior wall where no one else was standing.

"Do you trust Sly Boy?" she asked.

"Oh seems. Seems like a stand-up guy."

"So, what do we do?"

"We wait and see if he comes back alone or with a bunch of those barbarian guys."

"And if he does?"

"Then we have an issue. What time is it?"

The sun was dropping in the sky. She looked at her watch, careful not to let anyone else see it.

"Six."

The generator noise was amplified by the closed space. It ran 24 hours a day, and some of the brothers had taken to stuffing bits of cloth in their ears to block it out. Hamid al-Afridi did so too. After all, he intended to survive what was coming and wished to preserve his hearing.

It also helped block out the screams, not that he cared about those anymore.

There was a knock at his door. He had taken over an office near the lab. There was no window, of course, but the power allowed them to run lights that cast a weak light in the darkness of the dungeon.

He opened it, expecting Azzam and dinner. Pure food was less a luxury than a necessity. But it was Dr. Maksimov. He gestured for the filthy Russian to enter.

Dried blood was splattered on his lab coat.

"It is working," the doctor said. "We have eight carriers currently. And perhaps forty subjects waiting."

Al-Afridi was pleased. The brothers who had carried the virus over from Munich in their bodies were the newest martyrs. Someday he would see them again in paradise, where they were now dining on grapes fed to them by virgins. He had administered the final mercy to them himself with his SIG Sauer P226. Now the bodies that savage had provided would incubate it. And soon, they would spread it.

"Excellent news, doctor," replied the Arab. "And we can begin when?"

The Russian seemed puzzled. "Any time," he said, his accent thick. His breath gave off the slight hint of the vodka ration al-Afridi allowed him. "The carriers are infectious, and they can spread it to the forty subjects with aggressive symptoms manifesting in just a few hours."

From beyond the door, back in the lab, there was a scream. Neither paid it any mind.

"It will not be long, doctor," al-Afridi assured him.

Another knock. He moved to the door and opened it.

It was Azzam, and he was agitated.

"Where is our food, brother?" asked the leader impatiently as his henchman stepped inside.

"I was at the meeting location, but he never came."

Al-Afridi considered it. "Perhaps he was merely late."

Azzam tilted his head backward. "No. I waited for him. He never came."

Troubling. This local man was reliable, a pious brother. He knew nothing of the specifics, of course, nothing of what they were actually here in the People's Republic to do, but he understood that his humble service of preparing *halal* meals was important to the cause. He had done it without fail as tasked – until tonight.

"Is it possible you did not see him?"

"No. I watched from a distance to see if he arrived and if he was followed. He never came. What will we eat?"

Al-Afridi smiled, amused at the pedestrian concerns of Azzam. He was suited for simple tasks and brute force, but not much else.

This development was a sign.

"Go, Azzam. Tell the others. It begins. Dr. Maksimov, make me an army of the infected."

"It's been an hour," Carter whispered. The sun was down, but the courtyard was bright with torches. The people were lining up, each carrying some kind of bowl.

Someone had literally rung the dinner bell.

But no one was eating yet. They were waiting.

Warriors began streaming into the courtyard. Somewhere across the space, people began to bang on drums.

A couple warriors were looking at them, causally, not too interested, but not completely disinterested. Turnbull did not return the eye contact. Fake submission might make them lose interest.

It seemed to work.

A silence descended on the courtyard. Those sitting or lying down stood up. The chant began.

"Hail to the King!"

"Hail to the King!"

"Hail to the King!"

The commotion was about 200 meters to the left, near the door on one of the five walls. Someone was coming.

"Guess who?" muttered Turnbull. The warriors were looking at him again. He stood up straighter and they returned to chanting.

King Leon IV followed by a dozen of his wives and many children, strolled out through the courtyard, acknowledging his subjects with nods and the occasional wave of his scepter. He carried his cavalry saber, as always.

"Bringer of light!"

"Bringer of eats!

"Bringer of juice!"

King Leon IV accepted their honors and accolades with regal alacrity. He stepped up to the cooks, who bowed and presented him with a large bowl. He took it in two hands and smelled it. Apparently, it passed the nose test, for he tipped it back and drank deeply from it then handed it back.

"This meal is fit for my subjects!" he bellowed, and the crowd cheered and closed in around him to take their places in line – the king, the royal household, the warriors, and then the peasants.

Turnbull pivoted toward Carter. "If he's not back...," he began but Carter's eyes grew wider.

Turnbull felt a hand seize his shoulder and swing him around 180 degrees. The warriors, and they were angry.

"How dare you turn your back on the King!" the one who grabbed him howled.

"An accident," Turnbull said. "I humbly beseech your forgiveness and the forgiveness of King Leon."

The warrior had a meat cleaver, and by the way he was raising it, forgiveness was not in the cards.

"The Fourth!" he shouted and swung, connecting with Turnbull's Kevlar vest. The armor kept him from being gutted, but it still hurt.

The warrior pulled back, surprised that his quarry had not been gutted, and prepared another blow, this one aimed at Turnbull's neck.

But Turnbull kicked him hard in the groin, knocking him backwards. His partner raised his spear.

Not a lot of options, so Turnbull went with his default move.

Kill 'em all.

Turnbull threw back the coat and brought up the MAC-10. Spear Man was a bit shocked to be facing a real live gun, but that only lasted for a moment. Turnbull put a burst into his thorax and Spear Man would never be shocked by anything again, at least not in this world. Turnbull pivoted to Cleaver Man. Another burst, and he staggered back with ten .45 caliber pits across is rib cage.

Because of the suppressor, the entire courtyard was not alerted immediately. But enough of the people around them scrambled and shouted. The crowd took notice.

Turnbull yanked Carter along with him back through the doorway and into the corridor.

"Run!" he yelled, dropping the mag and reloading. She complied.

They raced down the hallway, past confused and frightened peasants. A man carrying a load of firewood –chopped up support beams from inside one of the Pentagon's walls – failed to move fast enough. Turnbull hit him like a freight train, sending wood scraps flying and him sprawling.

Behind them, the warriors were coming.

And in front of them, illuminated by orange torchlight at maybe 20 meters range, were three with clubs charging, eager to be the ones to capture them and receive the resulting honors.

Turnbull brought the MAC-10 up squeezed the trigger. The action clattered and shells flew out of the open bolt. The warriors were not expecting the swarm of lead. Spouts of plaster flew across the hallway and across their bare chests. It sounded like a buzz saw and lasted less than two seconds before the 30-round mag went dry.

The three were splayed out on the floor; Turnbull and Carter leapt over them.

There was a right turn, perhaps a crossing to an interior ring. They ran as hard as they could, but the riotous rumble behind them was gaining.

There was a doorway, and inside, darkness.

"Find Sly Boy," Turnbull said as he pushed her inside the pitch-black room. And then he kept running.

He went left at the next ring, sprinting as best he could while reloading. Two warriors to his front. He took them down with a burst. But maybe twenty beyond them. He stopped, and turned back around. Maybe thirty that way.

He dropped the mag and slammed in another. Then something hard hit him on the back of his head – a club, thrown from behind – and he staggered. They mobbed him. He squeezed the trigger and it buzz-sawed and someone got hit because someone was screaming and then they simply piled on top of him until he was crushed to the floor.

King Leon IV appeared puzzled by the man trussed up before him. He stared, and thought, and stared some more.

Turnbull looked around. His wrists hurt from being tied up for what had been at least a few hours – there was no way to mark the passage of time in here. A couple dozen warriors lined the ornate throne room. Above the throne on the wall, a round seal with an eagle clutching lightning bolts on a light blue background. This freak had taken over the Secretary of Defense's office.

Well, reasoned Turnbull, that made more sense than anything else he had seen in here so far.

"Who are you?" asked the King. His chest was covered in bad tatts, the kind you get on a cellblock to kill time while doing time.

"I'm guessing you're King Leon," Turnbull said. "The Fourth," he added.

"I know who I am," said the monarch, his face painted bone white to resemble a grinning skull. "Who are you?"

"I'm the guy who is going to make you a very great King."

"I am truly a great king already."

"I can make you even greater. I have connections."

"Connections?" The King laughed. "What does that even mean?"

"Well, your army, for example, they seem a bit under-armed. I could change that."

"But you have already brought me these," the King said. He walked to a table near the throne and picked up the Wilson .45 and the Mac-10. The rest of his gear and knapsack were on the table.

"I mean *a lot* of guns," Turnbull said. "You know the police forces. I work with them."

The King laughed. "The police are not popular around here, cop."

Turnbull was beginning to think he had taken the wrong tack.

"You see, I spent almost my whole life in their jails," the King went on. "After they Split, they overthrew the prison-industrial complex, and people like me were freed. And many of us came here, to our kingdom, our utopia. But once again, they imprison us. They give us a pittance, enough to survive. So we don't much like cops."

"How about if I could get you more than a pittance?"

"For your life?" The King found this amusing.

"That's part of it, but there's something I'm even more interested in. And you ought to be interested in it too."

"And what is this?"

"I want to know where the Arabs are."

That got a reaction. King Leon IV tented his fingers and paced back and forth for a moment.

"Arabs? What Arabs?"

"You know what I'm talking about," Turnbull said.

"What do you want with these Arabs?"

"I want to find them."

"And then?"

"I want to kill them all. And if you were smart, you'd help me."

The warriors around him were taken aback by the disrespect.

"Let me do him, Your Majesty!" shouted one with an axe and a dried hand hanging from a string around his neck. King Leon IV held up his palm.

"Do you know what they brought me as tribute?" asked the monarch.

"Hummus?"

"Horse. Smack. Heroin. Enough to ease the pain of my kingdom for a week. And next week they will bring me more."

"There won't be a next week. Do you have any idea what they are brewing up down there?"

"I already know," said the King. "I already told you. Heroin. Juice."

"It's not a drug lab, you royal dipshit. It's a plague, and your people are going to be the ones who spread it for him."

"I was going to be merciful," the King said. "I was going to be kind and kill you quickly. But your disrespect, and your lies about our friends…"

He paced some more.

"No, I am giving you to them. You and your toys, all to them. To show that I keep my word."

"You're discovering honesty now? At this moment?" Turnbull said.

"A king's word is gold."

"Well, I got a word too. I'm going to see you again, and I'm going to try it out when I do."

The warriors seized him from behind as others gathered up his equipment.

"What's your word, dead man?" asked His Majesty

"Regicide," Turnbull said as they hustled him out.

16.

Turnbull's hands were tied behind him, and the two biggest of the warriors had firm grips on his upper arms. One walked out ahead of them with a torch. Another followed, carrying a sack with all of Turnbull's gear. They packed a collection of rudimentary axes, clubs, and spears.

The four warriors took him down, into the dark – at least, mostly dark. The corridors and stairwells were lit with the familiar torches mounted on the wall, though they were few and far between – about 70 meters apart. Apparently, there were drones who ran around the corridors doing nothing but ensuring that King Leon IV's lights kept flickering. That's how they earned their man-gruel.

The flames gave the labyrinth a black and orange feel that reminded Turnbull of Halloween. Except all these guys were going as skinnier, dumber versions of the extras from *Road Warrior*.

It was five levels down, so Turnbull figured he was in the second basement level. There were no windows down here, of course, and clearly it was not the high-end neighborhood. The denizens of these forgotten rooms glanced out of their doorways at the passing band, puzzled and afraid at the same time. Obviously, they didn't see much through traffic. Usually, one of the painted and snarling escorts would shout at them and they would withdraw back into the darkness.

"How far is it?" Turnbull asked, conversationally.

"Shut up," said the escort leader. "And all you, I'm taking those boots before we push him inside. They're mine!"

There were mumbles of discontent and the band kept walking.

There was a large fire door ahead closing off the corridor. A couple more warriors lingered in front of it. It was barred through the handles with a 2 X 4 hunk of wood.

One of the door guards stepped up.

"What you want?" he shouted, his chin up. Dominance pose.

Great, Turnbull thought. Here comes the battle of the supra-geniuses.

The band stopped and the escort with the torch stepped up. "This one's going in," he announced.

"King says nobody goes in!"

"Well, King says this one does."

"Bullshit! Ain't fooling me. I got my orders!"

"New orders!" shouted the escort.

Turnbull, pinned by his captors, surveyed the tableau skeptically. It reminded him of something – oh right, that stupid book, *The Runewench of Zorgon*, one of the dozens in the *Elf-Blade of Noxim Saga*. There was a part where an elf-mage held captive by ogre-goblins and the ogre-goblins fought over him and in the confusion the hero escaped the dungeon into the Forest of Doom. Of course, in the book the elf-mage had an invisibility rune, so he had that going for him.

The battle of wits escalated and drew back his attention.

"You best open the door!"

"I ain't seen no orders! The King commanded no one who ain't one of our guests goes through that door without his say so, and no one is!"

"Well," Turnbull said. "Guess we gotta turn around."

"Shut up, you!" hissed the escort leader, wheeling about.

"You dumbasses going to kill me or bore me to death?" Turnbull said.

The escort leader made a face and then a dot appeared in his forehead and a puff of pink expanded behind him. He staggered back, dropping his torch.

The guy holding his left arm went limp, so Turnbull drove right, dragging his remaining captor off balance and into the mildewed wall. There were cries and shouts now; out of the corner of his eye, he saw another warrior stagger.

But the one still grabbing his upper right arm was his focus. He slammed the man into the wall again, and it was not plaster. It was concrete, and the force knocked the warrior loose. Turnbull pulled back, and kicked the side of the man's left knee with the flat of his combat boot sole. There was a crack, and the man crumbled.

More noises behind him, but Turnbull was fixed on finishing with his target. He kicked again, this time at the man's face. His steel toe connected with the man's jaw, and the man's jaw lost. Blood splattered the wall and teeth clattered across the floor.

It was quiet.

Turnbull reeled about.

"Sly Boy ding ding," said Sly Boy. Behind him, Carter was slamming home a fresh mag into her suppressed Glock. All the warriors were down; half were still moving.

"Finish them," Turnbull said, walking over to the sack, which lay next to a dead warrior. He could hear the *pffts* as Carter complied.

He did a chamber check on the Wilson .45 and slid it into the holster at the small of his back, then picked up the MAC-10. Loaded and ready. He began gathering the rest of his gear.

"Sly Boy found me. We thought you were dead, but then we found out that they took you up to the throne room so we staked it out. We figured they would take you out of there one way or another," Carter explained. "We followed you down here. Took my target of opportunity. But it was their adherence to a patriarchal power structure of toxic masculinity that forced me to do it. Sad, but necessary."

"Nice job anyway," Turnbull said. "See, I was right to bring you along."

"I could not have done it without him."

"But you don't have to tell me, over and over again," Sly Boy rapped, proud of himself.

"I like how you have a little song about yourself, Sly Boy," Turnbull said. Their guide beamed. "Not really. Stop singing."

"How do we find the Arabs? We're out of time," Carter said.

"That's who King Leon – *the Fourth* – was having this brain trust take me to see. Apparently, they bought his protection by giving him a bunch of heroin and promising him more."

"Bringer of juice," said Sly Boy.

"Yeah, except their next delivery is going to be a little different and not quite as much fun."

Turnbull steeped over to the barred fire doors and put his ear to it.

"Humming, like a machine."

"Generator?" asked Carter. Turnbull nodded.

"Sly Boy, you stay here, and you make sure no one bars this door. When we come back out, it's going to be fast. You got me?"

"Sly Boy got ya!"

"Now, if it isn't us, if it's something, something like a crazy, or *worse* than a crazy, that means we're dead. You get as far away as you can go. You got me?"

"What's worse than a crazy?" asked Sly Boy.

"You just do what I say and make sure this door opens when we need to come back through." Turnbull removed the bar and turned on the flashlight on his MAC-10. Muzzle leading, he pulled open the door. Nothing. He entered and Carter followed, Glock in hand.

"What's worse than a crazy?" Sly Boy muttered again as the door shut.

This corridor was in significantly better shape than the others they had walked through – the door had probably been shut for a long time, and few of the locals had infested this wing of the basement. It was hard dark, like the air itself was pitch black, with no torches and only the flashlight on the machine pistol to illuminate their way.

It would draw attention, if there were guards. But there was no real choice.

They followed the noise, the mechanical humming that slowly grew louder as they walked into the blackness. And then, at a T-intersection, light at the far end down to the left.

White light, from bulbs.

And another noise. Screams and howls.

"I think we found the lab," Turnbull said, turning off the flashlight on his weapon. But he kept the gun up as they slowly approached.

It was a long walk, at least 100 meters. The lighted area was a central corridor with at least a dozen closed doors. Wires and cables ran on the floor alongside the baseboards. The illumination came from a multi-bulb flood light panel mounted on a cart.

"We know where they are now," Carter said. "We can pull back and inform the Director."

"We're already here, we –"

The door to the left opened. It was an Arab man with a pack, and he was surprised.

Turnbull ripped him stem to stern with the MAC-10. The shells clattering on the linoleum were louder than the report. The man collapsed backwards into his room. Turnbull charged in, covering left – nothing – and right – man on a cot fumbling for a MP5. Turnbull sprayed him across the chest, putting several rounded into the cinder black on either side of him. He fell forward and onto the floor, the wall behind him splattered and pockmarked.

Turnbull dropped the mag and reloaded. Carter came inside the room and shut the door behind her. He looked over the two dead guys – neither was al-Afridi.

They waited.

Nothing.

The room was spartan, but a palace compared to the rest of the Pentagon's accommodations. A couple of cots, some ancient desks; one had a Koran on it. They were living out of their backpacks.

There were bowls of water on the desks, and towels. They were cleaning themselves up for something.

"What were you up to?" Turnbull muttered at the corpses.

Both had submachine guns. Turnbull handed one to Carter.

"I hate movies where the protagonists leave better weapons than they have behind. Find all the mags you can, just in case we need to stop with the silent mode."

She nodded and began putting loaded 9mm magazines in her pockets.

Turnbull went to the door and slid it open a crack. The corridor was empty, but the yelling was getting louder.

Turnbull went out the door, weapon up. The ruckus was coming from inside the door at the end of the hall. The one with red Arabic script painted on it.

He couldn't read the language, but he was pretty sure is said "Stay the hell out."

He put his left hand of the door and pushed gently, then threw his weight against it and rushed inside, gun up.

A lab. Tables, racks, cabinets. Cages, maybe a dozen, empty. And men. Three targets, all stunned and still. One was near the back door, which was painted red and had a push bar. Another a frazzled older man who reminded Turnbull of the guy in *Back to the Future*. And Hamid.

All still, staring at him.

Turnbull restrained the urge to smoke the lot of them. At least for the moment.

Hamid has a SIG on his hip, Dr. Maksimov had no weapon. And the third guy, he was in a white robe and looked like he had just showered.

From the door behind the clean man came a scream, and a howl, and a whole cacophony of shrieking.

Turnbull knew those shrieks.

"You've bred carriers," Turnbull said.

"So many," al-Afridi said, smirking. Turnbull put the red dot on his forehead.

Dr. Maksimov looked around, desperate. "I was kidnapped!" he shouted in Russian-inflected English. Turnbull put the dot on him next.

"Is there a vaccine?" Turnbull asked. Dr. Maksimov swallowed.

"No," he said. "No vaccine. But I am the only one who can produce the Marburg X. Take me with you. I will work for you instead of these animals."

"No vaccine?" Turnbull said. "And you're the only one who can revive it?"

"Yes," said the Russian, nodding eagerly.

"Well, that makes it easy." Turnbull squeezed the trigger and sent five rounds through the scientist's forehead.

Al-Afridi dropped behind a table, and Turnbull finished off the mag in his direction, wrecking beakers and shattering instruments.

Turnbull dropped to his knee, drew out another mag and slammed it home. Now al-Afridi was yelling something.

The clean guy yelled something too.

"*Allah ackbar.*"

Turnbull rose with the MAC-10 ready but it was too late. The clean man was pushing down on the bar and shoving the back door open. It was hard at first, until the infecteds behind it realized that this was how they would escape. Bloody arms reached though the opening and grabbed and tore at their liberator. He struggled and collapsed under them, screaming as the bloody madmen poured through.

There were more than Turnbull could count.

BAM BAM BAM!

The rounds ripped by Turnbull's head – too close, and he dropped again under the table as al-Afridi ran past suppressing him with his SIG pistol.

The horde saw the running man and shrieked as one, and those not actively engaged in tearing the clean man limb from limb clambered after him.

Al-Afridi was out the door. And the horde was coming.

Four of them – maybe men, maybe women, it was hard to tell – were at the vanguard of the mass. Turnbull rose and leveled his weapon, empting the whole mag into them.

The .45 rounds slammed into their skinny bodies, tossing and jolting them even as they tried to force their way through the storm of hollow points. They fell, a slick, twitching obstacle to the dozens behind them.

Turnbull bolted through the door into the corridor. The door slammed behind him.

Al-Afridi was ahead, firing into the room where Carter was. His SIG locked back empty and he ran on. A burst of submachine gun fire answered from inside, missing him. The Arab disappeared into the darkness as Turnbull slammed in a fresh mag.

Carter staggered out and into his line of fire at the fleeing Arab. Turnbull caught her and pulled her along. He would have fired, but he needed the rounds.

The carriers were pounding on the inside of the lab door; it would be only moments before they figured out how to pull it open.

"I'm hit," Carter said. "Lower left rib. The vest took it. It didn't penetrate."

"We need to move," Turnbull said.

"Is that what I think it is?" Carter said, hearing the horde assaulting the door.

"Yeah, but a lot more than you can imagine." The door shuttered. They shuffled forward.

"Help's coming," Carter said.

"Help?"

"Yeah. The Director gave me a beacon. I activated it."

"A beacon?"

"Yes, so the tactical team could find us."

"Where's this beacon?" The lab door shuttered again. They stumbled forward.

"I left it in the room," Carter said, annoyed and scared all at once. The howling from the lab was getting wilder.

"What did it look like?"

"Look like?"

"The beacon," Turnbull said, pulling her along. They were passing the light rack and heading toward the darkness. More howls – the horde's fury at the door imprisoning it was reaching a crescendo.

"Green."

"Like OD green?"

"OD?"

"Like Army green?"

"I guess."

"Did it *say* anything?"

"What?"

"Was there anything written on it?"

"Yes, I think."

"Like 'USAF'?"

"Yeah," Carter said. "There was."

"Old United States Air Force. It's a targeting beacon. We need to get the hell out of here." Turnbull raised his MAC-10 to the bank of floodlights and squeezed the trigger just as the lab door opened and the scarlet, mad horde spilled out.

"Equality three-three, this is Matriarch one-seven, over," blared the squawk box in General Zisk's tactical command post at Fonda Air Force Base in Maryland. The general was assuming personal operational control of this mission, with only his executive officer, targeting officer, and diversity officer assisting.

"Matriarch one-seven, go ahead," the general said into the mic. He had picked his two best F-15 crews to fly two of the six remaining operational fighters at the base. Luckily, his diversity officer was cooperative and ignored how the commander had ignored every characteristic except flying ability in choosing who would undertake this vital mission.

"Xoe have my full support," the diversity officer told xim. General Zisk would certainly return the favor in the future.

There were only a few BLU-118/B bunker busters left in the People's Republic Air Force inventory. Each aircraft carried two.

The flight commander responded. "We have the beacon. Transmitting data, over."

The targeting officer examined the stream of data on his screen and compared it to the digital model of the facility. It would take a few minutes to program the exact detonation point for each to ensure total sterilization.

Turnbull and Carter inched forward in the dark. The corridor in front of them was pitch back, but with the light set shot out it was almost the same to the rear, except for few tendrils of light coming out of the ruined lab door.

The infected were spreading, not with any kind of plan, just wandering. But noise or light...

And al-Afridi was somewhere up front ahead of them, with a SIG.

They walked slowly and quietly. They came to the T-intersection. After that turn, it was utterly black.

Grunts and groans behind them. Infected, wandering in their direction at a trot. No purpose to it; nothing, of course, except the mad motion picture going on in their inflamed brains.

They pressed up against the wall, and felt the air move. Someone – at least one – passed them.

Maybe 100 meters to Sly Boy.

They stepped forward, with Carter able to move on her own. Or so it seemed.

She fell, the MP5 clattering on the ground.

Turnbull dropped to the floor as three loud shots erupted maybe 20 meters ahead. The ricochets echoed in the hallway. And there were howls from outside the lab.

Turnbull fired off an entire mag at thigh level ahead of them, and he was already reloading as he heard someone fall and a metallic clatter. As the mass somewhere behind them screamed and charged, Turnbull flicked on his flashlight to their front.

A woman with blood pouring from her eyes, ears, nose, and mouth turned at his light and hissed. Turnbull fired and it sprawled. Then more footsteps, fast, from the front.

The flashlight found the bloody man charging at perhaps five meters. The MAC-10 roared and the rounds impacted across his chest, but he kept coming. The creature tackled Turnbull and sent him sprawling backwards, clawing at his face. Turnbull punched him in the cheek hard, but it hardly registered. The creature howled, spraying him with a spray of saliva and blood.

Carter stumbled forward, smashing its head with the stock of her submachine gun. Blood from its ripped scalp splattered them both. It rolled off Turnbull and turned on her, allowing Turnbull to bring up the MAC-10 and fire again. The last burst sent him backwards, leaving him dead on the floor.

"Go," Turnbull said, wiping the red goo off his face and reloading. Just six mags left. Enough?

He turned the flashlight to the floor. Hamid al-Afridi had taken two hits in his thighs. He was crawling for the SIG a few feet away on the linoleum tile.

Turnbull walked ahead and kicked the pistol down the hall.

"You won't be needing that," he said. In the darkness of the corridor, they could hear the horde coming fast.

"Oh, wait, you really, *really* need that right now. Oops" He took out his LED flashlight. "But you can have this."

Turnbull turned on the light and tossed it to al-Afridi, illuminating him.

The horde down the hall howled and charged.

"Say 'Hi' to your pussy brother in hell."

Turnbull turned and trotted away as Hamid al-Afridi cursed him in Arabic until the horde overwhelmed him and finally silenced him by eating his tongue.

Carter got to the doors and pushed. Firm. She pounded and shouted.

Nothing.

Turnbull trotted up.

"Where is he?" Turnbull muttered, pounding the door.

Nothing.

He turned, his weapon's flashlight on, aiming into the darkness. Carter lifted her MP5.

They were coming.

"Save one for yourself," Turnbull advised. He opened fire, and so did she, and the noise from her weapon was deafening. Shells clattered on the tile and the infected screamed, but more came clambering over the shredded bodies of the dead and wounded.

The door opened, and Turnbull pushed Carter through and then went himself.

A warrior pushed the door closed and barred it, then relieved Carter of her MP5.

There were at least 50 warriors, and King Leon IV stood before them. Their torches bathed the chamber in orange light.

Sly Boy was on his knees before him with a bloody nose.

"I thought you were dead," he said before a warrior kicked him.

There was pounding and screaming from behind the doors.

"What did you do?" asked His Majesty, enraged.

"I don't suggest you open the doors and find out," Turnbull said, raising the MAC-10 and aiming it at the King's face.

The King laughed.

"From all that shooting we heard, you're empty," he laughed.

True. Turnbull lowered the weapon. He had neglected to take his own advice and save one for himself.

"What now?" Turnbull said.

"What now?" repeated the King. "What now is I kill all of you for defiling my hospitality to my guests."

"They were bad guests."

"They were still guests."

"Killing us doesn't work for me," Turnbull said.

The King laughed, and then so did his warriors.

"But I don't see that you have a say in the matter. Take him."

"Wait a second," Turnbull said. "I challenge you."

The King laughed again. A hearty belly laugh. But Turnbull was not laughing.

"I want to be King Leon V. I have a right to challenge you. Anyone does. And since you want to kill me anyway, what's the big deal? I mean, you're not afraid of me, are you?"

"Oliver," Carter said.

"It'll be all right," Turnbull assured her. "Hold this for a minute." He unclipped the MAC-10 from the swivel and handed it to her. Sly Boy was now looking at Turnbull the way Turnbull usually looked at him.

King Leon IV's laughter phase had ended. He was annoyed now. His eyes darted around his warriors, and he knew they were watching.

"I accept your challenge," he announced, and his warriors cheered.

"What are the rules?" Turnbull asked.

The King drew the saber he had liberated from the wall of an office that had formerly been occupied by the commander of the First Cavalry Division before the Split. It gleamed; he had one attendant whose entire job consisted of keeping it razor-sharp.

"There are no rules," King Leon IV laughed.

"Good, because I *hate* rules." Turnbull squared off with the King,

"I will hang your heads from the doorways," the monarch announced. His warriors laughed. The saber's blade caught the orange light of the torches.

Say, you spent most of your life in jail before your coronation, right?" asked Turnbull.

The King waved the saber through the air.

"I was falsely imprisoned for many years. Are these the last words you want to utter?"

"I'm just thinking that you missed a lot of classic movies, being locked up and all."

"I grow weary of you," the monarch said, slashing the air.

"So, you probably never saw *Raiders of the Lost Ark*?"

"No," King Leon IV said, stepping forward to finish the duel before it started.

"Then this will be a *big* surprise." Turnbull reached behind his back under his jacket, drew out the Wilson .45 and shot King Leon IV in the forehead.

The sovereign's body fell onto its back and twitched twice. The warriors looked down at their fallen ruler, and then up at Turnbull, who held the .45 at face level, sweeping the audience.

The crowd stood silent, stunned.

"Would anyone else like to discuss the royal line of succession?" Turnbull inquired loudly.

No takers.

"Well, as King Leon V, here's my first command. Move aside, because we're leaving. And then my second is get everyone out of this building. Now."

"Everyone?" asked one warrior who had been standing behind King Leon IV and was now wearing a film of red goo that had been his majesty's cerebellum.

"Everyone." Turnbull took the MAC-10 from Carter and reloaded as he led her and Sly Boy down the hall between the silent warriors. Once past them, they broke into a run.

A couple of warriors who had not gotten the word about Turnbull's coronation tried to impale the trio with spears as they sprinted out of the exit into the shantytown in the south parking lot. The MAC-10 solved those two problem individuals, and no one else molested them as they bolted away from the enormous building.

The moon was up, and the inhabitants were tending their fires throughout the shantytown. They ran. Turnbull glanced back and saw that his subjects had heeded his command. The inhabitants were streaming out of the building.

There was the roar of aircraft engines and whistling that got louder and louder until it sounded like a train and then thuds, three or four of them.

The four 2000-pound BLU-118/B thermobaric bombs that the F-15s dropped were individually targeted to exact GPS coordinates located around the beacon in open spaces depicted in the Pentagon plans. The fuses were programmed for a slightly greater time lapse to account for having to punch through five or six floors to get down to the right depth. At a precisely calculated spot, their bursting charges expelled a chemical mist of fuel that filled the open spaces in the underground complex. Then they each detonated, creating a combination of heat and blast overpressure that simultaneously crushed and burned to a cinder everything in those tunnels.

The entire corner of the Pentagon that they had just fled glowed orange for a moment, then the windows erupted outward in ribbons of flame. A section of the concrete structure lifted into the air, then expanded like a balloon filled with fire, then collapsed back down upon itself with a hideous roar. Flames leapt up from the rubble.

Turnbull, Carter and Sly Boy watched for a moment. The people were coming out of their shanties to witness the destruction.

"I gave the flashlight to somebody," Turnbull said. "Sorry."

"Take this," Carter said, handing over the MP5 and her remaining mags.

Sly Boy took his pay and tried to hide it under his vest.

"Thanks," Turnbull said, and he and Carter trotted off into the crowd.

Sly Boy just stood watching the Pentagon burn, singing his Sly Boy song.

17.

"It is over," Martin Rios-Parkinson told the Vice-President in the new office that replaced the Oval Office – the Oval Office "manifested a legacy of hetero-normative imperialism" and was torn down and replaced with a memorial to the hate crimes committed there by the presidents of the old United States. The new office was plush, but generic. Harrington did not care much – he had no intention of staying in the swampy backwater of Capital City any longer than he must.

"Congratulations," Harrington said, cradling a tumbler of imported Glenlivet Whisky. "You've eliminated the Marburg X plot and outmaneuvered your rival Stenz. And you've forged a bond with the military – you and the generals share a common interest now in creating an explanation for the Pentagon airstrike. You have made them allies. How are you going to consolidate your victory?"

"Methodically. The PIA complex is fortified. I can hardly send my agents to arrest the Chameleon and her henchpeople."

"Of course, you incinerated the proof of her plot with your bombs."

"We know the truth."

"Truth is a bourgeois conceit, Director."

"I agree."

"There's another truth that I have become aware of."

"What is that?"

"That you brought a United States operative back from Mexico as your right-hand person."

"Of course, I deny these slanderous lies. But even if they were true, I incinerated the proof with my bombs."

"No loose ends," smiled the politician. "This is why I bet on you."

"You bet on both of us, me and the Chameleon. So, whoever prevailed was irrelevant. You won either way."

Harrington smiled, and lifted his tumbler in a salute.

"And you were willing to kill thousands, maybe millions," Rios-Parkinson said.

"You disapprove?"

"No," the PBI Director replied. "I admire your focus and determination. You told me about Siberia, and then you told the Chameleon that I was going to arrange to eliminate the terrorist cell."

"One should always keep his options open, and not be afraid to change course."

"You arranged this competition between us. Tell me, have I won it?"

"You seem to be winning," the Vice-President replied, sipping again. "But there is still the question of the Chameleon and her rogue agency."

Rios-Parkinson considered for a moment. "I will bide my time. She is trapped."

"Be careful, Director," Harrington said, sipping his whisky. "Trapped animals are often the most dangerous."

"How do you feel?" Turnbull asked. They were in the back of a People's Security Force patrol car. The two officers up front had been stunned when the pair of derelicts walked up to them as they watched the Pentagon burn. They had been even more stunned when they produced ID and demanded a ride back into the Control Zone, but not so stunned that they couldn't laugh. And one of the two wet himself when the male produced a machine gun and told them if they wouldn't drive them, he would splatter them all over the checkpoint and drive the damn car back to the PBI headquarters himself.

They were counting on the male to keep his word and give them back their Berettas when they got to their destination.

A Plexiglas screen walled off the front seats from the back. It provided privacy for a whispered conversation. And it kept the front seat occupants safe from contagion.

Carter looked down. She was splattered with blood, but nowhere near as bad at Turnbull.

"I feel okay, not counting my rib," she said. "You think we're infected?"

"It's only been forty minutes. It takes a few hours."

"I feel fine."

"You will until you don't. We need to get out of here."

"What do you mean?" she said, perplexed. "We can go to the infirmary."

"They won't know what to do. But I know who will. You have to trust me."

"The Director will get us the best care in the PR," Carter said.

"The Director tried to flash fry us."

"He had no choice."

"He didn't *want* any other choice."

"We can discuss it when we see him at headquarters," Carter said firmly.

"Yeah," Turnbull said. "I intend to hold an in-depth discussion with Martin Rios-Parkinson when I get back." He did not anticipate that chat lasting very long.

The vehicle crossed the old Arlington Memorial Bridge and entered the city. Turnbull reassembled his European phone. With the battery in, it lit up. No signal. He waited. There was a signal. He hit the familiar number. If he was right, the European chip would route the call back through Europe and frustrate the PBI monitors.

Silence. Then ringing. Another ring.

"Broadsword," Clay Deeds said. His voice was still thin.

"Danny Boy," Turnbull said. "Time for a ride. DC is making me homesick."

"Everything all right?"

"We're coming out dirty."

"We?"

"Roger."

"Dirty?"

"Roger."

"Time and place in five minutes."

"Roger. See you soon, Danny Boy."

"Out here, Broadsword." Turnbull hung up.

"What was all that?" demanded Carter. "I didn't understand a word of it."

"Good. Then it worked. Look, we go to the headquarters, take care of business, and then you come with me and we make sure we get fixed up. There's a special facility. I can't say anymore."

"I don't understand any of this."

"Just trust me."

He watched the Pentagon burn through the open door as they descended. On a positive note, Turnbull was certainly dead. But the Chameleon's plan had been blown apart too. So he made a new plan, one which he hoped would result in him being richly rewarded.

Adam Marshall and his two operators from the Direct Action Department hopped out of the PIA's newly-repaired Blackhawk helicopter, though it was never referred to as a "Blackhawk." That was racist. They moved swiftly across the helipad to the access door to the PBI headquarters. As promised, it was unlocked.

No one expected an attack to come from above.

They moved down the stairs, pistols hidden under their jackets, to the door to the seventh-floor corridor. Marshall walked through, as he would on any other occasion when he went to meet with the PBI Director in the large office at the end of the hall.

At the double doors he knocked, and Blue Hair opened them for him, smiling and gesturing for the trio to come into the antechamber

"He's not here," she said.

"When is he coming back?" the PIA Deputy Director asked.

"Soon," Blue Hair assured him.

"Then we'll wait for him."

"I thought you were dead," Ernie Smith said, looking them up and down.

"I've been getting that a lot," Turnbull said.

"You look awful You smell worse."

Turnbull put the MAC-10 on the counter and took off the tattered coat.

"That all your blood?" Smith asked.

"Not most of it. Can we get our old clothes back?"

"You need showers too."

"Later."

Smith disappeared into the back and returned with their old clothes. He walked up and put the pile on the counter. Then he picked up the heap of clothes Turnbull had taken off.

"No!" Turnbull shouted. "Stay back."

Smith looked shocked at the outburst.

"We may be infectious. Give me a plastic trash bag and I'll put them in and tie it off."

"Plastic garbage bags are illegal," Smith explained.

"It's an earth-crime," Carter said.

"Just get me something I can put these in."

Smith found him a burlap sack. They stuffed the deadly duds inside.

"You need a medic?" Smith asked.

"Yeah. That's where we're going." Deeds had texted him coordinates to a location about an hour out of town in rural Virginia.

The rendezvous was in about four hours. That might not be enough time.

"You both got whatever it is?"

Carter nodded. "Maybe. We don't know. We feel fine now."

"It incubates for a few hours, then it affects you. You start to lose control. You become wild, dangerous, almost rabid," Turnbull said.

"Then you need someone to help you get where you are going." It was not a question.

"I can't ask you to do that, Ernie," Turnbull said.

"You don't need to."

They entered the one unbroken elevator and hit the "7". There was no security measure to keep people from going up there besides fear of the inhabitants. At the third floor, the door opened and what appeared to be a male with bright purple hair and a diaper entered. Neither Ernie nor Carter batted an eye. Diaper Man got off on the fourth floor.

The MAC-10 hung down under Turnbull's jacket. He tried to look nonchalant as he imagined the many ways he had to choose from with regard to shooting Martin Rios-Parkinson.

Maybe he would start at the bastard's toes and work up. But he still was not sure how Kristina Carter would react to him blowing away her mentor. Ernie Smith would probably be cool.

The elevator door opened at the seventh floor, and the hall was empty. Even though all hell was breaking loose across the river, there was no unusual sense of urgency at the PBI headquarters that night. The trio walked down the hall and went through the door into the Director's anteroom.

Blue Hair jumped up at her desk, surprised. She was watching government television on the screen across from the desk with the sound turned up.

"This is CNN. Racist forces caused a fire at the People's Housing Complex in Virginia. Local volunteers are responding and promising to rebuild," intoned a wizened reporter, slurring his words as if he had stopped for a drink before going before the camera. The chyron gave his Journalist License Number in the lower right corner of the screen.

Good to see Don Lemon was still getting work, Turnbull thought as he brushed past Blue Hair to the door to the Director's office. He figured he'd ask a few questions of the Director, then splatter him all over his desk set. Then he would work it out with Carter.

Blue Hair seized the remote off her desk as they passed and shut off Lemon's yapping. That was the signal.

Turnbull pushed open the door and was greeted by three Glocks.

Adam Marshall and two thugs held them; Marshall seemed surprised.

"You?" he said. Then he smiled. "I thought you were dead. Shut the front door," he ordered, and Blue Hair ran across the antechamber and complied.

Turnbull, Carter and Smith stood still.

"Why are you pointing guns at us in the Director's office?" Carter demanded.

Marshall gestured to one of his operators and he relieved the three of their weapons. He handed the MAC-10 to Marshall, who admired it. Ernie Smith had a very nice Colt Python .357, and the operator paused to examine it.

"Be careful," Smith said. "It's loaded." The operator smashed him on the side of the head with it and Smith staggered and fell.

"Don't even, Captain Turnbull," Adam Marshall said, raising the MAC-10 for emphasis.

"That's the PBI Director's Chief of Security," Carter said. Marshall laughed.

"Oh, your little friend doesn't know, does she, Turnbull?"

"I don't appreciate your sexist invalidation of my –," Carter began.

"Shut up!" barked Marshall. He looked at Turnbull. "Tell her."

"I'm really offended by your toxic masculinity and white privilege," Turnbull said.

Marshall laughed. "Like you of all people buy into this bullshit. Agent Carter, your friend here is one Kelly Turnbull. He's an agent of the United States of America. A spy, here, working with your boss Rios-Parkinson."

"No, I identify as People's Republican," Turnbull said.

"Is this true?" asked Carter.

"Go ahead, Turnbull. Tell her," Marshall said, the submachine gun dancing in their faces. "Do you remember me? From when you were in the American Army at that damn basic training base and you had that sergeant drag me away when I refused to continue? I told you I was going to come here to the PR, where they aren't knuckle-dragging Jesus freaks. Do you remember that?"

"Nope," Turnbull said, shaking his head. "I mean, I have a pretty good memory, but you just don't ring a bell. I guess you didn't make much of an impression."

"Oh, you're still a smart guy. Let's see how smart you are after I get you back to the complex. We came here for Rios-Parkinson, but you – you're even better. You're all living, breathing proof of his treason. There won't be a PBI when this is all over."

Inspector Cooley pushed open the main door to Blue Hair's antechamber and stood shocked at the scene before him. Behind him was a familiar figure – Martin Rios-Parkinson.

"Get him!" Marshall yelled.

Marshall kept Turnbull and Carter covered, but the operators opened up with their Glocks. Cooley staggered under the impacts; there was no way he could even make a viable play for his weapon. He fell back, hit a half dozen times.

Behind him, Rios-Parkinson turned and ran, squeezing off unaimed rounds to his rear from his Walther PPK as he bolted down the hallway and into a stairway. A moment later, the alarm sounded, a series of horn blasts.

"He ran away," one of the operators reported, exasperated.

"Yeah, he does that," Turnbull said. "He's like a freaking roach when you flick on the lights."

"Bring that one," Marshall said, gesturing to Smith's crumpled figure. He used the MAC-10 to gesture for Turnbull and Carter to move out of the office and down the hall, to the helipad access corridor.

"Pretty audacious, breaking into the PBI and trying to snatch the Director," Turnbull said. "I was just going to shoot him myself."

"Shut up," Marshall said, forcing them up the steps.

They went out through the access door onto the helipad. It was cold and very windy with the chopper revving up. Across the river, they could still see the fire burning in the corner of the Pentagon.

The group loaded in, PIA agents with Marshall in the middle and Turnbull, Carter and Smith across from them with their backs to the pilot and co-pilot. Carter had to help buckle the woozy Smith in. Blood was running down the side of his head.

As the helicopter rotors started accelerating, Turnbull leaned forward.

"Nope, still don't remember you," he shouted over the noise.

Marshall glared, leveling the MAC-10. The bird left the ground and rose as it swooped forward over the Control Zone and north toward the PIA compound.

They were out over the city, then over the river, moving fast. Cold wind buffeted them through the open doors.

"Are you really a red spy?" Carter said loudly, over the engine noise.

"It's a long story," he said.

"He'll tell it all once we get back to the complex," Marshall said, smirking.

"So, I guess your Marburg X virus plan kind of went to shit. Sorry," Turnbull said.

"I have new plan. You."

"I really wish I remembered you, but you're just not that interesting."

The flew on over the countryside until they crossed over a wall and into the airspace above a large government complex. Marshall looked out the open door. The PIA helipad was below.

That moment was when Turnbull flipped open his harness and lunged, pushing the submachine gun's suppressor to his right and back hard so that when Marshall squeezed the trigger it was pointed into the lap of a thug sitting beside him. The man howled as his groin and thighs were shredded.

The MAC-10 fired for a bit over a second then went dry, and the operator went limp and fell forward.

Turnbull brought his elbow back and savagely slammed it into the other operator's face once, then again. There was blood, and a couple teeth came tumbling out of the ruins of his mouth. Turnbull's hand found the latch on the man's harness and tripped it. The buckle came free and Turnbull gave a shove and the operator fell out the open door.

Carter got out of her belt and dove toward the shredded operator, plunging her hands in the pool of red and white goo that had once been his groin.

Marshall attacked, viciously, grabbing Turnbull by the throat and face. He got head-butted hard in the nose for his trouble but kept grappling. His right hand moved up over Turnbull's mouth with the objective of gouging out his eyes. Turnbull opened his mouth and bit Marshall's extended index finger, hard, until there was a crunch, and then he threw back his head and tore.

They call it a degloving injury, when the skin and flesh of an extremity is pulled off, leaving a bare white bone and spurting blood from the severed vessels. Marshall held up his bone-finger and screamed once, then twice, forgetting about fighting, unable to look away.

Turnbull spit out the pinkish finger-sheath.

The helicopter touched down on the helipad, and by that time Carter had found what she was looking for, the Glock, covered with blood and gore. She pulled it out, dripping and red.

Marshall was still staring at his mutilated finger, still shrieking, as Turnbull flicked open the wounded man's harness latch and took the empty MAC-10 back.

Carter pointed her dripping Glock at the PIA deputy director, but Turnbull shook his head. "Make them get us out of here."

He grabbed Marshall, bringing him in close.

"I do remember you," Turnbull said. "You were a fucking asshole."

He threw the howling man out of the chopper and into a heap on the helipad.

Carter was shouting "Go, go!" to the pilots. The pilot did not take off, so Carter shot the co-pilot. Ernie Smith was right – the Glock would fire no matter what it was covered with. The pilot complied, and as they rose, veering south, they watched Marshall run hunched over to the access door, cradling his ruined right hand.

Carter took aim, but Turnbull pushed her arm down, shaking his head and smiling.

18.

Carter kept an eye on the pilot, passing on Turnbull's instructions about where to go. Turnbull, for his part, attended to Ernie Smith, who had a golf ball-sized knot on his right temple where the operator had slammed him with the big revolver.

They set down at a neighborhood park, which was really just a vacant lot occupied by derelicts. The pilot waited, terrified, as the rotors spun while Turnbull got out of the helicopter with his MAC-10 and ran down the street.

The locals came out to see what the ruckus was, but they left the man with the scary gun alone as he went up to the one neatly kept house on the street and opened the front door. Then he came out with a dog.

The helicopter landed in an open field that would have been growing something – corn, tobacco, hemp – if the people to whom the People's Republic had decided to redistribute it to had any kind of incentive to actually work. They did not. In fact, they did not even come out of the rotting farmhouse where they spent their days watching TV shows like *People's Justice* and *Fairness Force Five* to see what the commotion was out on the property they had stolen.

"You need to run," Turnbull said to the terrified aviator. "Run that way, which is north, and keep running. Don't be stupid and try to get one of the locals to call the PSF. These are country folk. They'll probably lock you up in the cellar and use you as a love slave."

The pilot nodded, and he took off his helmet, leapt out of the chopper and ran north.

"Do all of you racist red people stereotype the rurally-inclined?" asked Carter.

"Yes," Turnbull said. "It's actually illegal not to."

His head was now feeling the familiar pounding. He felt a wave of nausea, and he staggered. Carter helped him stabilize.

"You're sick," she said.

"Wait until I puke blood," Turnbull said. "That's the test."

She looked serious. "I'm starting to feel sick too," she confessed. "Maybe it's just my rib."

"Look, the rendezvous is two klicks south and one hour out. If I get, you know, like them, you do what you have too with that Glock. Got it?"

She nodded. "And vice versa."

It was Turnbull's turn to nod.

He put out his hand.

"Give me your phone."

She looked at him quizzically.

"Your phone."

She handed it over, and he went to the directory and hit the one number.

Martin Rios-Parkinson picked up.

"Agent Carter, or Agent Warren."

"Kelly Turnbull, Marty."

"Are you calling from captivity at my rival's compound?" Was there a hint of nervousness?

"No, Plan B failed too. But I left them with a little surprise. I'd make sure that those walls around PIA headquarters keep everyone inside. You don't want what I left in there with Deputy Director Marshall getting out after all the trouble you went to contain it at the Pentagon."

"But I did not manage to contain *you*."

"And I didn't get you either. Maybe the third time is the charm."

"Maybe. Well, it has been a challenging evening. Sadly, Inspector Cooley gave xis life to protect mine. A true hero of the People's Republic."

"I think Carter and I may be the only two people who ever worked for you who didn't end up dead."

"Well, it is not too late for that, Kelly. I assume Clay Deeds is arranging your exfiltration. Tick tock, how long do you have before the infection manifests? And how long does your little friend Agent Carter have?"

"We're hard to kill too, Marty," Turnbull said. He swallowed, trying to combat the nausea. "Know this. One day I'm going to smoke your ass and even Clay Deeds won't be able to stop me."

"You do not sound well. Perhaps Wildfire will do what I could not. Good bye, Kelly Turnbull."

The line went dead.

"Let's get him up," said Turnbull. Carter helped him carry Smith as the three headed south. The dog trotted behind them.

The United States Air Force special operations Osprey MV-22 appeared over the trees, taking them by surprise – the noise suppression technology was that good. It was painted all in black for night ops, with no insignia or symbols and all sorts of weird bumps and pods on the fuselage housing the special electronics and weapons systems that made it possible for it to penetrate enemy airspace. The dual rotors were already moving into the hover position – upright – as the plane slowed above them. When they were vertical, the plane descended into the clearing. Turnbull covered his eyes from the debris. It was loud now, all right. Remarkably, the dog didn't try to run away.

He fought the urge to puke.

The dust swirled up around them as they each took one of Ernie's slack shoulders and dragged him toward the V-22's open rear deck ramp. There was an unmanned .50 machine gun mounted there – the weapon was the first thing that drew Turnbull's eye. Then the interior of the craft. It seemed to be wrapped in plastic. Then he saw two figures, strange and bulky, in orange suits with helmets, coming down the ramp. Flight surgeons.

Turnbull and Kristina silently handed off Ernie to them; they pulled him aboard.

"Come on," Turnbull said loudly, over the noise.

She hesitated. Her eyes were bloodshot.

"I can't," she replied, shouting. "I can't leave." Up the ramp, one of the docs appeared and gestured for them to hurry. The engines began to rev.

"I get it," Turnbull shouted back. "I totally respect that." Then he grabbed her right arm and twisted it hard behind her shoulder, forcing her up the ramp in spite of her protests and resistance. The dog came along behind.

One of the docs spoke into the intercom and the plane lurched then leapt upwards. Behind them, the ramp pulled closed and the nacelles groaned as they returned to the forward position for horizontal flight.

"You son of a bitch!" Carter shouted. "You had no right!"

"You might be contaminated," he said. "I had every right."

He sat down on one of the canvas benches and buckled in. Carter reluctantly did the same across from him. The dog settled in on the metal floor.

The medic came over with a syringe and Turnbull bared his right arm. Another appeared with a needle in front of Carter, who looked over at Turnbull, both angry and confused.

"Anti-virals," Turnbull said over the noise. "Trust me, you want them." The techs plunged the needles in. Now his arm hurt too; his body was one-hundred percent pain.

The doctors withdrew to tend to Smith. Turnbull pulled out his Wilson X-TAC and checked to make sure there was a round in the chamber.

Of course there was.

"I think I'm going to keep this handy," he said. "Just in case. I'd give it to the docs and let them watch me, but they'd probably hesitate, thinking they could fix me before I ripped you all apart."

"Give it to me," Carter said.

"Not quite yet. You'd probably shoot me now."

"I probably would," she said.

Turnbull laughed, sort of. Then he threw up a gusher of red.

19.

The nurse tapping her foot outside the plastic barrier was an Army major, and distinctly unimpressed with the mysterious Lieutenant Colonel Sawyer, who was lying inside the isolation chamber. The last time he had been there he was a full colonel named Anderson. She did not have much use for whatever secret squirrel games were going on, but after a decade at the United States Army Medical Research Institute of Infectious Diseases – USAMRIID, which they pronounced "you sam rid" – the nurse had learned not to ask questions that were unrelated to the specific medical issues at hand.

The last time, her patient had been there for a couple months with the same hemorrhagic fever. Now he was back, but it was much, much milder this time. The docs were fascinated. It looked like while the 4.7% of victims who survived Marburg X were not entirely immune to reinfection, the virus was much less virulent in patients who were re-exposed. This LTC Sawyer was going to be the star of a dozen classified medical journal articles.

"You get the phone when I get the blood," the nurse said through the solid plastic wall that separated the patient from the rest of the room.

"How about I get treated like a colonel?" the man said. He was testy; his head hurt.

"How about I treat you like a lieutenant?"

The man gave up and submitted to the remote blood draw apparatus, just as he had done for a half-dozen times every day since he arrived. It scanned for a vein, then inserted the needle and drew out the blood, which went directly to the analyzers. Then it pulled the needle out.

"Any idea when I am getting out of here?" asked the patient.

"You are two days out of a coma," snarled the nurse.

"And?"

"When your blood is clear for two weeks," she said. "Maybe."

"Well, how clear is it now?"

"We haven't tested it yet, but yesterday's numbers were an improvement. There," she said, pushing a button on her panel. "Your outside line is activated."

The nurse left the room and Turnbull picked the telephone handset up off the table by his bed. She did not have to tell him to be discreet, or that people would be listening. He swung his legs over the side and sat up on the edge of the hospital bed and dialed the number Clay had provided.

It rang. Lorna answered.

"Hi Kelly. I guessed it was you from the 'NO ID' that came up on my phone."

"Yeah, I'm still somewhere off the grid," he said. It would probably surprise her to know he was only a few hours away, in San Antonio inside the most secure part of Fort Sam Houston.

"I'd ask you where, but you'd probably have to kill me," she said.

She did not know the half of it.

"Well," Turnbull said. "I just wanted to check on the dog."

"The dog is still fine," she said. "You are really bad at this. I hope you're better at what you actually do for a living."

"The jury is out on that."

"*I'm* fine too," Lorna said.

Turnbull detected the sarcasm, but was not sure how best to respond. He went with: "Um, I think I'll be a few more weeks. Can you keep watching him?"

"Sure," Lorna replied. "But you know, when you get home, you are taking me out. Somewhere nice."

"Sure," Turnbull said. "Uh, where?"

"Are you really going to make me plan our first date, Kelly?"

Outside the barrier there was a familiar figure.

"Lorna, I have to go."

"Kelly, you..."

"Really. Bye." He hung up and put the handset back in the cradle.

Clay Deeds walked up to the plastic barrier. He looked thinner, but healthy. He had come by several times already.

"How are you feeling?" he asked.

"Better. I'd like to get out of here."

"They tell me soon. Your friend Ernie Smith is out. He did not have any virus even after two weeks. We placed him in a defector transition facility that allows pets. It's hard coming over from the People's Republic, like when North Koreans defected into South Korea before the unification."

"They mess with your head over there in the blue," Turnbull said. "But I think Ernie will do all right. You know, his dog is named after you."

"I heard."

"What about Kristina? She still mad at me?"

"Ask her yourself," Clay said, stepping back to open the door to the main corridor. Kristina Carter stepped inside wearing jeans and a blouse, not quite a Texas girl but on the way. It also looked like she had put a little weight on her skinny frame.

"Hello, Kelly. It's still weird not calling you Oliver. How are you?"

"I'm good. Little bit of a headache. You?"

"They say I'm clear of the virus. If I had it, the anti-viral intervention early stopped it. I understand you were the template for the treatment protocol. Anyway, I'm out of isolation. They are sending me to a program for new arrivals. I'm leaving here today."

"Check out the sights in town," Turnbull said. "You're going to love the Alamo. When you find out who the good guys were, it will blow your mind."

"Okay, I will."

"Look," Turnbull said. "Sorry about back there on the airplane."

"I understand. But...," she paused.

"But what?"

"I don't know if I can stay here, Kelly. It's not home."

"Give it a chance. All you've been in is a hospital. It gets better. I promise."

"Oh, it's wonderful here. Everyone is nice. The food is incredible," she said. "But it's not home. I wish someone had told me that you don't share your pronouns and ask theirs when you first meet someone here."

"Yeah, I can see it being an adjustment. Freedom takes getting used to."

"I don't know if I even want to be free."

"You do. Everyone does, even if they don't know it."

"I just don't know if I can fit in here. It's nothing like we were told, but it's still so different."

"They'll probably kill you if you go back."

"I can explain what happened. Rios-Parkinson will understand."

"He may be standing in front of a wall as we speak. It's falling apart over there, Kristina."

"It's my home though, Kelly."

"Give the USA a chance, then you decide."

"Would they really let me go back if that's what I wanted?"

"Our walls are to keep people out, not to keep them in. You just have to decide what you want. You have that freedom, like it or not."

"Thanks for everything, Kelly."

"Thanks for saving my ass."

"Not bad for a 110-pound girl. See, maybe Kimba isn't so far off."

"Now my headache really is back."

"See you around, Kelly." Kristina went out the door into the corridor.

Clay turned back to face Kelly and pulled out an iPad. "Check the monitor."

The monitor inside the isolation chamber came on. It was clearly a satellite video of some sort of large, walled compound surrounded by green fields. Dark shapes darted about the open spaces inside the wall, chaotic, mindless, like ants on a hot griddle.

"PIA headquarters in Langley," Deeds said. "Keep watching."

Suddenly, the compound was covered in orange bursts.

"Incendiary bombs," Deeds said. "An airstrike. They incinerated the whole thing, just like the Pentagon. Whatever was in that compound, they wanted it to die there. Anything you want to tell me?"

"Well, I don't want to ruin my debriefing for you with spoilers, but yeah, I probably had something to do with it." Turnbull's head was beginning to throb.

"I'm not shocked. Anyway, it worked. There's been no Wildfire outbreak. Except for you, there does not appear to be anyone else left alive with the virus in his bloodstream. And you'll be clear of it within a couple of weeks."

"Until someone makes it again from scratch. Though that seems unlikely."

"I'm guessing Dr. Maksimov is out of the picture."

"Yeah, he's super dead." Turnbull lay back on his pillows.

"Then I guess we're safe, at least from that threat. But the People's Republic is getting more unstable. It's bad, Kelly. I don't have to tell you."

Turnbull relaxed into the pillow. "No, you don't have to tell me."

"Get well. I may need you again."

Turnbull shut his eyes and put his head on the pillow.

"Clay," he said, shutting his eyes. "Stop talking."

Author's Note

Naturally, most of this is fiction. Except the parts that are coming true.

Don't let any of it come true.

KAS

November 2018

Kelly Turnbull will return in

CRISIS

About the Author

Kurt Schlichter is a senior columnist for *Townhall.com*, where his work appears twice a week. He is also a Los Angeles trial lawyer admitted in California, Texas, and Washington, DC, and a retired Army Infantry colonel.

A Twitter activist (@KurtSchlichter) with over 170,000 followers, Kurt was personally recruited by Andrew Breitbart, and he is the Senior Columnist at Townhall.com. His writings on political and cultural issues have also been published in *American Greatness, IJ Review, The Federalist*, the *New York Post*, the *Washington Examiner*, the *Los Angeles Times*, the *Boston Globe*, the *Washington Times*, *Army Times*, the *San Francisco Examiner*, and elsewhere.

Kurt serves as a news source, an on-screen commentator, and a guest on nationally syndicated radio programs regarding political, military, and legal issues, at Fox News, Fox Business News, CNN, NewsMax, One America Network, The Blaze, and with hosts such as Hugh Hewitt, Larry O'Connor, Cam Edwards, Chris Stigall, Dennis Prager, Tony Katz, John Cardillo, Dana Loesch Show, John Gibson, and Derek Hunter, among others. Kurt also does twice-weekly video commentary for *The Rebel Media*.

Kurt was a stand-up comic for several years, which led him to write three e-books that each reached number one on the Amazon Kindle "Political Humor" bestseller list: *I Am a Conservative: Uncensored, Undiluted, and Absolutely Un-PC, I Am a Liberal: A Conservative's Guide to Dealing with Nature's Most Irritating Mistake*, and *Fetch My Latte: Sharing Feelings with Stupid People*.

In 2014, his book *Conservative Insurgency: The Struggle to Take America Back 2013-2041* was published by Post Tree Press.

His 2016 novel *People's Republic* and its 2017 prequel *Indian Country* reached No. 1 and No. 2 on the Amazon Kindle "Political Thriller" bestseller list.

His non-fiction book *Militant Normals: How Regular Americans Are Rebelling Against the Elite to Reclaim Our Democracy* was published by Center Street Books in October 2018. It made the USA Today Bestseller List.

Kurt is a successful trial lawyer and name partner in a Los Angeles law firm representing Fortune 500 companies and individuals in matters ranging from routine business cases to confidential Hollywood disputes and political controversies. A member of the Million Dollar Advocates Forum, which recognizes attorneys who have won trial verdicts in excess of $1 million, his litigation strategy and legal analysis articles have been published in legal publications such as the *Los Angeles Daily Journal* and *California Lawyer*.

He is frequently engaged by noted conservatives in need of legal representation, and he was counsel for political commentator and author Ben Shapiro in the widely publicized "Clock Boy" defamation lawsuit, which resulted in the case being dismissed and the victory being upheld on appeal.

Kurt is a 1994 graduate of Loyola Law School, where he was a law review editor. He majored in communications and political science as an undergraduate at the University of California, San Diego, co-editing the conservative student paper *California Review* while also writing a regular column in the student humor paper *The Koala*.

Kurt served as a US Army infantry officer on active duty and in the California Army National Guard, retiring at the rank of full colonel. He wears the silver "jump wings" of a paratrooper and commanded the 1st Squadron, 18th Cavalry Regiment (Reconnaissance-Surveillance-Target Acquisition). A veteran of both the Persian Gulf War and Operation Enduring Freedom (Kosovo), he is a graduate of the Army's Combined Arms and Services Staff School, the Command

320 | KURT SCHLICHTER

and General Staff College, and the United States Army War College, where he received a master's degree in strategic studies.

He lives with his wife Irina and their monstrous dogs Bitey and Barkey in the Los Angeles area, and he enjoys sarcasm and red meat.

His favorite caliber is .45.

Made in the USA
Columbia, SC
13 July 2020